THE GRAYWOLF ANNUAL NINE:

STORIES FROM THE NEW EUROPE

1992

Previous *Graywolf Annuals*
Edited by Scott Walker

THE GRAYWOLF
ANNUAL NINE

STORIES
FROM THE
NEW
EUROPE

Edited and with an Introduction by
Scott Walker

GRAYWOLF PRESS : SAINT PAUL

Copyright © 1992 by Graywolf Press
Introduction copyright © 1992 by Scott Walker

Publication of this volume is made possible in part by grants from
the National Endowment for the Arts, the Minnesota State Arts Board
through an appropriation from the Minnesota State Legislature,
the Andrew W. Mellon Foundation, the Lila Wallace/Reader's Digest
Fund, the McKnight Foundation, and from other generous
contributions to Graywolf Press from corporations, foundations,
and individuals. Graywolf Press is a member agency
of United Arts, Saint Paul.

ISBN 1-55597-169-5
ISSN 0734-7471

9 8 7 6 5 4 3 2
First Printing, 1992

Published by Graywolf Press, 2402 University Avenue, Suite 203,
Saint Paul, Minnesota 55114. All rights reserved.

Cover art is a detail from a man's wedding apron from Hungary.
Courtesy of Textile Arts International, Inc.

ACKNOWLEDGMENTS

Most of the stories collected in this *Graywolf Annual* have appeared previously in publications, as noted below. We gratefully acknowledge the cooperation of editors, agents, and the authors for their permission to reprint stories here. We have made every effort to contact all of the authors represented in this anthology, but due to circumstances beyond our control some of the material appears here without the author's explicit consent.

Dubravka Ugrešić's "A Hot Dog in a Warm Bun" originally appeared in a 1989 issue of *Formations,* which is published by Northwestern University. English translation is copyright © 1989 by Michael Henry Heim.

The selection from Danilo Kiš's 1975 novel *Garden, Ashes* is reprinted by permission of the publisher (Harcourt Brace Jovanovich). William J. Hannaher's English translation is copyright © 1975 by Harcourt Brace Jovanovich.

Ladislav Dvorak's "Swords 'n' Sabers" was published in *The Writing on the Wall—An Anthology of Czech Literature,* edited by Antonin Liehm and Peter Kussi (Karz-Cohl Publishing, 1983). Suzanne Rappaport's translation is copyright © 1985 by Readers International, Inc.

Ivan Klíma's "Monday Morning: A Black Market Tale" is from his book *My Merry Mornings* (Readers International, 1985). George Theiner's translation is copyright © 1985 by Readers International, Inc.

Teet Kallas's story "Back to the Rocks" was published in *The Sailors' Garden,* edited by August Eelmäe (Perioodika, Tallinn, 1984).

Regīna Ezera's "Man Needs Dog" is from *The Glade with Life-Giving Water: Stories from the Soviet Baltic Republics* (Progress Publishers, 1981).

Juozas Aputis's "The Glade with Life-Giving Water" is the title story of *The Glade with Life-Giving Water: Stories from the Soviet Baltic Republics* (Progress Publishers, 1981).

Rita Kelly's "The Cobweb Curtain" was first published in her collection *The Whispering Arch and Other Stories* (Arlen Press, Dublin, 1986). Copyright © 1986 by Rita Kelly.

CONTENTS

INTRODUCTION

I

THIS ANTHOLOGY of short stories offers a way to begin to understand the realities of the new Europe. The subject of "multi-culturalism" versus "Eurocentrism" has been much debated in the United States, most often as if "Europe" were a single cultural entity. This notion is encouraged by the development of the European Economic Community, with Euro-currency and unrestricted travel and trade between "countries," and by the triumph of consumerism, which has resulted in identical products and services, from soap to hotels, found everywhere.

However, study of European cultures reveals some simultaneous, contrary developments: Eastern Europe's fragmentation into smaller cultural states, and widespread independence movements among separate cultures and regions in almost all of western Europe as well.

The short stories included in this *Graywolf Annual* illustrate the particularities of the remarkable variety of European cultures, from the individual voices of the former Soviet Baltic states to the nuances of Croat/Serb and Czech/Slovak voices, and the surprising strength of Euzkadi (Basque), Icelandic, Irish, immigrant, and Catalan cultures. Ancient, deep-rooted cultures and languages have managed to survive despite political pressures to unify under artificial boundaries, the economic pressures of the EEC, and a mass market and communications system that threatens to overwhelm localized customs and concerns. In a precise counterbalance to the strength of mass culture, regional identities are blossoming throughout Europe.

The "European" parts of American culture are much more diverse than is usually acknowledged. The concept of the state – an arbitrary boundary which our leaders often rush to defend against what they perceive to be internal or external "aggression," as in the case of Kuwait – is one that has shifted and which will continue to change over time. By acknowledging this fact, we may learn something of how our own multi-ethnic culture, one built for the most part of immigrants from every country of the world, can both celebrate its diversity and maintain a vital political unity.

II

MOST OF THE "other" European cultures have demonstrated an amazing resilience in the face of a long history of military and/or political repression. When the large nation-states formed – over half of all nations were formed in the past forty years – so too did the practical need for a single language among their inhabitants; subsidiary languages and cultures were directly or indirectly discouraged and often banned.

For instance, during Franco's regime, Spain canceled autonomy for Spanish Catalonia, outlawed Catalan culture and language, burned Catalan books and closed Catalan newspapers, and sent a half a million Catalans into exile. Estonians, Latvians, and Lithuanians have fought to keep their cultures alive despite deliberate and massive transfers of Soviet people into their territories. Until the most recent generation, which grew up watching television, more than half the citizens of Italy spoke Italian as their second language – their first being one of sixty regional dialects.

Despite and perhaps because of repression, these cultures, though often on the point of extinction, kept their language intact and their traditions alive. When a language is banned it is given a remarkable power; even to speak such a language is an act of rebellion. One of the first signals of impending cultural upheaval is the revival of a repressed language, be it Gaelic, Breton or Yiddish; Catalan, Basque or Romany; Spanish, Navajo or rap.

In the recent past, those who desired to maintain their languages and traditions often turned to poetry, a compressed form that lends itself to subtle implication and to memorization, which made it easier to avoid the censors. Citizens were accustomed to listening for the larger meanings and context behind narrative and lyrical poetry, and poetry became the language of subversion. This in part explains the enormous popularity of literature in the former Soviet Union and in Eastern Europe: to these people as to any citizenry of repressed cultures, language and art are an important part of daily life.

III

EUROPE IS an integral part of the North American past and future, and it is important to understand its many boundaries. Europe is, at once: 1) a part of the transnational economy of multinational corporations, some of which are as large as a nation; 2) the European Economic Community, acting at times as one economic entity; 3) a group of separate states divided into historical geographic boundaries; and 4) many ethnic nations and regions, which often cross district and state boundaries. (Breton culture, for instance, may be found in France, Cornwall, and Wales.)

Benjamin Barber, in an *Atlantic* magazine article, echoes the thoughts of other observers when he writes, "The old interwar national state based on territory and political sovereignty looks to be a mere transitional development." An earlier *Atlantic* article by David Lawday quoted the leader of the

Lombard League (an Italian separatist party) as saying, "Europe has three levels now—the EC, the state, and the region. The weakest of these is the state. The state may well disappear."

Perhaps we should not have been so astonished by the swift reunification of Germany, the fracturing of Eastern European states into roughly their former tribal boundaries, and the quick revival of nationalism within the states of the former Soviet Union. Clearly, artificial national boundaries have at best a tentative hold if they extend beyond a single linguistic/cultural group.

Americans who have a "European" heritage may think of themselves in a more complex way. Rather than being Italian or French, Spanish or Yugoslavian, we may find a more resonant cultural past by identifying the regions, languages, and dialects of our ancestors.

Despite the strength of the mass market culture, of a universal televised "norm" that is broadcast everywhere, individual cultural identities will thrive. The mass market culture is based not, as we like to think of it, on democracy, but rather on an economic system of consumption of manufactured goods. Local cultural revivals are partly a response to homogenization and standardization, and partly because of our search for community and individual identity. Being cut off from our cultural roots may be the one common characteristic of the American national identity: we are all exiled from our pasts, and in our individual and community-wide striving for cultural identity we may perhaps find common understanding.

IV

LITERATURE is a complex and particular way to evoke, imply, and preserve the subtle essence of a culture's language, lifestyles, and turn of mind. In repressed European cultures, there are many strong poetic traditions, and though the prose story is a rather recent development it has become one of the most vigorous and popular of literary forms. Because of its length, the short story is easily reproduced, hidden, and transported, and so lends itself to these creative acts of defiance and cultural preservation. Paying close attention to certain aspects of the narrative reveals remarkable depths of allusion, reference and complexity.

In one way or another, all of the New European stories included in this anthology reflect or resurrect a repressed cultural tradition. They display a remarkable diversity of form, tone, and setting, but in each we sense the psychological gap between the mainstream culture and the writer's own.

As might be expected, a citizen's relationship to authority is a common theme in these stories. Ivan Klíma, a Czech writer, is represented here by a banned "underground" story called "Monday Morning: A Black Market Tale," in which we watch citizens work themselves through a thicket of deceptions and schemes. In Ladislav Dvorak's "Swords 'n' Sabers," which subtly defines the tensions between Czechs and Slovaks, we encounter the relative incompetence caused by unqualified, educated people who have been placed in menial jobs. (In this and other stories we see that inter-tribal tensions are subdued when both groups are united against a common enemy.) The Latvian writer Regīna Ezera's story, "Man Needs Dog" is on the surface a story about a man who has lost his job and who is attempting to sell a batch of puppies; it is also a parable of the responsibilities of one country or individual which possesses another, and a story about how an ordinary man feels the constant pressure of authority.

One common method of calling up a national tradition is to place a story in a rural context. Many of Nobel Prize-winner Halldór Laxness's finest stories are set in rural Iceland, and Laxness, like many Icelandic writers, is very consciously preserving Icelandic culture. Rita Kelly, a young Irish writer, does a masterful job of evoking the persistence of Irish culture despite an onslaught of change and "development."

V

FINDING AN appropriate range of stories proved much harder than expected. It was difficult to find stories written in repressed languages or set in repressed cultures, or to find authors catalogued by their "true" nationality. These cultures and their literatures, for such a long time hidden from view for fear of imprisonment or exile, are now beginning to come into the open. By studying them, we enlarge our understanding of Europe and of our North American heritage, and we witness the remarkable revival of true national communities.

The editor of this anthology was greatly aided in his efforts by Anne Czarniecki, an editor at Graywolf Press, Chris Hubbuch, and other Graywolf staff members who helped to refine and modify the idea for this anthology. To them I owe continued gratitude.

SCOTT WALKER

MAY 1992

Serbia

DANILO KIŠ

from *Garden, Ashes*

Translated by William J. Hannaher

THE BOOK of my life, the book that had such a profound and far-reaching effect on me, the book from which my nightmares and fantasies were recruited, the discovery that pushed my father's incriminated *Travel Guide* into the background, the book that was absorbed into my blood and my brain over the years along with the sinful picture magazines from Budapest, in between the likes of *The Captain of the Silver Bell, The Beauties in the Cage,* and *Man-Horse-Dog,* was the *Small School Bible,* published by the Society of Saint Stephen, "arranged for school-age children by Dr. Joannes Marczell, *vicarius generalis.*" They bought the book for me when I was in the third grade, along with the *Small Catechism,* from Anna's classmate Ilonka Vaci, who had written her name in it in indelible red ink. This Bible was the quintessence of all miracles, all myths and legends, great deeds and terrors, horses, armies and swords, trumpets, drums, howls. Tattered, with its covers gone, like peeled fruit, like bittersweet marzipan removed from its tin foil, the book began on page seven, *in medias res,* with the first sin: "... straightaway after the first sin, people found out that someone would crush the head of the serpent one day." Engravings in which the faces of angels, saints, and martyrs speak with pathos serve to point up the divine conciseness of the anecdote, this essence of essences stripped of eloquence, these events bared to the bone, this story line brought to white heat. This is an army of bad persons and good, the sinful and the innocent, people trapped in that instant of eternity that shapes or at least decides character, people marked with character like a trademark, like the brand of the divine farmstead to which they belong. Adam's face as he is about to bring the apple to his mouth: he is secreting mythic saliva, like a Pavlovian dog, as a conditional reflex provoked by the sour-sweet juice of the apple, his face puckered into a passionate grimace. Eve, our primal ancestress, is taking the stance of a village seductress offering the gingerbread cakes of her nakedness as she leans against the tree in the provocative pose of a fashion plate, sticking out her swelling hips. Her hair falls all the way to her ankles as if she were standing under a waterfall, her breasts are small and entirely out of proportion to her hips and thighs, she resembles the idealized female specimens in the illustrations of anatomy textbooks. A jet from that dark waterfall, a single lock from her abundant head of hair, has detoured abruptly from its course, twirling like a mustache, circling around her thighs like a creeper of some living organism, defying the laws of gravity, guided by an inspiration both divine and sinful concealing the nakedness of the primal ancestress, whose navel peers out from her fertile belly like an enormous, Cyclopean eye.

I stand bending over these engravings not as if I were watching a horror movie of history and myth, but rather as a witness, as if I were in some sort of transcendental time machine, attending the events themselves. Bathed in sweat, aware of the far-reaching and painful consequences of Adam's action, I whisper, "No! No!" every time, because he still has time to release his grip and let the apple drop to the ground. I wink to him to turn around and see what I see: the python curled around the tree branch above Eve's head. But this eternal moment continues, finished yet repeated every time, and whenever I turn the page, I catch a new whiff of the sweet smells of paradise, paradise lost, the sweet smell of tropical fruit, I am illuminated by the balm of the sun and the azure of the bay (reminding me of our trip, when we stopped along the coast and I saw the sea for the first time). The landscape of paradise in the engraving, that brilliant work of divine inspiration, was not a picture or representation of events so far as I was concerned; it was for me a window onto eternity, a magic mirror. These engravings, these biblical landscapes, were no more than frozen, isolated moments in man's history, fossils preserved through all the cataclysms, in the honey-yellow amber that coils around the wing of the dragonfly, along with smoke from the sacrificial altars, the sound of the trumpet of Jericho, the bellowing of the lions and the bleating of the sheep of paradise, the frantic hubbub of the biblical mob, the roar of the raging sea, the odors of myrtle, figs, and lemons, the hoarse voices of the prophets.

I suffered in my childhood the destinies of all the Old Testament personages, the sins of the sinners and the righteousness of the righteous, I was by turns Cain and Abel, I was idling on Noah's ark and drowning in the sea with the sinful. *People had become more and more numerous and were full of iniquities. God then said to Noah: Build yourself an ark, for I am going to flood the entire earth. The Lord waited a hundred and twenty years for people to reform, but they did not reform. In the meantime, Noah was building himself an ark. Noah and his wife, and their sons and their wives, thereupon entered the ark. They took with them all manner of creatures, as God had commanded them. They also took along a considerable amount of food. Rain then poured down for forty days and forty nights, and a flood covered the earth. The water rose higher and higher. Higher than the mountains. People and animals perished. Only Noah, and those with him on the ark, survived. . . . When the water had completely receded, Noah disembarked from the ark, built a sacrificial altar, and made a burnt offering to Him. The burnt*

offering was pleasing to God. And He promised that there would be
no new floods. From that time forward, the heavenly rainbow has be-
come a sign of the covenant between God and man.

I experienced this biblical drama of the flood as my own
personal drama, conscious in moments of sincerity that I had
no place in the ark, so I would imagine myself trembling in
my mother's lap, wrapped in a wet blanket, or on the roof of
some house with that handful of survivors, aware that this was
our final refuge, and the rain kept pouring down, biblically. I
was consumed by the flame of repentance like the rest of the
people on the roof, as if on a coral reef in the middle of the
sea, while the swollen corpses of animals and people floated
all around us and the bodies of newborn infants glimmered
like fish next to the wrinkled, hairy bodies of old men and
women. And that man wrapped in a caftan with the insane
glow in his eyes, with his arms raised to heaven, that must be
my father, the sinful prophet, the false apostle. And while the
water inexorably rises, inch by inch, turning everything into
one grand liquid nothing, Noah's ark is floating in the gloomy
distance like an enormous fruit from which people will
sprout, and beasts, and trees; that great laboratory of life is
sailing away, full of human and animal sperm, of specimens
of all species classified and labeled with Latin inscriptions as
in a pharmacy, with a fresh crop of onions and potatoes, with
apples sorted in wooden crates as in a fruit market, with oranges and lemons that conceal within themselves a grain of
light and eternity, with birds in cages that will soon enrich the
air with the tiny seedlings of their chirping and will ennoble
the wasted emptiness of the sky with their skillful flights.

Once I accepted in my soul the day of reckoning, recon-
ciled myself to my own death and my mother's, understood
that everything is finished, that we are no longer suffering,
that we are no more than swollen corpses in the sea, and ignoring for the moment the sorrowful consequences to which
my soul will be exposed (I generously allot myself – at least in
moments of supreme optimism – purgatory), I also experi-

enced the joy of surviving, the Columbian joy of the righteous man. Once the water recedes and the ark has touched the earth after so many days of senseless floating in the waves, I experience the most brilliant hours of my own fantasy and human history. The joy of living becomes so concentrated in me that I want to scream. I do my best to forget that this is not my joy, I abandon myself to this fantasy, this lie, I mix my shouting with the shouting of those getting off the ark, I gaze upon the triumphal flight of the birds streaking out of their cages, I listen to their singing, I listen to the roaring of the lions who are leaving claw marks in the still-moist, cracked earth, I listen to the deafening thud of the hoofed creatures that are trampling soil sprouting freshly with grasses and flowers, new onions and sorrel, while the figs and oranges just brought onto land are bursting like berries, swollen with the weight of their juices and their role in life.

But there is an interlude in the ecstatic moment of my best fantasies, a divine entr'acte, halfway between the void and vital exuberance. This demiurgical instant, full of the most explosive fertility, as just before an erection – that is the point where the circles of nothingness intersect with the arc of life, that infinitesimal moment when one thing ends and another begins, the pregnant silence that rules the world before birds disperse it with their beaks and before creatures and beasts trample it with their hoofs, the postdiluvian silence not yet swallowed by grasses or penetrated by the winds. This is the unique, pregnant silence, the climax of its history, the peak of its own fertility, from which the hubbub of the world is to be born.

On the next page the silence has already been shattered by horses' tails, trampled by the dusty sandals of Noah's sons, torn apart by the shrieking of birds and beasts, by the neighing of biblical donkeys, by the wails of righteousness and criminality, by the birth pangs of the numerous biblical mothers, of whom not one was barren, and their wombs opened up all the time like the school door, with clusters of Noah's powerful descendants issuing forth, chubby and clumsy fellows who just barely found time in their historical haste to bite off their umbilical cords, and they in turn multiplied like flies or rather like bacilli, by the simple division of primitive organisms, rushing to fulfill their great, messianic role. They grew like incarnations of divine concepts, like characters in some grand farce in which the protagonists have their foreordained roles to play, the proud pride, the modest modesty, while criminals and patricides were being born with knives under their belts. They lifted their Promethean gaze arrogantly to the sky, forgetful of the mercy bestowed upon them, and built high towers, defying the will of God: *Come on, let us build ourselves a tower that will touch the clouds with its roof and make our name a glorious one.* Then a swarm of angels flies in, swooping low over their heads, and with a single movement of their hands sow confusion in the languages below. Teams of master builders flap their arms hysterically, uttering gibberish, unheard-of words, fainting from fear and falling from the tower that is disintegrating in the midst of this universal, apocalyptic chaos of languages, of concepts, of words.

By the fifteenth page, the deluge is no more than a remote, mythical memory, the lesson of the Tower of Babel a utilitarian, urbanistic, architectural achievement: houses and towers are built without divine ambition, for human, worldly use, hugging the ground, occasionally as high as two stories. The descendants of Noah and Abraham are settling into them, numerous as ants, whole legions of bearded, sunburned males, hairy as sheep, talkative as magpies, lazy and dirty — packs of drunkards who have preserved only their masculinity from among all the divine attributes of the righteous, their biblical bullish fertility, and forced to the level of a principle, to the level of a vice, they attack women and spill their fertile slime in abundance while the women, constantly pregnant, bring into the world future sinners in clusters, like roe.

Knowing myself, aware of my guilt, of my sinful thoughts and acts, knowing that curiosity is the fundamental trait of my character, curiosity that borders on sin, curiosity that indeed is sin itself, in my case at any rate, I experienced horrible crises at the gates of Sodom. In the false role of a righteous person, I assigned myself the role of Lot's wife, because her behavior seemed the most human, the most sinful, and therefore closest to mine. Consumed by curiosity, I was drawn to the magnificent, horrible sight of fire and disaster as houses collapsed and towers folded like dominoes amidst human wailing that rose to the sky. My curiosity, brought to an explosive point by the divine warning, was suddenly transformed into my sole trait, overwhelming reason and the feeling of fear, turning me into a weakling of a woman, unable to resist my inquisitiveness, and I would turn around abruptly with my whole body as if rotated by the centrifugal force of my curiosity, which had passed through me like a sword.

And when my brothers sold me in Egypt, I stood humbly among the strict, dark-complexioned slave traders, full of the quiet joy of the martyr, conscious that I was fulfilling my role of the righteous person and victim. The babble of the Egyptian marketplaces, blacks, Arabs, Jews, mulattoes, the sound and gurgling of strange tongues, the smell of exotic fruits, the dust of the desert, the camel caravans, the sun-baked faces of the Bedouins, the color of different climates, the adventure of travel through the desert climates, the adventure of travel through the desert sands in the company of slaves—all this was merely the backdrop for my divine destiny, compensation for all my sufferings, the first act of my biblical drama.

By the twenty-seventh page, my role as Joseph is played to full satisfaction. There is a splendid ending of trumpet fanfares, the desert sands have settled, the babble of the Egyptian marketplaces has faded away. Yet, a new role has been assigned to me in this biblical farce, a very passive role, a secondary role if you will, perhaps even insignificant, the role of Moses, and I experience what is surely the strangest of my metamorphoses, a quasi-anthropomorphic flashback to my earliest childhood. Of course, I once more become a victim,

the most innocent victim in the world, victim of victims (like
my father): one of the male children of Israel thrown into the
waters of the Nile by command of the cruel and almighty
king. As always, however, I am the shining exception, the
mortal who will evade death, the lost one who will be found,
the sacrificial victim who will come back to life. My mother
places me in a basket of reeds sealed with pitch, she leaves me
on the banks of the Nile, and in the insignificant but dignified
role of the foundling, I become an orphan, a divine *enfant
trouvé*. When the pharaoh's daughter, a dark beauty accompanied by her ladies-in-waiting, hears me crying on that blazing
afternoon on the banks of the Nile, in the shade of the swaying palm trees, I experience a sinful ecstasy quite out of keeping with my role. I forget that I am a newborn infant. I forget
that of all vital sensations, human and divine, the most that I
can feel and experience is the scenic effect of the sun, which
suddenly blinds me when the pharaoh's daughter raises the
lid on my cradle of reeds, in which I have been awaiting the
fulfillment of my role, and playing a secondary role consisting
of whimpering as piercingly as possible to attract the attention
of the royal strollers. But that is altogether unimportant to
me. Exceptionally sensitive to all scenes that include emperors
and kings, royal heirs, princes and courtiers, and their female
consorts, especially the female consorts, equally sensitive to
the atmosphere of the exotic countries in which these royal
tales take place, Spain, China, Egypt, I experience in an almost erotic way the dramatic moment when the pharoah's
beautiful daughter, moved to compassion by my whimpering,
embraces me, when her slender companions begin intoning
some lachrymose accompaniment on their lyres and lutes. I
inherited their weakness for royal themes from my mother, in
all of whose stories the protagonists were kings, princes, and
princesses, while the rest of the characters had to settle for
roles as standbys, a crowd of anonymous folk, from which
only an occasional person – usually a beautiful gypsy woman
or handsome gypsy man – would attain a more elevated role,

on which the dramatic woof of her tales depended. My mother had been heavily influenced in youth by Chateaubriand's *Last Abencérage,* freely translated by King Nikola of Montenegro, and that influence remained undiminished throughout her life. For me, the happy ending to the whole drama of Moses is right there in that encounter, the drama evolves no further, remains frozen in the eternal moment of the blazing Egyptian afternoon, which to me is the climax of the drama. The future destiny of Moses no longer affects me. The continuation of the story simply lists unimportant scenic directions, printed in nonpareil type, apart from the framework of the dramatic action: the departure of the regal procession, the chanting of the princess's companions, the rhythmical swaying of their hips under the multicolored tunics, the sound of their stringed instruments.

The true end of everything is not depicted in an engraving. I say "the true end" because this is truly the irrevocable and horrible end, a sudden and unexpected cataclysm for all living things, although we are only on page thirty-three. But, as I said, this is indeed the true end: for me, for my book (I can read no further), for this biblical chapter. Death arrives altogether unexpectedly, interrupts my reading, cuts the thread of my fantasy with the scissors of darkness, and that darkness, that gruesome darkness, is above and beyond the powers of the inspired engraver, who abdicates in the face of the grand, apocalyptic theme. The darkness is carried over into the ingenious picturesqueness of the text itself and the typeface, which are gradually drained of meaning, and then into the divine omnipotence of bare words, into the neurotic frenzy of italics, which now replace the curlicues and arabesques of the engraving. The blatant italic captions disrupt the cathedral-like restraint of the nonpareil like a shriek, leap out from the routine order of things, disintegrate in some sort of internal fever, burn up in the flames of rebellion and anarchism, are prone to exaggeration and excesses but are frustrated by the packed rows of loyal nonpareil, combining to become the divine Word, carried along by the senseless, Promethean idea of speaking out, of saying something about which there is nothing to say, which forced even the gifted engraver to abdicate: about the End.

But what I call the end is simply my eschatological conviction that my end is the end of everything. I am now allotting myself the final role, the role of the firstborn (even though my sister Anna is older than I am), the firstborn whom the divine angel-murderer is going to kill. The idea of perishing at the hand of an angel appeals to me enormously, of dying as humanity's martyr, as victim of victims, a tenfold death, because a tenfold death best suits my fantasies, bearing witness to my obstinacy, my strength, my steadfastness, satisfying my thirst for knowledge (truly useless) even in death. But let us turn, finally, to the Book, and let the Word be fulfilled: "Moses and Aaron appeared once more before the Pharaoh. But in vain did they turn a staff into a serpent so as to prove the divine origin of their mission, since the Pharaoh would not listen to them at all. Then God punished Egypt with ten terrible plagues: (1) The waters of the Nile turned into *blood;* (2) *frogs* swarmed over everything, including houses; (3) swarms of *mosquitoes* and (4) *poisonous flies* tormented people and animals; (5) a *pestilence* afflicted the cattle; (6) *ulcers and boils* broke out on men and beasts; (7) a *frightful rain* ruined crops; (8) *swarms of locusts* devastated the remainder of the harvest; (9) a profound *darkness* settled over Egypt for three whole days; (10) the divine *angel-murderer* flew through the sky at midnight and slaughtered all the first-born. *A terrible wailing and lamenting then ensued, for there was no house without a dead person.*"

We shall not retell all the sorrowful consequences of the divine comedy begun by a childish and seemingly insignificant intrigue. We shall settle for the most fundamental points.

Julia's parents gave me to understand one day that I was no

longer welcome in the house. Their excuse was the loathsome suspicion that I had stolen Julia's watercolors, which was their way of discrediting our liaison. "No one except you has been here the last few days, little gentleman," Mr. Szabo told me. "Those watercolors were here, right here, nobody ever touched them." My oaths and my eloquent defense did not sway him. On the verge of hysterical weeping, I declared that I was going to take my case to God if necessary, that I would unmask the disgraceful schemers behind this plot and force them to confess. Righteous punishment will not pass them by.

But that was only the beginning of the misfortunes that came crashing down upon me. My sister received an anonymous letter describing the intimacy of my liaison with Julia with amazing exaggeration (in which I recognize, behind the altered handwriting, the sick fantasies of Laszlo Toth). This vile letter also contained a threat of murder by ambush unless I left Julia alone, which under normal circumstances would make me laugh, because Laszlo Toth is the incarnation of cowardice. Scared by the threat, Anna showed the letter to my mother, who fell into a deep despair, afraid for my life and touched by my sinfulness. Despite my desire to unburden my soul, of course, my confession does not go beyond this (which might be called an ordinary lie): Julia and I hid in Mr. Szabo's stable, in the same stall. That's all. Everything else is a product of a sick and jealous fantasy. Yes, I swear by her life, by my mother's life, that our relationship had not exceeded by an inch the boundary of the permissible and the honorable.... My mother, while suspicious, promised to say nothing about the scandal to my father, who had fallen into his quiet pre-spring depression.

The golden dust of time has slowly settled over this event. Julia's watercolors saw the light of day, in the pockets of her apron, where they had been drowsing in the form of a dozen button samples, in the form of multicolored wax seals impressed on my indictment, which burst on their own in contact with the light and freed me of suspicion. . . .

On All Saints' Day, Julia received her first communion, and, cleansed of sin, as if emerging from a warm bath, she left the chapel dressed in white, a small mother-of-pearl prayer book in her hands, her braids gathered at the back of her neck, pink-cheeked from the shameful confession that she had just made to the Reverend Father. Did she recount to him the sequence of events, the craftiness of my schemes, and her own role as well? Had she mentioned the name of her seducer?

Exceptionally sensitive to the setting and *mise-en-scène* of church rituals, to the tinkling of the bells and the smell of incense, I was kneeling along with the other boys on the threshold of paradise, briefly equal with them, at least ostensibly, yet apart, marked by the brand that was burning into my forehead. I would not have been able to make that final step from pew to sacristy had it not been for the good graces of the Reverend Father, who had given permission for me to attend this solemn ritual of confirmation, during which our class – like a flock of black sheep – entered the divine steam bath and departed, bathed and bleached, leaving behind a pile of sins like a heap of contaminated pus. I sit there, overwhelmed by the frightful burden of my sins, I kneel on the chill concrete like a martyr, like a constipated sheep, the sin of envy that I feel toward my classmates coming out of the sacristy with faces lit up, a postlaxative glow and freshness on their cheeks, drips like vitriol onto my soul, constipated with sins. The solemnity of the moment prevents me from breaking into loud sobbing and from transferring my despair into a public confession before the entire congregation, before my classmates and their parents, so as to attract everybody's attention and pity and attribute to myself a full measure of importance; yet, at the same time, I don't venture to bare my incorrigible sinfulness, which is conspicuous enough as it is.

The solemn words of the liturgy, from the *Ad Deum* to the

Gloria Tibi, trickle in their divine, incomprehensible Latin, interrupted by the dense silence of two-quarter pauses, like the white space between paragraphs. They continue to trickle, these sublime passages, paced by the rhythm of the little silver bell in the hands of the altar boy. A sacred dialogue — *Kyrie eleison, Christe eleison* — is under way, like divine rhymes put to human words. And I kneel in front of the nave of the church stunned to dizziness by the smell of incense, which in this universal feast of the soul conjures up the calm of evergreen forests, the smell of pines and resin, and facing me, high above the nave, above the flickering, sputtering candles, a round stained-glass window is blazing away in a display of fireworks, like a hand of playing cards, kings, queens, and jacks. Mrs. Rigo sits at the reed organ with her head thrown back and eyes shut, strumming the keyboard, strangely youthful in a dark dress with white collar, the tips of her big eyelashes set off by a violet glow. She draws a whole scale of minor-key sighs muffled and high, out of the black polished to a high gloss like the old-fashioned carriages, pressing the pedals as though riding a bicycle in her dreams along a straight wide road.

Croatia

DUBRAVKA UGREŠIĆ

A Hot Dog in a Warm Bun

Translated by Michael Henry Heim

I

ON THE twenty-fifth of March a truly unbelievable thing took place in Zagreb. Nada Matić, a young doctor specializing in plastic surgery, awoke in her room and looked at the clock. It was 6:15. Nada jumped out of bed, jumped into the shower, squatted under the stream of water, then, lighting a cigarette, jumped into a terrycloth robe. It was 6:25. She pulled on her gray spring suit, daubed some rouge on her cheeks, and grabbed her bag. It was half past six. She locked the door, finished the cigarette in the elevator, and hurried off to catch her tram.

By the time Nada Matić stepped off the tram, it was ten to seven. And just then, right in the middle of the square, Nada Matić was overcome by a sudden, unusually intense hunger. She rushed over to the Skyscraper Cafeteria, which served hot dogs in warm buns, nervously called out to the waitress, "More mustard, please!" greedily grabbed the hot dog, and impatiently threw away the napkin. (That is what Nada Matić did. That is what I do too: I always dispose of those unnecessary and shamefully tiny scraps of paper waitresses use to wrap hot dogs.)

Then she set off across the square. She was about to bring
the hot dog to her lips, when—was it some dark sense of fore-
boding or a ray of the March morning sun alighting on the
object in question, illuminating it with its own special radi-
ance? In either case, to make a long story short—she glanced
down at the fresh pink hot dog and her face convulsed in horror. For what did she see peering through the longish bun
and ocherish mustard foam but a genuine, bona fide...!
Nada came to a complete and utter halt. No, there could be
no doubt. *Glans, corpus, radix, corpora cavernosa, corpora spon-
giosa, praeputium, frenulum, scrotum,* our heroine, Nada Matić,
thought, running through her totally useless anatomy class
knowledge and still not believing her eyes. No, that thing in
the bun was most definitely not a hot dog!

Utterly shaken, Nada resumed her journey to the Municipal Hospital at a much slower pace. It had all come together
in a single moment: the anatomy lesson, plastic surgery, the
desire to specialize in aesthetic prosthetics—it had all flashed
before her eyes like a mystical sign, a warning, the finger of
fate, a finger that, if we may be forgiven the crudeness of our
metaphor, peered out of the bun in so tangible, firm, fresh,
and pink a state as to be anything but an illusion.

Nada Matić decided to give the "hot dog" issue top priority.
Taking the "hot dog" to the laboratory and dropping it in a
bottle of Formalin would have been the simplest solution, of
course, but what would her colleagues have said? Nada
looked here and there for a litter basket; there were none in
sight. As she'd thrown the napkin away and had no paper tis-
sues, she tried to hide the "hot dog" by coaxing it into the bun
with her finger, but smooth, slippery, and springy as it was, it
kept sliding out, the head gleaming almost maliciously in
Nada's direction.

It then occurred to Nada that she might drop into a café
and just happen to leave the "hot dog" on the lower shelf of
one of the tables she often stood beside—she had said good-
bye to three umbrellas that way—but in the end she lost her

nerve. For the first time in her life Nada felt what it was like to
be a criminal.

Oh, before I forget, I ought to tell you a few things about
our heroine. Nada Matić is the kind of shortish, plumpish
blonde that men find attractive. But her generous, amicable,
amorous character kept getting in her way, and men disappeared from her life, poor thing, without her ever quite understanding why. Abandoned by no fault of her own, she naturally and periodically found herself involved in hot and
heavy escapades with married medical personnel of the male
sex.

Suddenly Nada felt terribly sorry for herself: her whole life
seemed to have shrunk into that grotesque symbol of bun-
cum-relay-race-baton. No, she'd better take care of it at once.
She gave the bun an unconscious squeeze and the hot dog
peeked out at her again, turning her self-pity to despair. And
just as she noticed a broken basement window and was about
to toss it away, bun and all, who should pass by with a cold
nod but one of the surgeons, Otto Waldinger. Quick as lightning, Nada stuffed the "hot dog" into her pocket, smearing
gooey mustard all over her fingers. The bastard! Scarcely
even acknowledging her, while not so long ago . . . !

And then she spied a mercifully open drain. She removed
the "hot dog" from her pocket with great care and flung it
into the orifice. It got stuck in the grating. She nudged it with
her foot, but it refused to budge. It was too fat.

At that point up sauntered a young, good-looking policeman.

"Identity papers, please."

"What for?" Nada mumbled.

"Jaywalking."

"Oh," said Nada, rummaging frenetically through her bag.

"What's the matter?" asked the policeman, looking down at
the grating. "Lost your appetite?" A good inch and a half of
the "hot dog" was sticking out of the bun. Nada Matić went
pale.

But at this point everything becomes so enveloped in mist that we cannot tell what happened next.

II

MATO KOVALIĆ, a writer (or, to be more specific, a novelist and short story writer), awoke rather early and smacked his lips, which he always did when he awoke though he could not for the life of him explain why. Kovalić stretched, moved his hand along the floor next to the bed until it found his cigarettes, lit one, inhaled, and settled back. There was a full-length mirror on the opposite wall, and Kovalić could see his bloated gray face in it.

During his habitual morning wallow in bed he was wont to run through the events of the previous day. The thought of the evening's activities and Maja, that she-devil of an invoice clerk, called forth a blissful smile on his face, and his hand willy-nilly slid under the covers. . . . Unbelievable! No, absolutely impossible!

Kovalić flung back the blanket and leaped up as if scalded. *There* he felt only a perfectly smooth surface. Kovalić rushed over to the mirror. He was right. *There* he saw only an empty, smooth space. He looked like one of those naked, plastic dummies in the shop windows. He pinched and pulled at himself several times; he slapped his face to see whether he was awake; he jumped in place once or twice; and again he placed his hand on the spot where only the night before there had been a bulge. . . . No, *it* was gone!

But here we must say a few words about Kovalić and show the reader what sort of man our hero is. We shall not go into his character, because the moment one says something about a writer all other writers take offense. And to point out that Kovalić was a writer who divided all prose into two categories, prose *with balls* and prose *without* (he was for the former), would be quite out of place in these circumstances and might even prompt the reader to give a completely erroneous and vulgar interpretation to the whole incident. Let us therefore say instead that Kovalić greatly valued – and wished to write – novels that were true to life, down to earth. What he despised more than anything were symbols, metaphors, allusions, ambiguities, literary frills; what he admired was authenticity, a razor-edged quality where every word meant what it meant and not God knows what else! He was especially put off by intellectualizing, attitudinizing, high-blown flights of fancy, genres of all kinds (life is too varied and unpredictable to be forced into prefabricated molds, damn it!), and – naturally – critics! Who but critics, force-fed on the pap of theory, turned works of literature into paper monsters teeming with hidden meanings?

Kovalić happened to be working on a book of stories called *Meat,* the kingpin of which was going to be about his neighbor, a retired butcher positively in love with his trade. Kovalić went on frequent drinking bouts with the man for the purpose of gathering material: nouns (brisket, chuck, flank, knuckle, round, rump, saddle, shank, loin; wienerwurst, weisswurst, liverwurst, bratwurst, blood pudding, etc.), verbs (pound, hack, gash, slash, gut, etc.), and whole sentences: "You shoulda seen me go through them – the slaughterhouse ain't got nothing on me!" "A beautiful way to live a life – and earn a pile!" "My knives go with me to the grave." Kovalić intended to use the latter, which the old man would say with great pathos, to end the story with a wallop.

We might add that Kovalić was a good-looking man and much loved by women, about which he had no qualms whatsoever.

Well, now the reader can judge for himself the state our hero was in when instead of his far from ugly bulge he found a smooth, even space.

Looking in the mirror, Kovalić saw a broken man. God, he thought, why me? And why not my arms or legs? Why not my ears or nose, unbearable as it would have been. . . . What good am I now? . . . Good for the dump, that's what! If somebody had chopped it off, I wouldn't have made a peep. But to up and disappear on me, vanish into thin air . . . ? No, it's impossible! I must be dreaming, hallucinating. And in his despair he started pinching the empty space again.

Suddenly, as if recalling something important, Kovalić pulled on his shoes and ran out into the street. It was a sunny day, and he soon slowed his pace and began to stroll. In the street he saw a child peeling a banana, in a bar he saw a man pouring beer from a bottle down his gullet, in a doorway he saw a boy with a plastic pistol in his hand come running straight at him; he saw a jet cross the sky, a fountain in a park start to spurt, a blue tram come round a bend, some workers block traffic dragging long rubber pipes across the road, two men walking toward him, one of whom was saying to the other, "But for that you really need balls. . . ."

God! thought Kovalić, compulsively eyeing the man's trousers. Can't life be cruel!

Queer! the cocky trousers sneered, brushing past him.

I must, I really must do something, thought Kovalić, sinking even deeper into despair. And then he had a lifesaver of a thought . . . Lidija! Of course! He'd go and see Lidija.

III

YOU NEVER KNOW what's going to happen next, thought Vinko K., the young, good-looking policeman, as he jaywalked across the square. Pausing in front of a shop window, he saw the outline of his lean figure and the shadow of the truncheon dangling at his side. Through the glass he saw a young woman with dark, shining eyes making hot dogs. First she pierced one half of a long roll with a heated metal stake and twisted it several times; then she poured some mustard into the hollow and stuffed a pink hot dog into it. Vinko K. was much taken with her dexterity. He went in and pretended to be waiting his turn, while in fact he was watching the girl's pudgy hands and absentmindedly twirling his billy.

"Next!" her voice rang out.

"Me? Oh, then I might as well have one," said a flustered Vinko K., "as long as . . ."

"Twenty!" her voice rang out like a cash register.

Vinko K. moved over to the side. He subjected the bun to a close inspection: it contained a fresh hot dog. Meanwhile, two more girls had come out of a small door, and soon all three were busy piercing rolls and filling them with mustard and hot dogs.

Vinko K. finished off his hot dog with obvious relish and then walked over to the girls.

"Care to take a little break, girls?" he said in a low voice. "Can we move over here?" he added, even more softly. "Yes, this is fine. . . ."

Squeezed together between cases of beverages and boxes of hot dogs, a sink, a bin, and a broom, Vinko K. and the waitresses could scarcely breathe.

"I want you to show me all the hot dogs you have on the premises," said a calm Vinko K.

The girl opened all the hot dog boxes without a murmur. The hot dogs were neatly packed in cellophane wrappers.

"Hm!" said Vinko K. "Tell me, are they all vacuum-packed?"

"Oh, yes!" all three voices rang out as a team. "They're all vacuum-packed!"

A long, uncomfortable silence ensued. Vinko K. was thinking. You never knew what would happen next in his line. You could never tell what human nature had in store.

Meanwhile the girls just stood there, huddled together like hot dogs in a cellophane wrapper. All at once Vinko K.'s fingers broke into a resolute riff on one of the cardboard boxes and, taking a deep breath, he said, as if giving a password, "Fellatio?"

"Aaaaah?!" the girls replied, shaking their heads, and though they did not seem to have understood the question they kept up a soft titter.

"Never heard of it?" asked Vinko K.

"Teehee! Teehee! Teehee!" they tittered on.

"Slurp, slurp?" Vinko K. tried, sounding them out as best he could.

"Teehee! Teehee! Teehee!" they laughed, pleasantly, like the Chinese.

Vinko K. was momentarily nonplussed. He thought of using another word with the same meaning, but it was so rude he decided against it.

"Hm!" he said instead.

"Hm!" said the girls, rolling their eyes and bobbing their heads.

Vinko K. realized his case was lost. He sighed. The girls sighed compassionately back.

By this time there was quite a crowd waiting for hot dogs. Vinko K. went outside. He stole one last glance at the first girl. She glanced back, tittered, and licked her lips. Vinko K. smiled and unconsciously bobbed his billy. She, too, smiled and vaguely nodded. Then she took a roll and resolutely rammed it onto the metal stake.

But at this point everything becomes so enveloped in mist again that we cannot tell what happened next.

I V

"*ENTREZ!*" Lidija called out unaffectedly, and Kovalić collapsed into her enormous, commodious armchair with a sigh of relief.

Lidija was Kovalić's best friend; she was completely, unhesitatingly devoted to him. Oh, he went to bed with her all right, but out of friendship; she went to bed with *him* out of friendship too. They didn't do it often, but they had stuck with it for ages—ten years by now. Kovalić knew everything there was to know about Lidija; Lidija knew everything there was to know about Kovalić. And they were never jealous. But Kovalić the writer—much as he valued sincerity in life and prose—refused to admit to himself that he had once seen their kind of relationship in a film and found it highly appealing, an example (or so he thought) of a new, more humane type of rapport between a man and a woman. It was in the name of this ideal that he gave his all to her in bed even when he was not particularly up to it.

They had not seen each other for quite some time, and Lidija started in blithely about all the things that had happened since their last meeting. She had a tendency to end each sentence with a puff, as if what she had just produced was less a sentence than a hot potato.

Lidija had soon trotted out the relevant items from the pantry of her daily life, and following a short silence—and a silent signal they had hit upon long before—the two of them began to undress.

"Christ!" cried Lidija, who in other circumstances was a translator to and from the French.

"Yesterday . . . " said Kovalić, crestfallen, apologetic. "Completely disappeared . . . "

For a while Lidija simply stood there, staring wide-eyed at Kovalić's empty space; then she assumed a serious and energetic expression, went over to her bookcase, and took down the encyclopedia.

"Why bother?" asked Kovalić as she riffled the pages. "Castration, castration complex, coital trophy—it's all beside the point! It's just disappeared, understand? Dis-appeared!"

"Bon Dieu de Bon Dieu!" Lidija muttered. "And what are you going to do now?"

"I don't know," Kovalić whimpered.

"Who were you with last?"

"Girl named Maja . . . But that's every bit as much beside the point."

"Just wondering," said Lidija, and said no more.

As a literary person in her own right, Lidija had often cheered Kovalić up and on with her gift for the apt image. But now her sugar-sweet sugar beet, her pickle in the middle, her poor withered mushroom, her very own Tom Thumb, her fig behind the leaf, her tingaling dingaling, her Jack-in-the-box had given way to—a blank space!

All of a sudden Lidija had a divine inspiration. She threw herself on Kovalić and for all the insulted, humiliated, oppressed, for all the ugly, impotent, and sterile, for all the poor in body, hunched in back, and ill in health—for every last one she gave him her tenderest treatment, polishing, honing him like a recalcitrant translation, fondling, caressing, her tongue as adroit as a keypunch, kneading his skin with her long, skillful fingers, moving lower and lower, seeking out her Jack's mislaid cudgel, picking and pecking at the empty space, fully expecting the firm little rod to pop out and give her cheek a love tap. Kovalić was a bit stunned by Lidija's abrupt show of passion, and even after he began to feel signs of arousal he remained prostrate, keeping close tabs on the pulsations within as they proceeded from pitapat to rat-tat-tat to boomety-boom, waiting for his Jack to jump, his rubber-gloved Tom to thump, he didn't care who, as long as he came out into the open!

Kovalić held his breath. He felt the blank space ticking off the seconds like an infernal machine; felt it about to erupt like a geyser, a volcano, an oil well; felt himself swelling like soaked peas, like a tulip bulb, like a cocoon; felt it coming, any time now, any second now, any—pow! boo-oo-oom! cra-a-a-sh-sh-sh!

Moaning with pleasure, Kovalić climaxed, climaxed to his

great surprise—in the big toe of his left foot!

Utterly shaken, Kovalić gave Lidija a slight shove and peered down at his foot. Then, still refusing to believe that what happened had happened, he fingered the toe. It gave him a combination of pleasure and mild pain—and just sat there, potatolike, indifferent. Kovalić stared at it, mildly offended by its lack of response.

"Idiot!" said Lidija with a French intonation, and stood up, stalked out, and slammed the door.

Kovalić stretched. The smooth space was still hideously smooth. He wiggled his left toe, then his right. The left one struck him as perceptibly fatter and longer.

It did happen, thought Kovalić. There's no doubt about it. It actually happened. Suddenly he felt grateful to Lidija. The only thing was, did he really climax in his toe or was his mind playing tricks on him? Kovalić leaned over and felt the toe again, then went back to the smooth space, and finally, heaving a worried sigh, lit a cigarette.

"Anyone for a nice homemade sausage?" asked a conciliatory Lidija, peeking in from the kitchen.

Kovalić felt all the air go out of him: Lidija's proposition was like a blow to the solar plexus; it turned him into the butt of a dirty joke.

Kovalić was especially sensitive to clichés; he avoided them in both literature and life. And now he was terribly upset. By some absurd concatenation of events his life had assumed the contours of a well-established genre (a joke of which he was the punch line). How could life, which he had always thought of as vast—no, boundless—how could life give in to the laws of a genre? And with nary a deviation! Kovalić was so distressed he felt tears welling in his eyes. How he loved—literature! It was so much better, more humane, less predictable, more fanciful. In a well-written story Lidija would have offered him nothing less than a veal cutlet; in the low genre of life, Lidija, she gives him—a sausage!

Suddenly Kovalić felt hungry.

V

ON SATURDAY, the seventh of April, Nada Matić awoke from a nightmare she had had for many nights. She would dream she was working in her office at Plastic Surgery. It was crammed with anatomical sketches, plaster molds, and plastic models – all of "hot dogs" of the most varied dimensions. Suddenly, in trooped a band of students who tore them all to pieces, laughing and pointing at her all the while. Nada thought she would die of shame, and to make matters worse she felt something sprouting on her nose – an honest-to-goodness sausage! At that point the scene would shift to the operating room, where she – Nada – and Dr. Waldinger were performing a complex procedure. But there was a round hole in the white sheet covering the patient, and she couldn't stop staring through it at his hideous smooth space. Then the scene would shift again, and she and Otto Waldinger were in a field pulling out a gigantic beet. She was holding Otto around the waist when suddenly she was attacked by a gigantic mouse! She could feel its claws on her thighs.

Nada Matić was drinking her morning coffee, smoking a cigarette, and leafing through the evening paper. She would seem to have acquired the fine habit of perusing the Saturday classifieds. Suddenly an item in the "Lost and Found" column caught her eye. She did a double take, stunned by a wild but logical thought: If someone were to lose something like that, it would only be natural for him to try to find it!

> On the twenty-fifth of March, I left a collapsible umbrella in
> the Skyscraper Cafeteria. Would the finder please return it.
> No questions asked. Phone xyz and ask for Milan.

Nada jumped out of her seat. The ad was perfectly clear! The umbrella was obviously a respectable substitution for *that*. The fact that it was collapsible made the whole thing absolutely unambiguous!

Nada grabbed the telephone and dialed the number. The

conversation was to the point: That's right. Five o'clock. See you there. Good-bye.

At five o'clock that afternoon Nada Matić rang the doorbell of a Dalmatinska Street apartment. A dark man of about thirty opened the door.

He could well be the one, thought Nada and said, "Hello, my name is Nada Matić."

"And mine is Milan Miško. Come in."

"Are you the one who lost his umbrella?"

"That's right."

"At the cafeteria?"

"The Skyscraper."

"Collapsible?"

"Yes, yes," said Milan Miško, the owner of the lost umbrella, in an amiable voice. "Do come in." Nada went in.

They sat down. The owner of the collapsible umbrella brought out a bottle of wine and two glasses.

"So, you're the one who lost it," Nada said tellingly and took a sip of the wine.

"That's right."

"God, how thick can he be?" thought Nada, beginning to feel annoyed. She took a long look at *that* place, but could make nothing out. She had to put it into words! But how?

"It must have been hard for you . . ." she said, trying a more direct approach.

"With all the spring showers, you mean? I'd have picked up another one, but you do get attached to your own . . ."

"What was it like? Your umbrella, I mean," she asked its owner nonchalantly.

"Oh, nothing special. . . . You mean, what color, how long?"

"Yes," said Nada, swallowing hard, "how long . . . ?"

"Oh, standard size," he said, as calm as could be. "You know — collapsible." And he looked over at Nada serenely. "The kind that goes in and out."

Now there could be no doubt. Nada resolved to take the plunge and call a spade a spade, even if it meant humiliating herself. After all, she had played her own bitter part in the affair. So she took the sort of deep breath she would have taken before a dive, half-shut her eyes, stretched out her arms in a sleepwalker's pose, and—jumped! I'm wrong, she thought as she flew mentally through the air, terribly, shamefully wrong. But it was too late to retreat.

And though at this point everything becomes enveloped in mist again, we can guess exactly what happened.

V I

THE WAITRESS switched off the light and shut the door after the other girls. For some reason she didn't feel like going with them. She sat down for a short rest and looked through the window at the passersby and the brand names atop the buildings. As she bent over to take off the slippers she wore at work, her hand happened to graze her knee. She let her hand rest on the knee and froze in that position as if listening for something. Then, heaven knows why, she thought of the dark handsome guy who'd left his umbrella in the cafeteria a week or so before and that young, good-looking policeman with the funny, kinky questions—both of them so attractive and somehow connected. . . . Or had she noticed them and had they registered with her mainly because they had—of that she was sure—noticed *her?*

Sheltered by the darkness, the cartons, and the glass, the girl sat with her legs slightly parted, relaxed, peering out of the window at the passersby, when suddenly her hands reached by themselves for one of the cardboard boxes, pulled out a few packages of hot dogs, and started tugging feverishly at the cellophane wrappers. God, what was she doing? What was she doing? What if somebody saw her? Nobody saw her.

She slowly brought a raw hot dog to her lips and quickly stuffed it into her mouth. The hot dog slid down her throat, leaving practically no taste behind. She grabbed a second and quickly chewed it up. Then a third, a fourth, a fifth . . .

There in the heart of the city, enslaved by the darkness, the cartons, and the glass, sat a waitress with her legs slightly parted and her dark, shining eyes peering out at the pass- ersby while she greedily downed hot dog after hot dog. At one point the image of a gigantic, ravenous female mouse flashed through her mind, but she immediately forgot it. She was following the movements of her jaws and listening in on her gullet.

VII

IN THE afternoon of the seventh of April there was a nervous ring at Kovalić's door. Kovalić was a bit taken aback to see a young, good-looking policeman carrying an unusual-looking bundle.

"Are you Mato Kovalić the writer? Or, rather, the novelist and short story writer?"

"I am," said Kovalić with a tremor in his voice.

"Well, this is yours. Sign here."

"But . . ." Kovalić muttered.

"Good-bye," said the policeman and, with a knowing wink, added, "and good luck!"

"But officer . . . !" Kovalić cried out. It was too late. The po- liceman had disappeared into the elevator.

Kovalić unwrapped the bundle with trembling hands. Out of the paper fell a bottle filled with a clear liquid, and floating in that liquid was his very own . . . ! Unbelievable! Kovalić was beside himself. For several moments he stood stock-still; then he went back and cautiously removed the object from the bottle and started inspecting it.

That's it, all right – the real thing! Kovalić thought aloud. He'd have recognized it anywhere! And he jumped for joy – though carefully grasping it in his hands.

Since, however, it is a well-known fact that nothing on this

earth lasts for very long, our hero suddenly frowned. He had
had a terrifying thought. What if it wouldn't go back on?

With indescribable terror in his heart Kovalić walked over
to the mirror. His hands were trembling. He carefully returned the object to its former place. Panic! It refused to
stick! He brought it up to his lips, warmed it with his breath,
and tried again. No luck!

"Come on, damn you!" Kovalić grumbled. "Stick! Stick, you
stupid fool!" But the object fell to the floor with a strange,
dull, corklike thud. "Why won't it take?" Kovalić wondered
nervously. And though he tried again and again, his efforts
were in vain.

Crushed, Kovalić was left holding his own, his very own
and now very useless part. And much as Kovalić stared at it, it
clearly remained indifferent to his despair and lay there in his
hand like a dead fish.

"Ba-a-a-a-astard!" Kovalić screamed in a bloodcurdling
voice and flung the object into a corner and himself onto his
bed. "No, I'm not dreaming," Kovalić whispered into his pillow. "This can't be a dream. This is madness, lunacy . . ." And
with that he fell asleep.

VIII

LIDIJA TYPED out the word *maladie* and paused. She was still on
page one. The translation of the report was due on Monday
morning at the Department of Veterinary Medicine.

She stood up, stretched, and switched on the light. She
glanced out of the window. It was still day, but the street was
gray and empty and smooth from the rain.

Lidija went into the kitchen and opened the refrigerator
door out of habit. She peered in without interest and
slammed it shut.

Then she went into the bathroom, turned on the tap, and
put her wrist under a jet of cold water. It felt good. She

glanced up at the mirror. All at once she felt like licking it. She moved in close to its smooth surface. Her face with tongue hanging out flashed into sight. She drew back slowly. A smooth and empty gesture. Like her life. "Smooth, empty, empty, smooth..." she murmured on her way back to the kitchen.

On the kitchen table Lidija noticed a few dried-out bits of bread. She touched them. She liked the way dry crumbs pricked the pulp of her fingers. She moistened her finger with saliva, gathered up the crumbs, and went into the combined bedroom and living room. Again she looked out at the street, preoccupied, nibbling on the crumbs from her finger and on the finger itself. The street was empty.

And then she noticed a young, good-looking policeman. He had a limber way about him and was crossing the smooth street, or so it seemed to Lidija, as if it were water. Suddenly she opened the window, breathed deeply, pursed her lips for a whistle, and stopped. What was she doing, for heaven's sake? What had gotten into her?

The policeman looked up. In a well-lit window he saw an unusual-looking young woman standing stock-still and staring at him. His glance came to rest on her full, slightly parted lips. He noticed a crumb on the lower one. Or was he just imagining it? Suddenly he had a desire to remove that real or imagined crumb with his own lips.

"What if she really..." flashed through his mind as he noiselessly slipped into the main door. But what happened next we really have no idea.

IX

KOVALIĆ AWOKE with a vague premonition. His head felt fuzzy, his body leaden. He lay completely motionless for a while when all at once he felt an odd throbbing sensation. He tore off the blanket, and lo and behold! — *it* was back in place.

Kovalić couldn't believe his eyes. He reached down and fingered it – yes, it was his, all right! He gave it a tug just to make sure – yes, it popped out of his hand, straight, taut, elastic. Kovalić jumped for joy and leapt out of bed, rushing over to the mirror for a look. No doubt about it: there it stood, rosy, shiny, and erect – and just where it had been before. Kovalić cast a worried glance at the bottle. He saw a little black catfish swimming about as merrily as you please. Intent on engineering clever turns within its narrow confines, it paid him no heed.

"Oh!" Kovalić cried out in amazement.

Then he looked back down below. Situation normal: stiff and erect! Trembling with excitement, Kovalić raced to the phone.

At this point, however, the events are temporarily misted over by censorship, and the reader will have to deduce what happened from the following lines.

Exhausted and depressed, her eyes circled in black, her mouth dry, Maja the invoice clerk lay on her back apathetically staring at that horrid black fish. It was making its two-thousand-one-hundred-and-fifty-first turn in the bottle. At last she picked herself up slowly and started gathering her clothes the way an animal licks its wounds. Suddenly her eyes lit on a slip of paper lying next to her left shoe. The paper contained a list of names in Kovalić's handwriting. *Vesna, Branka, Iris, Goga, Ljerka, Višnja, Maja, Lidija.* All the names but Lidija's (hers too!) had lines through them.

"Monster!" she said in a hoarse, weary voice, and slammed the door.

Kovalić stared apathetically at the lower half of his body. *It* was in place, sprightly, and erect as ever. He flew into a rage, bounded out of bed, bolted to the bottle, and smashed it to the floor. The catfish flipped and flopped for a while, then calmed down. Kovalić gleefully watched the gill contractions subside. But *it* was still erect.

"Down, monster!" Kovalić shouted and gave it a mean

thwack. It swayed and reddened, but then spryly, with a rubberlike elasticity, sprang back into place and raised its head at Kovalić almost sheepishly.

"Off with you, beast!" Kovalić screamed. The object refused to budge.

"I'll strangle you!" Kovalić bellowed. The object stared straight ahead, curtly indifferent.

"I wish you'd never been found," Kovalić whimpered, and flung himself onto the bed in despair. "You bastard, you! I'll get you yet!" And he burst into sobs, mumbling incoherent threats into the pillow. Then, wiping his tears, he raised his fist into the air, heaven knows why, and muttered, "I'll put you through the meat grinder!" And all of a sudden the old butcher's saying went off like an alarm in his brain: *My knives go with me to the grave!*

And the fear and trembling caused by this new piece of data sent Kovalić reeling—and into a dead faint.

X

WELL, dear readers, now you see the sort of thing that happens in our city! And only now, after much reflection, do I realize how much in it is unbelievable—starting from the alienation of the object in question from its rightful owner. Nor is it believable that authors should choose such things to write stories about. First, they are of no use either to literature or to the population, the reading population, and second, they are of no use . . . well, either. And yet, when all is said and done, there is hardly a place you won't find similar incongruities. No, say what you will, these things do happen—rarely, but they do.

For my part, I have a clear conscience. I have stuck to the plot. Had I given myself free rein, well, I don't know where things would have ended! And even so, what happened to Nada Matić? Who is Milan Miško? What became of Vinko K.?

And Lidija and the waitress and the butcher? To say nothing of our hero Mato Kovalić? Is he doomed to spend his life getting it – down?

But I repeat: I have stuck to the plot. Though if the truth be told, I did insert two nightmares from my own childhood, to wit: 1) the sausage dream ("Watch out or a sausage will sprout on your nose," my grandfather used to say when he got angry with me), and 2) the beet dream (I call recall no more terrifying story from my childhood than the one in which a whole family gathered to pull out a big, beautiful, and completely innocent beet!).

In connection with said plot may I suggest the following points as worthy of further consideration:

1. How did the object alienated from its owner, Mato Kovalić, find its way into the bun?

2. How did Vinko K. discover its owner?

3. Miscellaneous.

All that is merely by-the-by, of course, in passing. I myself have no intention of taking things any further. . . . But if you, honored readers, decide to do so, I wish you a merry time of it and a hearty appetite!

Czechoslovakia

LADISLAV DVORAK

Swords 'n' Sabers

Translated by Suzanne Rappaport

Five cars moved the tender...

Wʜᴇɴ ᴅᴏᴄᴛᴏʀ ᴅᴏᴄʜᴛᴇʀ and I weren't just snarling at each other, we would share what was on our minds before the shift began. There in the storeroom behind the metal lockers — before getting into our overalls, which smelled of oil and sweat and over which we put on some ghastly protective coats made of sackcloth — we had enough time to talk about what had happened at our respective places the day before.

At that time, Doctor Dochter was anxious about his wife's treasured watch. He had ascertained that she had not been wearing this family heirloom on her wrist for some time now, and he was trying to find out whether she had sold it or only pawned it. And since he knew what that watch meant to Miladka and how attached she was to it, he was horrified to think of what hot water he must be in with the new order for her to have given it up without telling him.

Well, if things had deteriorated at their place, it was just as bad at ours.

We would offer each other these "tidbits," these daily slivers like candies or cough drops, like medicinal pills to fortify us for the bloodletting, which awaited us each day as we piled up the metal plates.

After Doctor Dochter had finished racking his brain over his wife's watch, it was my turn to serve something up from my current serial concerning the sudden disappearance of the heating pipe hole in my small student room. This, however, was a peppermint candy. When I offered this one to Dochter, I could be certain that all his cares would immediately dissolve, and he would become exhilarated, as if having downed at least two jelly jars of rum. He was in ecstasy, and straightway he fell into a fit of his legendary laughter. He became especially boisterous over the contradictory and awkward position into which the situation was clearly forcing me.

Last summer, during which I spent my vacation as usual at my home in Vysechina, my landlady, Mrs. Piskachek, had had this hole in my room filled in. She had but a single goal in mind: she wanted the back part of her four-room apartment, which she rented to students, declared unfit for habitation. As I found out later, it was our house painter and caretaker, Mr. Brugelhof, who had executed the filling in of the hole.

After returning from my vacation, I of course did not notice the structural changes in my room. I had other things to attend to besides carefully examining my walls. Only out of politeness did I listen to Mrs. Piskachek's complaints about the troublemakers from the housing committee, with whom she had been conducting a savage war for several years and who once more for no reason at all had something against her. And I was only vaguely aware of the existence at the housing office of a thick volume containing demands and counterdemands, complaints and praise, which was marked MPB (Mrs. Piskachek's Boardinghouse) and which was ever expanding. I myself though, with good intentions, must have contributed to it too, and quite recently in fact, when at Mrs. Piskachek's request I had testified before the housing committee that I thoroughly froze in that small room in winter.

"Now you see," she cried out joyfully to the committee, "and you say that I'm a liar! There's no chimney! And there never was one!"

It's true that I used to freeze, but she had never admitted this fact for all these years, until now. Whenever I complained about being cold, she would retort that my room was as warm as a nice bath and that if I was cold there must be something wrong with my blood circulation, and she would always send me to the clinic for a checkup.

In November I got married, and the housing committee designated my room as a family apartment. I now searched all over for the concealed heating pipe hole, tapping the walls with my hammer.

But it was no use. Everything sounded hollow at that time, not only the walls, not only things, but the people too: the decision makers, the teachers, the radio announcers reporting on where Slansky's conspiracy was headquartered. They all sounded hollow. It was clear from people's voices that behind the words, in their chests and hearts, all human feeling for one's neighbor or oneself had become extinct. It was strange and inexplicable that there were so many people who could not hear that desolate, terribly hollow and empty booming.

Doctor Dochter, choking with laughter, declared that old lady Piskachek was a modern genius, demonic perhaps, but all the more in keeping with our contemporary way of life. So the crux of the matter was that I would now have to retract my assertion to the committee about freezing in my room—to the contrary, I must claim that the heat in my room is stifling—and sue both Piskachek and the sly caretaker. Otherwise I would not find the opening for the heating pipe and would most certainly freeze to death together with my wife and child. He would add philosophically that though in my case this only amounted to a silly hole in the wall and, to put it bluntly, the death of three rather unimportant people, still it throws a penetratingly sharp light on our everyday life, which has been reduced to basic survival, and testifies to the hollowness of people's characters today, just as powerfully as Marie Majerova's novel *The Siren** did yesterday.

Having changed into our dirty, smelly rags, the mere sight of each other filled us with sorrow and bitterness. Consequently, we normally finished the ordeal of changing with a round of drinks. This was done partly to improve the bitter taste in our mouths from eating many pralines and peppermint candies on an empty stomach, partly to make our eyes grow misty, and to help us look at each other more mercifully than sober people usually do.

The bloodletting, which Dochter was determined should be ended once and for all, normally took place soon after the steam engine had managed to push the cars with their thrice-accursed metal plates from the freight station to the ramp of our factory. The engine, which, to use a metaphor from the world of livestock, butted them in our direction, was clearly in an unfavorable position vis-à-vis the freight cars. The herd of cars returned each of its butts with a furious counterattack. It went all right when the cars were moving down the hill from the railroad station, but it got worse when they were to be butted up from the valley to the ramp of our factory.

"A metal circus," said Doctor Dochter, as he glanced at the caterpillar of cars overloaded with metal plates. This remark was laced with the same mockery and scorn with which the Czechs and Poles used to yell at the German armored cars entering their territories. And the magic formula had as much effect now as it did then: the apparition did not go away, the cars did not disappear; on the contrary, they were closing in.

At that time Doctor Dochter had a large, lilac-blue bump on his forehead, and his whole face was mangled, as if he had collided with an entire collection of those cars, from which we daily unloaded the metal plates.

But it couldn't have happened to him at work, or I'd have known about it. For we constituted an inseparable pair, and

The Siren (1935) deals with life in a coal mining town.

one of us could not get hurt without the other's knowing about it.

One fine day he simply appeared at work with it, jutting out from his forehead like a tennis ball and surrounded by a rainbow of bruises and bloody scars. I had been waiting the whole day for an explanation, but in vain. He acted as if it was not there at all. Even in the shower at the end of the day, when he couldn't help but be reminded of it, he said nothing. So I also pretended not to see the bump, which was difficult. If only it would disappear if I tried not to look at it! But, on the contrary, and perhaps on account of my efforts, it grew and turned purple! It seemed as if it would rise up between Doctor Dochter and me like a huge, insurmountable mountain. The fact that there had been no secrets between us until now made me even more upset.

When that hellish steam engine had finally managed to push the freight cars to our factory, a black man by the name of Hajredin, who had formerly been a top salesman in coffee beans, walked out unsteadily onto the ramp. He was an almost seven-foot giant, and in his hands the twenty-pound pole looked like a toothpick. He rolled his eyes, as all blacks do, and flashed his dazzlingly white teeth, like those of a real cannibal. Behind him was his co-worker, skinny little Doctor Kraus, who had once been a lecturer on Shakespeare at Charles University. Kraus was also carrying a twenty-pound pole. He staggered from the warehouse to the edge of the ramp, and he had to rest and catch his breath at every step, standing the pole between the planks on the ramp and leaning on it as if it were a crutch or the mace of a university professor. Then all you needed was to hang the university insignia around his neck and intone "Long live the groves of academe, long live the professors" to make the picture complete. Together the two looked like David and Goliath or rather, in those coats of theirs, like Laurel and Hardy.

One could not watch these two former pillars of rotten bourgeois society unload the metal plates without breaking into fits of laughter. Opinions differed regarding which one was clumsier. Some thought the profiteer Hajredin, a representative of the extortionate wing of the bourgeoisie, was more awkward; while others believed that the lecturer Kraus, a representative of the even more treacherous wing, far outdid Hajredin in clumsiness.

Thinking of Kraus, Doctor Dochter would often say, "All that we go through on this ramp could be easily made into an authentic Shakespearean play. It has all the requisite magnificence and drama, yet as it is, our tragedy is quite different. To begin with, a Shakespearean hero would have a servant to carry such heavy things as the pole. Indeed, would Lecturer Kraus look as ridiculous on the ramp if the pole was carried by an armor-bearer? He would not. No, no, our tragedy is different, quite different!"

Of course, Doctor Dochter and I speculated about why it was necessary to select precisely such unqualified people as ourselves for such roles. Doctor Dochter thought that this made sense, and he supported his view by telling me about his uncle, a forester, who in 1938 escaped the Germans by going to Brazil. On returning home after the war, he went to work as an administrator in the Shumava forest region. In the course of his job he learned that bark beetles were destroying the forest. In order to pursue the matter further, he conferred with county officials and then, frustrated by the response, he went on to the regional capital. Having similar luck, he left for Prague. Well, he was an expert, a nitpicker. But in Prague a deputy to the minister of forests, waters, and hillsides finally told him: "Comrade, you must have really taken leave of your senses. You have been talking to me for a whole hour about a two-hundred-and-fifty-acre forest somewhere in the Shumava region being turned into a glade, as if you did not know that we would like to turn the whole country into such a glade."

And so Doctor Dochter's uncle is now playing havoc with the forests. He is a woodcutter and clears the forests, just as the university students, lecturers, and professors unload metal plates, and with equal finesse.

Although these two, the nouveau-riche coffee merchant, Hajredin, and the bamboozler of university students, Lecturer Kraus, worked together like genuine laborers ("Heave ho, m-o-o-ve it, shit, m-o-o-ve it"), every time one of them would pull, the other one would let go, dropping the plate through the yard-wide space between the freight car and the ramp. The manager of the warehouse would then directly enter it into the column for waste instead of for incoming material. As it fell the metal plate sounded like a gong, and it ended up on the railroad tracks with one or both pairs of greasy mittens, sometimes including one of the two protagonists of our tragedy, if he did not manage to tear off his mittens in time. And thus one day the ambulance would leave with the coffee king, and another day with the lecturer, and this happened again and again.

But best of all was when it left with both of them. According to the ambulance drivers, they would mercilessly abuse each other for the whole trip, tearing at each other's bandages and trying to strangle each other.

But we know them as quite different men! For instance, while taking their showers they would in a brotherly manner (and how carefully!) pinch out the stitches from each other's skin. This would leave lighter, pinkish spots on the African's body after the wounds healed. They used to call them hickeys.

"If you go on like this, blackamoor," the lecturer chuckled, "your skin may completely clear up."

Doctor Dochter, who liked to explain one incomprehensible event by another similarly incomprehensible one, compared the behavior of friends who had been cut and slashed by the metal plates to that of postnatal mothers who had been subjected to forceps and Caesarean sections. Supposedly, one could not imagine how vicious they could be with their nearest and, only yesterday, dearest lovers and husbands.

"I'm telling you," he said, drawing close to me and in a beseeching tone, "if your old lady or a girlfriend you have on the side gives birth, don't try to make it with her during the postnatal period!"

We were in the showers at the time, washing with the smelly paste and paddling about in our birthday suits, which must have been what inspired Doctor Dochter to recall this heartrending episode from his life, and he added in a whisper and somehow very strangely and gently: "Send grandma to the hospital with flowers and a box of chocolates, but don't go there yourself! Wait until your dear ones forget the pain; then you'll be like turtledoves again, like Hajredin and Kraus over there."

Right after we returned from the shower to the cloakroom, Doctor Dochter mixed two jelly jars of his favorite drink, which since time immemorial has been called "Swords 'n' Sabers."

This truly intoxicating beverage, loved and cursed, praised and blamed, comes from the blending of cherry brandy and rum. I had the best ones I remember with Doctor Dochter in the little suburban taverns in Smichov, and I imagine that that is where it originated. But we also found it in all the various Prague neighborhoods, everywhere the wind had swept us. In doing the rounds we made a discovery, and it might well be the discovery of our age for Czech philology, namely that the Vltava River forms a kind of borderline or, as linguists would call it, an isogloss for two different names for our delightfully intoxicating beverage. The name "Swords 'n' Sabers" is established, as Doctor Dochter and I verified and repeatedly tested, on the whole left bank of the Vltava. Koshirzhe is its epicenter and it spreads out through Brzhevnov, Vokovitse, Dejvitse, and Podbaba far inland to Hradets on the left side of the river and venerable Budech of Ludmila and Vaclav, which precisely traces the whole territory originally inhabited by the Czech tribe. You can simply enter any tavern in this area and simply say, "Swords." Yet on the opposite bank of the Vltava, among the denizens of Slavnik or Vrshovitse, you can get it only by using the name "Half-Ox, Half-Bee."

"Swords 'n' Sabers" or "Half-Ox, Half-Bee" is, in addition, the drink of truth. Only when downing his second glass did Doctor Dochter confess to me how he had gotten that lilac-blue bump on his forehead. He had gone to visit his wife, his beloved Miladka, in the maternity ward with some flowers in his hand and a can of orange juice in a string bag. As soon as he fished the can out of the bag and placed it on the bedside table, Miladka whacked him in the head with it.

"She immediately apologized and told me that she didn't mean it and that her fellow sufferers had put her up to it, but how could anything she say help after that?"

He clinked his glass against mine, which was still full, and I had to down it like he did and start mixing another round. It was clear to me that he needed to get it out of his system.

"It was a terrible blow, you know, not so much the fact that she hit me, but rather why she hit me. Was it me who thought up this way of entering the world? And those other postnatal women, those new mothers on the beds around her, how they carried on. They would have torn me to pieces if the nurse had not come in. She led me out and kept asking me how I felt. She must have thought that I had suffered a concussion. I felt sick all right, but not because of my head."

As the alcohol level in his blood rose, Doctor Dochter's confession became a lament. He needed to talk it out, and I knew that no comforting words would help here, nor were they expected. He needed a silent confessor, to whom he could pour out his heart. And I became that silent confessor. He began his confession in a low voice, as befits a true confession, but gradually he got carried away. Right behind our lockers, that other pair from the heave-ho squad—the wholesale coffee merchant, Omar Hajredin, and the lecturer Kraus—were changing. They must have overheard something about wounds, and since wounds—whether it was a matter of cuts, gashes, or lacerations—were their specialty and they couldn't have mistaken the sound of clinking glasses, they moved over to our area both still in their birthday suits. They then swiveled around like two elderly recruits before a draft board, so that we could examine all the places where they had been cut. Scabs, scratches, and bumps covered both their bodies. There were wounds that were already healed as well as fresh wounds still wet with blood.

"A great *amour*," the good-natured Hajredin grinned at Doctor Dochter, "*c'est toujours* a great *douleur*." And Lecturer Kraus began discoursing about Shakespeare–Ophelia, Romeo, and Juliet–pointing out that pain and love are one.

But Doctor Dochter was not looking for consolation, as I have already mentioned.

"First get dressed, you damned Sodomites," he snarled, "or you won't get a single drop."

Implying or rather telling Doctor Dochter that his bump was nothing compared to their own wounds, incurred for no reason whatsoever while stacking metal plates, would lead to no good. Besides which, Doctor Dochter was in no mood for Hajredin and Kraus and had not reckoned on their being in the cloakroom at this time. The ambulance had usually taken them away before the shift was over. That Hajredin and Kraus's performance on the ramp today had not ended in the spilling of blood was a rare exception.

"And why aren't you in the ambulance?" Doctor Dochter asked.

"*Demain*," said Hajredin in his deep bass.

"Morning," said our Shakespeareolog.

Well, this seemed to pacify Doctor Dochter somewhat, and he poured them drinks.

The following day an atmosphere of immense excitement and expectation descended upon the whole factory again, as soon as the caterpillar of freight cars appeared below the ramp. The warehouse manager alerted the ambulance as soon as he saw the caterpillar, which triggered the transmission through the grapevine telegraph–consisting of metal-shavings sweepers, snack distributors, departmental clerks, planners, and even machines—of the following four words: the rodeo is beginning.

Suddenly, all the machines were idling. The lathes were humming, but their knives were cutting invisible chips from an invisible piece of wood held fast by clamps, and the milling machines and conveyor belts created imaginary parts from transparent material, perhaps from antimatter. The blows of the hammers shook the empty halls with a rumbling noise. It was like a scene from the folktale in which an ax hanging from a tree in the forest is being tugged by the wind.

The lathe and milling machine operators, the toolmakers, the maintenance people, and all the apprentices had long since taken up their usual places around the ramp. Fat women crane operators and the even fatter women electric-cart drivers were for some reason assigned to the first rows, perhaps as a gesture to their femininity, which was otherwise frowned upon by their foremen, due to their contact with men on the job. If one of them came to work wearing a pair of rather tight-fitting pants, ones that sharply defined the two halves of her behind, she was immediately forced to take them off and put on a baggy pair. Right behind them were the planners in their spotless white coats, and behind them the typists, who were immediately recognizable from their somewhat rounded backs. And it went on and on, row upon row, filling the sold-out theater.

And anyone who had not got the message that the rodeo was beginning from the grapevine telegraph found out from the deafening blows made by the pole on the sliding door of the warehouse. It was Hajredin himself, the main actor and male lead. These blows sounded, at least to me, like the beginning of Beethoven's Ninth Symphony. And if for the public the blows meant something like the first call at the theater, signaling them to take their seats and compose themselves for the artistic event, for us, Doctor Dochter and me, it was the cue to lean against the sliding panels of the warehouse door and open the curtain before these two public favorites.

Lecturer Kraus appeared, and amidst laughter and cheering he dragged his pole. His face was livid, and looking completely exhausted he thrust the pole between the planks of the ramp with each step and then leaned against it deadbeat, like a clown or mime. His eyes narrowed to a slit, looking, begging, for someone to take this cross from him. And now came the moment for the doctor's walk-on part. He himself called his act, which lasted only a second, playing the bailiff. Using a pole, he handed up to Lecturer Kraus a glass of our blended drink. This was no easy trick, and Doctor Dochter looked great. He looked just like Pilate's bailiff when he lifted his lance with the sponge soaked in vinegar and gall to the tortured lips of Christ.

"Swords-s – 'n' Sabers-s," roared the public, composed obviously of members of the Czech tribe.

"Half-Ox-x – Half-Bee-ee," boisterously yelled the Slavnikovci and Vrshovitsi, who at this time had not been completely suppressed. And steins filled with the same golden liquid were raised above their heads to propose a toast. And I, huddled against the warehouse door, suddenly had the feeling that somehow, without realizing it, we were reenacting the medieval passion plays about the crucifixion and martyrdom of Christ.

Then came the moment when the two leading actors, Hajredin on one side of the car and Lecturer Kraus on the other, pounded on the steel lock. It would certainly have been easier to lift the catch of the lock by hand, but then the important sound effects would have been lost.

And then came the real performance, that is, the somersaults, headsprings, handsprings, and other acrobatics in order to avoid the pole, when it would accidentally get between the legs of one or the other, or to avoid tripping on their dangling coattails.

"Let's go! Let's go!" roared the impatient public, wanting to keep the overture short and get something more titillating and spicy under way, something like a little jet of spurting blood.

"Stab him, cut him, let's see some blood flow," chanted the metal workers in unison.

But all in vain. Hajredin and Kraus would never start until the ambulance and medics arrived. From the ramp they would both furtively keep an eye out for it, and in the meantime Lecturer Kraus would appease these impatient people by improvising.

Though he performed alone, he successfully played the role of two stretcher-bearers: the pole served as a stretcher, on which he first carried himself out and then returned for Hajredin, in this way intimating to the public that both of them would be taken to the hospital, thereby assuring the crowd that blood would flow like a river when the time came.

It was Hajredin who first caught sight of the medics approaching, and he lifted the pole above his head as a signal to Lecturer Kraus. I couldn't watch and shut my eyes. When I opened them, both Hajredin and Kraus were writhing in a freight car among blood-stained metal plates.

"Enough! That's enough already! Stop it!" screamed Doctor Dochter next to me. He yelled like an enraged director, whose actors had ruined a key scene by playing it without any feeling. He grabbed me by the hand and dragged me down to the railroad tracks, ordering me to jump onto the last car. He then disengaged the brakes and jumped up after me. Solemnly and triumphantly, the cars slowly began to move before the hundreds of astonished spectators, wide-eyed at this new, unexpected element, ingeniously introduced into our tragedy by Doctor Dochter. It was not Mrs. Piskachek but him whom I now saw as a genius—a bright, shining genius. From that moment on our little vale of tears was suffused with light.

"Five cars moved the tender . . ." intoned the ancient quavering voice of an old lady called Auntie, who distributed snacks at the factory. The janitor, called Ferda the Swab, joined her with his drunken voice. And like two old-timers who would lead the singing in a procession of pilgrims they roused the exhilarated crowds to sing.

The medics ran after us with stretchers, their white coats flapping around them like angels' wings. Hajredin and Kraus sucked the blood out of each other's wounds and spat it at them.

Our little train picked up speed, and as it rolled down into a little valley it snorted like a real train with a locomotive. Luckily or unluckily, after passing through the valley the rails began to curve up a hillside. Puffing halfway up, our little train paused for a moment and then rolled back down into the valley and nearly back up the ramp. This time the female crane operators and electric cart drivers jumped on board; after all, they well knew the value of a nice ride. During the next shuttle stop near the ramp even the bashful planners in their spotless white coats let themselves be persuaded to ride with us, and then the typists and finally, of all people, even the personnel managers joined us.

The comrade director, not knowing how else to stop our universally popular swinging, ordered that the rails and ties under the frolicking cars be torn up. But there was no one to execute it for him, since the typists as well as his right-hand man were all swinging together with us.

And we would be rocking with Doctor Dochter in that valley to this day if toward evening we had not spotted our nearest and dearest in front of the security station. Doctor Dochter's Miladka was there as well as my Veronika, both with baby carriages. So we had to stop our frolicking for that day, and we quickly washed and changed. Anyway, now that that *perpetuum mobile* had been set in motion and worked fabulously, there was no stopping it.

"You sure took a long time, are you working overtime again?" Miladka asked us as we walked up to the security station. And she conspicuously drew up her sleeve to look at her watch, at that family heirloom, there unmistakably on her wrist, where it was supposed to be and where it hadn't been for the last several days. Next to Miladka, Veronika smirked: "Imagine that, the heating's already on!"

"Is that so?" I said. "Did Brugelhof's or Piskachek's conscience finally start bothering them?"

Veronika shook her head no and laughed, and pointed at Majka sleeping in the baby carriage.

"You know her, she was making up stories with her tongue on the wall above her little bed and discovered the hole."

"This calls for a celebration," said Doctor Dochter.

We stopped at the first tavern we came to, the Charles the Fourth, and we sat outside in the garden with the baby carriages and ordered four "Swords 'n' Sabers," I mean "Half-Ox, Half-Bees." I'm so happy that I don't even know which side of the Vltava I'm on.

Czechoslovakia

IVAN KLÍMA

Monday Morning: A Black Market Tale

Translated by George Theiner

IT WAS ON a Monday morning that little Freddie landed on my terrace. I was sitting at my desk, writing, when suddenly I thought I could hear someone out in the hall. I could not understand it because my wife and children were long gone and I had locked the front door as usual.

"Anybody there?" I called out.

Silence.

Puzzled, I went out, and in the hall I found Freddie, standing there with a little blood and a rebellious expression on his face.

"How on earth . . . ! How did you get here?"

"I jumped." He was smearing the blood all over his face with his hand, but he didn't cry.

Freddie is five years old and belongs to the people upstairs in the attic apartment, which doesn't really qualify as an apartment at all. He has very dark, Jewish eyes, elongated ears, and the jaw of a pugilist – all inherited from his father. There he stood, still spreading the blood over his face, silently regarding me. Our hall is completely windowless, no way can anyone jump in there.

"You *jumped* in here?"

"I jumped out the window." Freddie has the imagination of a poet and the guile of a professional criminal. Both inherited from his father. When Freddie sees a little girl playing in the sand he pees on her back. Not that his father does *that* anymore. At least, so I supposed.

"You couldn't *possibly* have jumped here from the window."

"I jumped on the terrace."

Well, I thought, he was certainly here and so it stood to reason he had to get in *somehow*. I strode through the bedroom, Freddie at my heels. The terrace was built of concrete. In the middle of it, among all the potted plants and cacti that my wife grows there, I found a brownish pool of blood. Looking up, I saw that the window just below the attic was open.

"You jumped from up there?"

"Yeah."

I couldn't understand how it was he didn't cry, but then maybe he was suffering from shock.

"Where's your daddy?"

"At work."

"And your mother?"

"She's gone shoppin'."

"Do you know where?"

"She locked me in," the boy complained, "and I was scared, so I jumped."

"Listen, Freddie, are you hurt?"

"Yeah."

"Where does it hurt?"

"Everywhere."

"Your head?"

"That too."

Now, needless to say, Freddie was no crybaby. His sadist of a father would wallop him with a leather belt and Freddie would just stand there, glaring back at him. The expression on both their faces was enough to frighten anybody. Freddie was either a brave little stoic, or he simply didn't feel any pain.

One thing I knew for certain—he completely lacked the instinct of self-preservation. The first time they took him to the swimming pool, his father boasted, Freddie just darted away from them as soon as he saw the water and plunged in at the deep end. They managed to drag him out, half drowned. "But, Mr. Vejr," my wife had protested when she heard this, "that's not normal. I think you should consult a psychiatrist."

"My dear lady," Freddie's father, the crook, rejected her advice, "*I* am his psychiatrist."

"Any idea when your mother's going to be back?" I asked the little stoic.

"She won't be back—she doesn't want me anymore."

I was sure he was making it all up. That child didn't know when he was making something up and when, by some accident, he was actually telling the truth (just like his dad), but we couldn't very well hang around waiting for his mother to return. Not to speak of his father.

Quickly, I scribbled a message:

> Mrs. Vejr,
>   Freddie has met with a slight accident, nothing serious. I've taken him to the doctor. I'll explain when I see you.

I signed my name and pushed the piece of paper under their door upstairs.

Our house has a history of misfortunes. The local pharmacist and his wife had it built before the war for themselves and their son. The son was an officer in the gendarmerie, and after the war he fled to America. The parents were punished by being forced to move into the two-roomed attic apartment, which was not officially recognized as such because the ceilings were ten centimeters lower than the state norm prescribed. Despite this, it has always been used to house people. As if to compensate, the bathroom is almost like something out of a stately home, with tiles all the way to that unapproved ceiling. They locked the pharmacist's wife up when she was seventy years old, allegedly for selling Tuzex coupons with which people can buy foreign goods in special Tuzex shops. And of course they confiscated her half of the house. When his wife went to prison, the pharmacist—whose shop had been confiscated a long time before without his having to do anything wrong—took an overdose. He was rushed to the hospital and never came back. The wife did come back, aged seventy-three. She inherited the other half of the house and the attic apartment, to which she brought a young man who played the accordion in a nightclub. People said he was her lover, but I doubt if anyone really knew what their relationship was.

She called him Pepi, cooked his meals, did his washing, and bought his clothes. Pepi was an extremely quiet and polite young man, who always greeted me with the words "Nice to see you, and please remember me to the wife." One day he just vanished. We might have come to the conclusion that someone had murdered him in the wood behind our house, which we all use as a shortcut to the bus stop, if it weren't for the fact that he took his accordion and his suitcase. Six months or so later I received a postcard from him, sent from Denmark. The card showed a restaurant belonging to a Mr. Hansen, and on the other side Pepi had written: "I'm doing fine and am free. Please remember me to all the tenants and to that mean old woman upstairs. Yours respectfully, Pepi."

That mean old woman upstairs lived for another five years, becoming quite senile toward the end. She was convinced everyone was out to rob her, and once a month she would phone the police to say all her savings books had been stolen. They would turn up at the house, find that everything was in order, and drive away again. When I expressed surprise that they fell for her fantasies every time, they explained that they were duty bound to investigate her complaints. What if one day it should turn out to be true?

Sad to say, they were right. But this time she did not have an opportunity to call them. We had no idea she was in there, lying quietly on her bed, until we realized that the house had been quiet for several days. And so this time we called the police ourselves.

They got into the attic by means of a ladder from our terrace. The place stank to high heaven, and there was a large pool of dried blood on the floor. The savings books had disappeared, and the police later discovered that someone had withdrawn twenty thousand from the old lady's several bank accounts.

All the tenants were called in for questioning, about half a year after the murder. I went too, but what could I tell them? Anyway, I had formed the impression that the case didn't particularly interest them. Younger people got themselves knocked off, and the theft of a mere twenty thousand no longer impressed anyone.

"Where are you taking me?" Freddie asked.

"To see a doctor."

"Will he be annoyed?"

"Of course he will." I decided not to try to bamboozle the child. "Why did you do it, anyway?"

"'Cos Mummy locked me in. And I wanted to make me dad mad."

"But you might have been killed!"

"I wish I had."

"You do?"

"Yeah, so they'd lock him up again."

Freddie's father was no stranger to prison. His last sentence expired just a year ago. On paper, he is a male nurse earning less than eighteen thousand. His real *métier* lies elsewhere—he is an expert at handling stolen goods. He is also something of a fantasist and poet, but chiefly a crook. If only things were different in this country, he believes, he would be a prosperous businessman, but he is wrong: he would be a crook whatever the regime.

When he moved into the attic apartment after the pharmacist's wife was murdered four years ago, he came to see me, pretending he wanted to borrow a screwdriver. His dark eyes

rested first on me, then on my books and furniture (he had
no doubt made enquiries about me and come to the erroneous conclusion that I was a potential customer), and I was fas-
cinated by those soft Jewish eyes, huge ears, and pugilsitic
jaw. As might have been expected, he wore his hair brushed
straight back and glistening with hair cream, and he gave off
a strong scent of aftershave. If we still had old maids with
dowries, I wouldn't need three guesses what his vocation
would be.

There followed his introductory monologue, such as no
self-respecting writer would invent and no actor perform, for
in all art worthy of its name, one has to keep within certain
bounds. I was to understand that he had been everywhere,
knew everybody, and could procure or arrange just about
anything. In the concentration camp he had shared a bunk
with Count Schwarzenberg. He was on first-name terms with
the prime minister's brother. He had once met Henry Ford
while visiting Niagara. He was trying to obtain a set of silver
platters for the Belgian delegate at the UN. He had rebuked
the deputy interior minister by saying: "You needn't think
you can pull the wool over *my* eyes, old boy, I can see right
through you!" When he visited Honza Schwarzenberg in Vi-
enna the other day, he was introduced to Otto Hapsburg, a
truly charming gentleman. An agent, of course. All those fine
gentlemen were agents. Agents were in charge the world
over – policemen of the world unite. Nixon and other clowns
like him – he wouldn't even bother to name our ones – were
just their lackeys. One of these days, when he had more time,
he would tell me more about all this.

After ten minutes I was supposed to feel like a country
cousin who has spent his life in total ignorance of the big
world outside. After twenty, I might begin to hope that despite all his knowledge and wide experience he might consider me worthy of notice.

The whole performance lasted a full ninety minutes. Dur-

ing that time he managed to reveal how he earned his
money – he would go to a secondhand shop and buy an ordinary carpet for eight hundred crowns, only of course it was
no ordinary carpet but a rare Persian that had gone unrecog-
nized, and he'd sell it for fifteen thousand – that he was having an expensive residence built in the university quarter, that
he had an absolutely stupid but beautiful wife, two sons from
his first marriage, a daughter from his second, and little Freddie with that absolutely stupid but beautiful third wife, that
his second wife had been a doctor and had once treated the
Shah of Persia, which he found amazing since his second wife,
too, had been basically stupid, like all women, that his eldest
son was such a stubborn bastard that when he had once tied
him to a table leg, the boy bit into the tabletop and hung on,
so that they had to prize him away, and what a job that was,
they had to throw water over him and that two-inch piece of
wood (nobody had wanted to believe this) was bitten right
through in five places. He also told me that he had been
meant to study law, but the war had intervened, that he had
written two books, although he had never had the time to re-
vise his manuscripts, but perhaps he could ask me to look at
them sometime, not that he thought there was much money
in writing (here followed the one and only, brief, pause in his
monologue in case I wished to express an opinion on this),
and he could get me a splendid set of silver cutlery that used
to belong to the Kolowrat family, a pewter teapot, genuine
Slavkov ware, several fine engravings, and a Louis XV com-
mode.

Furthermore, he managed to describe his arrest in the fif-
ties, which he glossed over with somewhat suspicious modesty
so that all I could gather was that he had taken part in some
kind of conspiracy together with Count Schwarzenberg and
the war hero General Kutlvašr, who had flown with the RAF.
I was not at all clear as to the aims of this conspiracy, nor did I
attempt to find out.

I learned later from his wife (who was neither stupid nor beautiful) that he got himself arrested because, while acting as an instructor at a school for waitresses somewhere in the border regions, he had had sex with some of his underage pupils. This figured, except that I couldn't imagine how anyone in her right mind could have ever allowed him into a classroom as a teacher.

At the hospital we were seen by a very strict staff nurse. I explained that Freddie had fallen onto my terrace, or, to be more precise, had flung himself onto it, possibly with suicidal intent.

"Are you his father?"

"No, just a neighbor."

She gave me a look that seemed to imply that in that case my part in the whole affair was highly suspicious.

"Does the child not *have* a father?"

"His father is at work," I explained.

"Can you give me his particulars?"

"I can try."

Between us, Freddie and I supplied most of the information required. Neither of us could give her his date of birth, but I promised to fill this in later. The nurse had an impressive bosom, and Freddie gazed at it with interest. And although I said to myself that I need feel no responsibility for him, I was filled with apprehension at what he might get up to.

Soon we were called into the examining room.

The doctor looked first at Freddie, then at me, finally again at the boy. He regarded Freddie with benevolence, me with a frown. "You the father?"

"No, a neighbor."

My reply quite obviously disgusted him, and he turned to Freddie again.

"So, young man, you jump out of windows, do you?"

"Yeah!" said Freddie proudly.

"And what would you like to be when you grow up?" asked the doctor, tapping the lad's forehead. "A paratrooper?"

"I'm gonna be a policeman," said Freddie.

"A policeman?" said the doctor, surprised. "Why a policeman?"

"So I can arrest me dad," explained Freddie.

The doctor gave me a dirty look, then realized that I was not the father, or if I was, Freddie did not acknowledge me as such, and he ordered Freddie to shut his eyes and walk five paces forward to the window and back again.

"I'd arrest everybody," mused Freddie with his eyes shut. "Grandad, granny, our teacher, *and* the cook at school."

"This child . . . ," began the doctor, giving me a reproachful glance. "Oh! . . . Now, how did you fall, Freddie? On your hands?"

"I first went to the door and when it was shut," related Freddie enthusiastically, "I climbed up on the roof and jumped."

The doctor wrote out instructions for an X-ray and told me to come back when it was done.

We sat together in a gloomy waiting room; next to us a dying old woman huddled in a wheelchair. Freddie looked amused. He wanted to know where the wheelchair had its motor. Then he offered to tell me a story. It was a very confused story, about a kind stepmother and an ugly father who was a merchant and a cannibal. This wicked father-cannibal sent his sons out into the world to bring him the biggest pearl. Those who returned empty-handed he would fry and eat with onions.

I don't know if he invented the story himself or heard it from someone else, but that bit about the sons fried with onions sounded to me like something his perverted father might have dreamed up. But before he could continue, Freddie was summoned inside.

I cannot help thinking that I have been somewhat less than

fair when describing his father. He certainly isn't as accomplished a villain as he would like to be. He lacks some of the attributes of the true professional, which must be counted in his favor, for to be amateurish is also to be human.

About a week after he moved into our house he invited me up to his apartment. He was wearing his Sunday best, his snow-white shirt equipped with a perfectly starched collar.

He had filled those two small attic rooms with old furniture, nothing of any particular value, but most of the stuff dated from the last century, and people pay quite a lot of money for that these days. Just by the door in the hall, hanging in a totally unsuitable place, there was a large canvas with a Cubist painting of a nude.

"This here is a Picasso." He opened fire with his heaviest guns. "Unfortunately, it ain't signed."

"This is no Picasso," I said, stopping him in his tracks. "Never has been and I don't expect it ever will be."

This quelled him a little. "But . . . but just look at those arms and those thighs! Who else could've painted them, I ask you?"

"Anyone could," I said.

"But Professor Matějiček . . ."

"Mr. Vejr," I said reproachfully, and he, without bothering to finish his sentence, drew me inside to show me his collection of precious stones. I protested that I knew nothing about precious stones, but that seemed only to encourage him. He took a canvas bag out of the escritoire, a bag such as ladies use to carry their suntan lotion and repellent cream to the beach, and shook out of it about a dozen small medicine bottles, taking out the corks and spilling the stones on the table. Here was a genuine South African twelve-carat diamond; while these two were artificial, this blue sapphire came from India. Then he showed me three rubies, an opal, and two bottles full of Bohemian garnets. One bottle tipped over, the stones came tumbling out and fell to the floor, making a rustling sound as they piled on top of one another. He knelt to pick them up, and as he did so his jacket rode up his back and I could see that his shirt had been patched at the bottom with a large red-and-white checked strip of material.

Then he brought out his son's numismatic collection, all the coins neatly arranged in a thick album with a copperplate inscription on its cover:

Frederick Vejr – Coin Collection
To Freddie, on the day of his birth
from his Father

I was almost moved.

In the course of the first six months he came at least twice a month to offer me something. "Maestro, how about a super baroque Christ? The carving's quite out of this world."

Reluctantly I went upstairs to look.

"But this is from the nineteenth century!"

"You really think so? Naw . . . just look at the folds in that garment. . . ."

But he did not insist anymore, leading me instead to the sideboard, there to show me a wrought silver dish that used to belong to the Piccolominis – genuine ninth-century work.

Next time he turned up to offer me a real Hamadan. I had not the slightest idea what a Hamadan was, my expertise in carpets being about on a par with that in diamonds. The carpet had been stowed under the stairs on the ground floor, a huge roll, at least four times five meters. He undid the roll to allow me a glimpse of the carpet itself, garish colors covered with a layer of dirt.

"Well, what d'ya say?" His face glowed with enthusiasm.

"It's dreadfully filthy, isn't it," I said.

"Oh, well," he waved my objection aside, "if only you'd seen how they had stored the thing! But the craftsmanship! First half of the century." He didn't say which one, to be on the safe side after his experience with the baroque Christ.

The following day I watched him as he dragged the Hamadan to the frame in the yard where the tenants beat their carpets. It was even larger than I had thought seeing it folded up under the stairs. Then he brought over a hose from the garden and began to spray the carpet with a mighty stream of water.

I stood on the terrace, watching him in amazement, which grew still further when I saw what was happening to the carpet. I had never seen anything like it, nor had I read about anything of the sort. Together with the accumulation of muck, the colors started to wash away from the surface of the carpet, which turned white in front of my eyes while trickles of discolored water snaked over the concrete down in the yard.

I believe that he too was stunned by the outcome of his cleansing operation, but having once started he didn't intend to give up. Then, right from the middle of the huge carpet, a piece of fabric dropped away; or rather, it didn't drop away, it dissolved and was no more.

When he finally turned off the water, a grayish-white rag with a gaping hole in the middle hung there in front of him. Mr. Vejr looked up at me, threw up his hands, and hid inside the house.

Soon after this incident he bought a five-ton truck.

"What do you need a truck for?" I wanted to know.

"Oh, it'll come in handy," he replied. "And it was dirt cheap, too. Six thousand." Then he added: "And a little on the side, of course."

For two days people came and swarmed around the blue truck, while he kept putting its canvas top up and taking it down again and sitting importantly behind the wheel. Like a little kid. Since then – and it's over two years now – the vehicle has been standing outside the house, gradually losing the air in its tires and its blue coat rusting.

Just a few months ago he bought a second-hand Morris – from the British Embassy, he said. For once, I suspect he was telling the truth, for who else in Prague would own an old Marina? The car was painted a light green and upholstered in yellow leather; it carried the British Leyland emblem.

"Dirt cheap, was it?" I enquired.

"A mere thirty thousand," he said proudly. "Try and get one for fifty, if you can!"

"I wouldn't. Try, I mean," I said truthfully. "I'd be worried about getting spare parts."

"Oh that! All I have to do is drop a line to old Alois in London and he'll send me whatever's needed."

I had no idea who old Alois might be, but I could appreciate that an enterprising trickster could use a Morris Marina. Silently he draws up outside the house of an old lady who has put an ad in the papers that she wants to sell a baroque angel. He gets out of his light-green car, takes off his leather gloves, and holds out his hand to the old lady, introducing himself as Dr. Vejr. He'll chatter on about the state of the world, about Renaissance sixteenth-century chests, about Gothic madonnas from the latter part of the fifteenth century, about Dr. Vojtíšek and Professor Bruncvík and other famous art experts, and then just by the way, drop a remark about his visit to Chagall. The old lady is quite carried away, and in the end it is left to him to fix the price. And he gives her three thousand less than a baroque angel would merit. So far, so good, but there are just two snags: first, the baroque angel will not be baroque, which Mr. Vejr won't even sniff, and second, if one is to alight from a light-green Morris Marina outside an old lady's house, this noble product of British Leyland has to be in working order. Mr. Vejr's was – for just six weeks; then the gearbox went kaput.

Ever since, the green Marina has perched on its blocks beside the blue five-ton truck, the two of them rusting away quietly in unison. And old Alois still hasn't sent a new gearbox from London.

Freddie was brought back by a young nurse.

"Well, Freddie, shall we tell Daddy what's wrong with us? That we've broken our wrist and bruised our fingers?"

"I'm not his father."

"You're not his father?"

"No. I'm his neighbor."

She gave me a scathing look, as if to say I should be ashamed of myself for repudiating my own flesh and blood, even if he *was* illegitimate. Having obviously decided not to waste any words on me, she turned affectionately to the young policeman-to-be. "Now, Freddie, you'll go along back to the doctor who gave you that piece of paper, won't you."

She thrust a metal rod into my hand with Freddie's X-rays threaded on it, and the two of us hurried back to the casualty department. As we sat down on the white bench in the waiting room I saw that the child, broken wrist and bruised fingers notwithstanding, was smiling, his face adorned with an expression denoting some inner joy. Unaware of my scrutiny, he was completely immersed in himself, his injured hand diving into one of his pockets every now and again, as if seeking something.

"What is it, Freddie?" I asked. "Is there anything you need?"

Freddie gave a start and shook his head silently, his hand still in his pocket.

"What have you got in that pocket?"

"Nothing!"

He hesitated for a moment, waging some inner struggle. Then he could resist no longer. "Look," he said, pulling a number of objects out of the pocket: a ballpoint, a pair of tweezers, a small ceramic dish, a tube of medicine.

"Where on earth did you get all this?"

"She had an apple there, too, but I hate apples," he announced.

The nurse received her property with a gracious nod. I could well imagine how she would hold forth at the earliest opportunity about the damage to a child's morals resulting from denial of paternity.

Then they led Freddie, now unburdened of contraband, away to have his wrist put in plaster.

His father had last been locked up in the period between the blue truck and the light-green Marina. They turned up one morning in two black Volgas, carried out a house search in the course of which they confiscated a number of antique objects, taking them away together with their owner. As there was no phone in their attic apartment (nor is there ever likely to be, seeing that it wasn't meant for human habitation), a terrified Mrs. Vejr came running downstairs to us as soon as the police cars had gone, asking if she might use ours.

"Of course, go right ahead," I said. "But do be careful – my phone is most likely to be tapped."

She nodded, but the word obviously meant nothing to her because she proceeded to speak on the telephone using highly libelous expressions to describe those who had just departed. Fortunately, the bugging is at the moment being done unofficially and is intended to monitor *my* conversations and not those of my neighbors.

After that, Mrs. Vejr would drop in to see me from time to time. Since her husband's arrest she had become more attractive to look at, having lost her habitual haunted expression. She would as a rule stand in the doorway of my study (she invariably declined to come in "so as not to disturb") and launch into a monologue. She was an animated speaker, shaking her head a great deal as she talked, her long, dyed hair dancing on her shoulders.

So it was that I regularly learned how her wily spouse was doing in his splendid isolation. Quite contrary to his habit, it appeared that he was keeping mum and had refused to confess to anything. His lawyer claimed that as long as he stuck it out, the police would have a hard time of it, as they had nothing on him. This surprised me quite a lot, and I think she found it equally astonishing.

At first I tended to placate her by saying that I was sure it would all turn out for the best and her husband would be home before she knew it, but then it dawned on me that far from placating her, I was giving her cause for worry. There was nothing she desired less than the speedy return of her lord and master.

"Oh, Gawd," she said in panic, "if he gets the feeling that he's put one over on them, he'll be more uppity than ever. As if he wasn't big-headed enough already..."

I learned that Mr. Vejr was twenty-five years older than his wife, a mangy kind of Casanova and a braggart, but he had managed to get her drunk and "well, *you* know how it is, I was silly and inexperienced, and I was afraid to have an abortion but couldn't tell me parents neither, like that I was going to have a bastard kid, you see. Anyway, they say a child without a father hasn't got a dog's chance in life, don't they? But what kind of a father is *he,* I ask you? If you only knew. He'll go a fortnight without so much as looking at the boy, and then all of a sudden he'll start playing the fool with him, tickling him, sometimes he tickles the lad such a lot that Freddie has a fit, goes all red in the face and can't catch his breath. And you should see what my old man gets up to with me...."

Next time she told me that her husband had arranged for his former associates, with whom he had sold all that junk, to give her ten thousand for household expenses. "Oh, they weren't very keen at all, you bet," the young woman narrated, shaking her head about as she spoke, "but he sent them a message from prison that he'd land them all in it if they didn't cough up. So they came round to see me last night, wanted me to write and tell him that I'd been well taken care of. But what I can't understand is how he can do all this when he's... well, you know, in the clink. Just imagine what he'll be like when they let him out, he'll think he's the master of all creation, so help me!"

"Oh, don't worry," I comforted her, "they won't let him out for a long time yet. I've never heard of anyone in our country whom they'd release just like that after six months in custody."

"You really think so?" she said, sounding hopeful all of a sudden. "Well, whatever, even if they do I can take it. I don't take any notice of his stupid jabber anymore. But Freddie, that's something else again, he's too young to know what's what and he always listened to his father as if he was preaching the Gospel. And as soon as the old man went out he'd be imitating him. He'd sit at the table and yell at me: 'Now, Mother, bring me this, give me that!' And his language! You know what he called me once? A silly old cow, that's what he called me. 'You want a smack around the ear-hole, you silly old cow?' that's what he said when I didn't hand him his spoon that he'd dropped. A child of four and he talks to his mother like that — I ask you. And once he told me he'd have everybody locked up because everybody was bloody stupid, only he and his dad weren't. How's he going to end up? With his father home he'd only turn into a criminal too."

The young woman dried her eyes. "Now in the last six months he's a different child, so sweet, and never a nasty word. He even helps me do the housework. If only they'd keep his father where he is for at least three years more!" That hopeful note sounded in her voice again. "The lawyer says it really looks like it."

Freddie's father spent eight months in custody before they brought him to trial.

That morning, she rang my bell. She was wearing a new two-piece, her hair was freshly permed, her hand moist as she shook mine. "Keep your fingers crossed," she said in a tremulous voice, "if only for Freddie's sake."

Two days later the scoundrel was back home. Acquitted for lack of evidence. True, the prosecutor had lodged an appeal, but . . .

It was quite incredible. I asked around among my lawyer friends, but none of them could remember anything like it in the last five, maybe fifteen years. Here was a man in police custody for eight months and he gets sent home for lack of evidence. At the very least, my friends said, you would have expected them to give him a sentence equivalent to the time he had spent in custody. "I hope you realize," one of the lawyers said to me, "that if they released him like this, it wasn't for nothing. I don't necessarily mean to say that he's being asked to spy on *you*, maybe they just wanted to plant their own man among the fences. But once he starts working for them . . ."

The following week he showed up, offering me a precious eighteenth-century vase. As if nothing had happened. I said I was not a china collector because it would not last long in my household. A week or so later and he was back with another suggestion: he had exhausted his financial reserves, apart from which, of course, he now had to watch his step, and so he had severed all connection with his former pals. Now I, he was sure, had some money to spare, while he had valuable experience and certain contacts. Why didn't we pool our resources—he could promise a twenty-percent return within a month on every crown I invested.

It was so blatant that I thought it couldn't be a provocation. More likely his own initiative. I told him I'd make a bad partner as I was under police surveillance already.

He seemed surprised that the police could possibly take an interest in someone like me, who was not involved in the antique business. But he offered to ask Vendelin about my case, a friend of his who was now working as secretary to the deputy interior minister.

The examination room door opened and the nurse came out.

"Could I speak to the boy's father, please," she said, addressing me.

I rose to my feet, and she beckoned me to follow her.

Freddie was sitting on a low white stool, his hand encased in plaster.

The doctor was so young and attractive I could hardly bear to look at her. "Mr. Vejr," she said severely, "are you aware that your boy shows suicidal tendencies?"

I nodded, resigned now to my mistaken identity, and wondered how I could set about making a date with her. It was so tempting—not just her stunning looks but this unusual opportunity to sail under a foreign flag.

"You really must take him to see a psychiatrist," said the stunning young doctor. "Now, you have to understand that any delay is to be avoided; a specialist will be able to advise you on how to prevent a repetition of what happened. Surely you don't want it to happen again one of these days?"

She crossed over to me and said in a whisper, so that Freddie should not hear: "Your son's life is at stake. He's such a lovely boy. And so brave. He didn't bat an eyelid, whereas many an adult will scream and carry on when we're setting their bones."

She smelled of freshly laundered linen. If only I did not have in tow the wretched offspring of the incorrigible swindler who, God forgive him, was now most probably earning a little extra by picking up gossip about my private life, I would have told her how enchanting I found her, or I might even have asked if I could wait for her outside when she finished work. As it was, I only managed to say: "You can rely on me, Doctor. Freddie mustn't be allowed to perish, for I believe he's destined for great things." I had thought of saying "crimes" but decided against it in case she felt I was making fun of her.

When we had sat down in the car, Freddie looked at his huge hand with evident relish. "When I get home," he said, "I'll thump me dad with this. And then I'll throw 'im out the window."

"Now, Freddie," I said quickly, "I must ask you never again to throw anyone or anything on our terrace."

"No, not on the terrace," he said, as if to put my mind at rest. "I'll throw 'im out into the street. So he croaks."

"Why should you want to kill your father?"

"So he don't tickle me anymore," he explained. "Nor me mum."

Mrs. Vejr saw us coming from her window. She raced downstairs, shouting "Freddie!" Then, turning to me: "I found the door locked and the window open and blood on your terrace! What have you done, Freddie?"

"It's nothing, Mrs. Vejr," I told her. "All's well."

"What *have* you done?" sobbed Mrs. Vejr, not to be consoled. "I expect the poor boy got scared his father would be back before I was, but I *told* him I'd be back in a jiffy." She pressed Freddie to her bosom, crying all the time. "You know your mummy loves you, your mummy couldn't live without you. Why, I'd have to jump out of the window too if anything happened to you."

I was looking at Freddie, clasped in her embrace, and to my surprise watched his face beginning to pucker up and tears starting to flow from his eyes.

He was crying at last.

Estonia

TEET KALLAS

Back to the Rocks

Translated by Tōno Onu

For a year now the man with the red beard had been a patient in the large psychiatric hospital; in other words, the nuthouse. In Latin his illness sounded complicated, elegant, even mysterious; in no way, however, did that make his situation any better. The red-bearded man's case was pretty bad if not altogether hopeless. For days on end he would lie on his freshly made bed without a word, a cough, or a sigh; with his hands pressed hard against his sides, his eyes fixed steadfastly to the ceiling. He had a Roman nose, an intellectual's high forehead, and there was the hint of an embittered mouth hidden behind the beard. In the evening, while the other patients watched television, the red-bearded man rose to walk back and forth on the tiny patch of floor between his bed and the narrow window. He rarely stepped outside his "territory." His bed was the third from the window. He walked and turned with military precision. Drugs were given at nine-thirty. The red-bearded man received a large dose of sedatives that were supposed to be good for the nerves, relaxation, and inducing sleep. Still, this did not prevent him from staring up at the ceiling with its dim light late into the night. The man's eyes shone yet were lifeless; they sent shivers up and down the spines of some of the cleaning staff.

The red-bearded man was called Mats. That was about all anybody knew about him. Mats ate up everything brought before him but never asked for seconds, lay for hours, walked in his corner in the evening, and changed pajamas every month like everyone else—that was all, that was the pattern of his life.

The department head, a generous and pleasant middle-aged woman with little specialized training to speak of, wrote discouraging comments in Mats's file from time to time: "Negative. No sign of improvement."

When the department head left for vacation in May, another doctor was temporarily assigned to Mats's case. The head left Mats's file with her junior colleague. On a slip of paper inside the file was written in slightly unsteady letters, typical of a man's handwriting, a simple, as a matter of fact a completely standard, prescription: "Aminasine, 3 times a day 100 mg" with a clearly jotted signature like a military order.

The young doctor's name was Rein Poom. He had finished university only a year before. On his first day as acting head, Rein Poom took a tour of the ward. The narrow windows were wide open and the fragrance of a lime tree's blossoms floated into the rooms. The windows had sturdy metal frames so that a full-grown person could not get more than halfway out.

Accompanied by nurses, the doctor walked through the huge ward. He felt a bit uncertain and even had the feeling that a couple of the nurses were laughing at him behind his back. Finally, Rein Poom arrived at the foot of Mats's bed. Ramrod straight, Mats with his russet beard lay on the bed cover, staring at the ceiling. He was wearing light green pajamas that blended in well with the dark green bed cover and its lime green stripes.

Rein Poom asked the head nurse: "How long has he been with us?"

The head nurse replied that it was now fourteen months. The thought flashed through Rein's mind that fourteen months ago he had still been a student in Tartu. Then he heard the head nurse's voice: "Let him leave? You must be joking, Doctor . . ."

Rein Poom blushed and quickly left the ward.

Back in his office, sitting alone, he doodled aimlessly on a piece of paper; he felt ashamed, depressed, and stupid.

The following day he made another visit.

The stern head nurse, with that uncompromising and vigilant look of a mother superior in a nunnery, the young nurses trying to be serious, huffing orderlies, authoritarian with the patients, while hypocritical about cleanliness and order, all gathered around the bed while the young doctor straightened the crease in his trousers and sat himself next to Mats.

Mats stared at the ceiling. He was powerful, dignified, and motionless.

"Jugar," said the doctor softly. "Jugar, I want to have a word with you."

"He doesn't talk," said the head nurse. "Nobody's heard him talk."

Rein Poom blushed, fidgeted some more, looked out the window, and said as cheerily as possible: "Jugar, don't you think it's pretty well time you left the hospital?"

The red-bearded Mats remained silent. Rein wasn't sure, but he had the impression that the man, just for a second, looked at him.

The next day Rein was back in the large ward. He talked with the other patients, asked how they were sleeping, who wanted to go out and work, joked with a young Jewish boy with huge childlike eyes who for days on end had been trying to learn Italian from a thin picture book—which was in Latvian. Suddenly the head nurse let out a gasp that betrayed surprise and indignation.

Rein Poom knew what was up. There, you mother superior, there! Still he could feel chills going up and down his spine. It was only with a great deal of effort that he was able to turn around without losing his composure. And there was

Mats standing right in front of him. Mats had left his territory – an unheard-of thing. An even more startling phenomenon was to follow immediately. Mats was a tall man. Rein waited nervously. He feared hearing disjointed sounds or the loud voice of someone deaf. He was prepared for both, yet still was edgy.

But then Mats said in a perfectly clear voice: "Doctor, yesterday you said I could go home. I should really go. I've got rabbits and a household there."

"There, you see, Jugar, we both think alike," Rein laughed. Without saying a word to those around him, giving an order or making a comment, he rushed out, crossed the hall, went into his office, and plugged in the kettle. Soon the yellowish kettle-odored water started to boil. Rein prepared a cup of bitterly strong coffee and drank it with gusto. He nearly burned his tongue but he didn't mind a bit. He took a pen, leafed through the calendar on his desk, and wrote on a page: "Redbeard leaves!!!"

A couple of weeks later, on a clear and promising June morning, the Volga reserved for the use of the hospital executives stood before the department. That morning the car was at Poom's disposal. He stood beside the automobile reading a newspaper. From time to time he glanced impatiently at the grayish-red building, which resembled a Prussian barracks.

An attractive female colleague from the children's ward rushed by and expressed her surprise: "On vacation but still on the job? What dedication, my Rein!"

"No vacation yet. It's the last day of work," Rein answered.

"Oh, really?"

Clip clip, pretty legs, scrunching sand, and the attractive colleague had disappeared behind the false acacias. At the same moment a heavy door opened and out stepped a squinting Mats Jugar. Beside him was a senior nurse. Rein could hardly contain his astonishment. Until now he had always seen Mats in clean light green pyjamas, washed and groomed.

Now Redbeard was wearing his own old soiled clothes. In fact, Mats was nothing more than a pile of rags, the likes of which the young doctor previously had seen only in films or on stage.

"Good morning, Jugar. Nice day, isn't it?" Rein said and opened the door of the Volga.

For a couple of hours they drove silently. By the side of the road early summer was in full bloom. Everything was bursting with green. At the edge of a village two people were mowing hay already.

Around one o'clock Mats suddenly started to swallow noticeably. Drops of saliva trickled into his beard. Rein then remembered that one o'clock was lunchtime at the hospital. Strangely enough, he started to feel hungry also.

In a little while a strange-looking rock stuck out of the roadside scenery. Somewhat timidly Rein asked the driver to slow down. At the edge of a field stood a boulder hewn into the shape of a plough's moldboard. Into the boulder someone had chiseled very simple, square, and noble letters: "PRAISE TO THE PLOUGHMAN, THANKS TO HIM WHO GIVES US BREAD!"

Mats looked out. When the boulder was behind them he mumbled, against his will a bit it seemed, "That's my work."

"Are you an artist then, Jugar?" Rein asked without wanting to. Mats's medical record made no mention of such a thing.

"I'm no artist," Mats responded indifferently. "How can I be an artist if I'm not? I simply look at them, the idea comes later."

"What do you look at?"

"Rocks," answered Mats with what seemed just a hint of superiority.

A bit later a country school appeared in a clearing by the road. Beside the gravel path that led to the schoolhouse stood a three-meter-tall boulder, looking like an old woman resting her feet here by the road, deep in thought. The car drove by that rock slowly also.

"LOVE YOUR MOTHER" was carved into the rock.

"For that I received three bags of wheat flour," Mats stated with a certain amount of pride.

"And for the plough?"

"For the plough I got sixty rubles."

They were getting close to the village council building. Sea gulls circled in the sky. The air was cooler. The sea was obviously nearby.

Rein knew that nobody at the village council was really going to be very thrilled about their arrival. Mats was the village fool. As long as his mother had been alive, things had not been too bad. However, once she passed away they had no choice but to send Mats to the hospital. He was a forty-one-year-old adult unable to look after himself. He couldn't do even the simplest of farm chores. Rein knew that Mats's house was on the shore and in a pretty pitiful state.

When the car drove up to the village council building, Rein could feel the anxiety in his heart, his mood became defiant, and his cheeks flushed. All he could think about was how in early spring he had driven by here with some friends to watch the arrival of swans on the bay of a wildlife sanctuary.

A few meters before the yellow wooden council building stood a high gray rectangular hewn boulder. "THE FUTURE LIES IN OUR HANDS" Rein could see in austere and high letters.

Mats's blank stare became warmer.

"I was offered a lot of money for that, but I didn't accept it. I wanted something else."

"Exactly what, Jugar?" Rein asked.

"You'll soon see."

As was to be expected, there were problems at the village council.

"He'll just mope by himself, he'll even forget to eat if somebody doesn't spoon-feed him."

"He doesn't know how to live!"

"Who's got time now during haymaking to look after him?" And so it went.

Rein didn't say anything and waited to see when he would lose his temper. He finally did.

"Here's the medical certificate," he said as he threw the papers onto the table. "Here's his disability certificate. Take the trouble to complete Jugar's pension application. If you think it's necessary, do something about getting Jugar admitted into a nursing home. That's within your responsibility. I can't keep him in the hospital any longer just for your sake; the hospital is meant for the sick and there's not enough beds."

Rein blushed, went out, sat in the car, and told Mats: "Show us the way, Jugar."

The Volga rattled over fallow ground and over ditches full of weeds until it reached the seashore. Far off were black fields, shrieking sea gulls, and terns diving with lightning quickness into the water. A stiff breeze tugged at their clothes. The car stopped beside three huge boulders lined up like three giant and slightly clumsy brothers. Rein didn't even notice Mats's house.

Redbeard, however, was back home. He stepped out and cast an inquisitive glance at the rocks, as his tattered clothes fluttered in the breeze and his long beard flew in two different directions in the wind. And then, with an unhurried step, he started to walk. Rein, the nurse, and the driver followed him. The ground was rough and covered by bits of rock.

"Here's my house," announced Mats seriously.

Rein stopped. What he saw was not a house. It was a sunken, completely rotted memory of a shingled roof, half of which had thoroughly decayed. In the tall grass, amidst nettles and fool's parsley, were strewn rotten logs.

With Mats leading the way and Rein Poom at his heels, feeling sorry for his new light summer suit, they made their way through some barely visible crack, which resembled the entrance to a cave. It was mad, sad, and fascinating. They literally fell into a room that years ago, probably about one hundred, might have been a kitchen. In one corner there were pieces of brick, in the middle of the room lay half a stove-ring, on the wall hung a gray wooden soup ladle. The floor was covered with some kind of thick and spongy material. Despite the fresh, crisp saltwater air outside, inside the air was so musty it was nearly impossible to breathe. Mats looked about absentmindedly yet longingly. Then unhesitatingly he forced his way through another opening into another room—also empty and without windows. It did, however, have enough light, which filtered through the countless cracks.

And they made their way into still another room, which was quite large. It even had a tiny window. The glass was broken and covered with dust.

Mats stopped.

"This is my room," he said, "my own."

A rusty metal bed stood in the room. On top of it lay a faded coat. A doorless, empty closet stood against a wall. That was all.

Mats bent over to pull out from beneath the bed a large metal-framed box. In it were some chisels, a couple of hammers, and a few other tools.

The old nurse, who had seen much in life, breathed anxiously on Rein's neck.

Mats also closely examined the floor. As in the other rooms, it was entirely covered by a spongy layer that was nothing else but rabbit droppings accumulated over the years.

"I've no more rabbits left," Mats said matter-of-factly. He was merely stating a fact, nothing more.

Then he announced: "Now I am going to show you my painting."

Mats stepped toward the moth-eaten and faded closet and from a dark corner pulled out a piece of plywood with worn corners. He brushed it with his sleeve and then suddenly, as in a fit of anger, handed it to the others.

It was an amateurish, yet striking painting of the sea. Rein carefully brushed away the lines of dust. A couple of streaks of light fell onto the painting from the cracks in the ceiling and they gave the effect of real saltwater bursting forth from under the dust; frizzy waves roared toward Rein, small, hesitating, energetic waves that neither roll nor crash but flutter like busy wagtails. Water, water and small waves were all that could be seen.

"Six years ago a painter spent his summer vacation here. I asked him to give me his old paints and a couple of brushes," Mats recounted with an air of importance. He took the painting back from Rein and again hid it in the closet.

Then he left the room.

The young doctor and the nurse with thirty years of experience avoided looking at each other.

Then the nurse said with some hesitation: "It really is hopeless. They were right at the village council. How can he survive? He doesn't even have a stove. He'll starve to death."

Rein shrugged and pointed in the direction of the dark corner where a small iron stove squatted. It hardly seemed usable.

The nurse, too, shrugged.

When they went back outside, Mats was standing by the big rocks. His beard down to his chest, a ragged old shoe set on a big rock, he was examining the earth and garbage-covered granite surface. Rein noticed for the first time that Mats was husky and well built, with a philosopher's forehead.

"So what are you going to do now, Jugar?" Rein asked.

Mats did not answer right away. A sly smile crept into his beard; he bit his lip and then spoke: "They wanted to give me money. That's what they wanted to do. But I was against that. I asked a tractor driver to bring those rocks..." and he pointed in the general direction of the sea, "into my yard so that I wouldn't have to walk needlessly. Needless walking is not good for the mind. Now they're here, those rocks."

The sea roared and the sea gulls shrieked.

Rein cleaned off the rabbit droppings from the soles of his shoes.

"Of course now the doctor wants to know what I'll do. Well, I'll tell you. Without the doctor, I wouldn't be here. First of all

I've got to look at the rocks. I don't know how long it'll take. Sometimes it doesn't take long, only a couple of weeks. Then an idea comes. And then I have to complete the work. That takes a long time. Sometimes it tires me out completely," Mats explained. He looked serious and thoughtful. He had never spoken about such things before.

"Uh, uh," Rein gulped.

In half an hour they started to leave.

"If you want . . . I can take you back to Tallinn . . . so that . . . in decent conditions . . ." Rein mumbled. In Rein's mind there was no doubt about the response or that Mats just must not be left there.

Mats did not say a thing. He patted the rocks, felt their protuberances, measured them in his mind. He had his own ideas. They were nobody's business but his. They were subject neither to words nor to people.

Rein pulled a ten-ruble bill out of his pocket at the same time that the nurse started to look in her purse.

"You'll probably need at the beginning . . . until the pension . . ." Rein mumbled. Without looking at it, Mats stuffed it into his pocket. The gesture was a picture of calmness. When they had climbed back into their Volga, Rein let out a sigh of relief.

Mats stood leaning on a rock with his beard in the wind. His eyes, which had motionlessly stared at the ceiling while he had been lying in the hospital for months on end, now narrowed with an owner's wise and thoughtful look as he sized up each rock. Three huge boulders sitting, waiting obediently; for a moment everything seemed wrong, as if red-bearded Mats was all-powerful, that the giant reddish-brown and gray boulders were his serfs, at his beck and call: do this, destroy that, fix that . . .

They drove to a restaurant in Haapsalu for lunch.

Sitting at the table, waiting for his pork chop dinner and gulping mineral water, Rein absentmindedly kept clicking his brand-new six-colored ballpoint pen.

Suddenly, thinking back on what had happened, he felt a bittersweet taste rise into his throat and his eyes getting moist.

"What are you ruining your pen for?" the nurse asked. "You'll still be needing it."

Rein gave a tense smile, blushed, and put away the pen.

In the evening the head doctor gave him a dressing-down. He had been away with the hospital's Volga for too long.

Latvia

REGĪNA EZERA

Man Needs Dog

Translated by Tamara Zalite

Of all the animals in the world the
dog is worthiest of man's undivided
attention, friendship, and love. One
may say, the dog is part of man.
— *Alfred Brehm*

I T WA S Sunday morning. Through the slumbering streets of
the city floated waves of pale lavender light composed of the
gleam of electric bulbs, still burning, the glow of the sun just
rising from behind the tall roofs, and the glitter of freshly fallen snow. Half-empty tramcars were clanging and creaking
past the marketplace, suburban trains rumbled across the viaduct heading for the seaside, also half-empty although the
day promised well.

An old man was standing at the edge of the canal, and on
the pavement at his feet was a basket covered with a woollen
shawl under which four pups – three dogs and a bitch – lay
huddled together. He had been standing like this for about
half an hour, listlessly watching the passing trams and thinking that he'd come early because he could never sleep long
these days though all his life he'd been starved for sleep, but
now, spitefully, sleep would flee at four-thirty and sometimes

even as early as four, which didn't matter so much in the summer when he could pick up a rake or a spade or a watering can and potter in the garden, but in winter all he could do was toss on his creaking bed, light a cigarette, scratch Gracia behind the ear, and dwell on memories of the past since the future held nothing for him, that much was clear, he had enough sense to see that, and was old enough to take a philosophical view on it.

These were the old man's thoughts as he stood with the puppies at his feet, while the sun slowly rose from behind the pavilion, and the trains clattered back and forth across the viaduct, and the hubbub of voices and the thumping of crates drifted toward him from the marketplace. A mixture of odors was wafted through the clear winter air – the dank, fusty smell of potatoes, carrots, swedes and turnips brought straight from the vegetable cellars, the appetizing aroma of sauerkraut and pickled cucumbers, hot dogs and meat pies that tickled the old man's nostrils. He'd left in the morning without a bite to eat, so now his Adam's apple began to work convulsively. There ought to be about a ruble and a half in his purse, he remembered, all in small change, but money was money, so he turned to face the pavilion, and as he did so the morning sun lit up his faded cap, transforming it into a kind of pinkish orange nimbus. A ripple passed over the woollen shawl covering the basket, and the old man pulled it off. Two of the puppies had woken up and were nuzzling the wicker walls of the basket and one another, groping for their mother. The old man lifted them out to forestall a general commotion in the basket. Happily, awkwardly, their tiny paws sinking into the freshly fallen snow, they toddled off along the pavement, straining away from their wicker cradle. The old man followed them, puffing and panting, snatching at them with stiff frozen fingers from which the sleek little bodies kept sliding like slippery black pebbles.

"Little devils," he muttered. "Little black devils!" But there was no anger in his voice, and he pursued his purpose with the single-mindedness of which only the very young and the very old are capable. Presently the puppies wearied and began to whimper, the snow was freezing their paws, and besides, they were hungry, like the old man himself.

He caught the fugitives and replaced them in the basket, hitched it onto his arm, and headed for the smell of hot dogs. But he didn't go straight to the eating place, he had to think of his basketful of warm life. So he made a detour, passing sacks of potatoes, barrels of sauerkraut, counters laden with fruit, and all the while his eyes were scanning the faces looking for somebody he knew and could entrust with his pups for a while.

The vendors stood mostly idle, the townsfolk were still sleeping their Sunday sleep. The old man with the basket over the edge of which four puppies were looking out drew everyone's notice, people laughed and called to him – "Are you selling them?" – but he plodded on unperturbed, his faded eyes brushing them indifferently. Clearly, all they wanted was a bit of fun, they'd never buy. Though he couldn't have explained it, the old man could always tell a prospective buyer from those who just stopped to fondle his little creatures for the pleasure of it. To the former belonged lonely elderly women who were easily moved because they had a surplus of love stored away, and also children who would crowd about him, spellbound, and tug at their mothers' skirts, and beg and plead until they had their way. Occasionally there were other kinds of buyers too, the pups were cheap enough, after all, but they were a lot of trouble, nobody knew it better than he did, though he would deny it staunchly, he'd even swear the reverse, which was the only lie he permitted himself in his commercial transactions – if it could be called a lie. Such were the old man's thoughts as he walked past and between the counters that were piled with shiny red apples, like piles of hidden life, oversize spawn about to engender enormous fantastic fishes; where cabbages and pumpkins raised their stupid bald heads, which were like pale

moons, and bunches of herbs exuded a variety of smells –
bitter, astringent, salty, honeyed, evoking memories of aches,
and sleeplessness, and distant summers, and sweet sins. The
rays of the rising sun turned the breath into plumes of pinkish steam, people were steaming little ovens framing the aisles
of the market through which the old man was walking, a little
cloud of steam hovering on his own lips, swinging his wicker
basket from which the four little puppies peered out at the
world.

After a while he found what he wanted. A familiar face was
looking at him from behind a cranberry stand, only he
couldn't recollect where and how he had met her. He racked
his memory, and the effort was crowned with the pleasant realization that the woman was not just an acquaintance but a
relative of sorts, on his late wife's side – a cousin once removed or something. True, they hadn't met more than a
couple of times, and only on very special occasions, but it was
good enough for his present purpose. The woman was looking at the pups, taking no notice of the old man, her plump
cheeks glistened in the frost like winter apples. The women
around her, all selling cranberries, were also looking at the
pups, and their cheeks were also a glossy red. They were none
of them young, but wholesome of complexion and firm of
flesh, and swathed in seven or eight layers of clothing against
the morning frost they resembled stocky, short-stemmed
mushrooms. The old man took them all in and fastened his
eyes on his relative. He was now impelled by a single sensation – that of unendurable hunger, because the cranberry
stand was right opposite the eating place whose door kept
opening and closing, filling the air with the aroma of hot
food. Neither the buxom women, nor anything else, was of
any consequence. And since his relative never took her eyes
off the puppies, he simply addressed her. Even then she
didn't raise her eyes to him, but murmured "What a pretty
little thing!" – which could hardly refer to the old man, especially as she reached across the counter with its cranberries

and tin measuring mugs, and with a blunt forefinger tickled
the throat of the nearest pup.

"Why not buy it?" said the old man in a hoarse voice – his
throat felt parched with the desire for something hot to eat.

At this she finally looked at him. It was clear from the expression on her face that she was in the same position in
which the old man had found himself a little while ago – his
face was familiar to her, but she couldn't find the connection.
He was about to remind her when she addressed him by his
name, so she'd remembered. They talked a little – not much,
of course, what was there to talk about for two people who
were almost strangers? They talked weather, market prices,
the mutual relatives who had died. The old man was not in a
mood for talk, he hadn't been looking for someone just to
gossip with, so he came straight to the point. The women
were responsive. Keep an eye on the pups? Why not? Here,
put them down. Buy them? Ah well, they all had dogs of their
own, two even, and his relative, it turned out, had three.
Maybe she did, maybe she didn't, how was he to tell, but if
they weren't going to buy there was nothing for it.

He set down the basket and walked unhurriedly to the eating place through whose door clouds of fragrant vapor hit his
nostrils. His frozen fingers fumbled for the coins that were as
cold as icicles though they'd been inside his purse. One
portion . . . no, better two, he'd have to take something to the
pups. Yes, two portions, and a glass of coffee. The sausages
were scorching hot, the milky coffee lukewarm but strong
and almost sickeningly sweet. What a man really wanted on a
winter day like this was a little snifter, and then it wouldn't
matter if he'd have to stand out-of-doors till doomsday. He
was always chilly these days, he never felt really warm, perhaps because he'd spent his life in sweltering heat, stoking the
ovens, and was accustomed to heat. Perhaps, but perhaps it
was because the old frame no longer held the warmth, like an
old oven too long in use. These were the old man's thoughts
while his large teeth, yellow like a horse's, bit into a hot sau-

sage, and he washed down each bite with a sip of lukewarm coffee. He also thought, as he broke bits from the slice of grayish-brown bread, that there wasn't a place in the world where rye bread tasted as good as it did in his native village; even Riga bread couldn't come anywhere near it, and if there was anyone who knew about bread it was he. Twenty years of work in a bakery wasn't to be sneezed at. True, he'd neither mixed the dough nor kneaded it, but the right kind of fire was the crux of the whole thing, so the man in charge of it was the second man after the baker—only then came the manager and all the rest of them.

The warm food slowly spread through the old man's veins like hot syrup. It made him a little giddy, he broke into a sweat, and then he felt very sprightly, as though he'd had a glass of brandy and not just coffee. When he stepped into the street it was like coming out of a bathhouse, he felt steaming hot, and the air seemed no longer as nippy as it had been before, he was wide awake, and his mind was full of pleasant thoughts. In his pocket he carried a sausage for the pups wrapped in a paper napkin, with a handkerchief tied around it to keep it warm.

But the cranberry women had fed the creatures, he could see it at a distance, they'd lifted them out of the basket and fed them. The counter looked like a table after a meal, it was littered with paper bags and greasy wrappings and scattered with bits of cheese, slices of bread, scraps of smoked fish, and chunks of sausage. Enough to feed at least ten more puppies in addition to the four that were now frisking about under the counter practically among the passing feet. People stopped, looked down and smiled, ignoring the cranberries and saleswomen, who didn't seem to mind a bit and also smiled. And although the old man knew that such a hullabaloo might end badly, that he could be driven out with his pups to the dog market, which was chock-full of purebreds and mongrels of every shade and hue, the spectacle made him feel warm all over, not only because now he was warm and replete inside, but mainly because his pups were eliciting all these smiles and all this admiration. So when his relative now beckoned to him and said to somebody "Here, you can talk to the owner himself!" he blew out his chest with pride and drawled "Anything wrong?"—just as if he'd only come up to put an end to the excitement and noise and not to sell these priceless little creatures that were worth more than all the money in the world could pay.

"What's the damage, dad?" The question came from a young man of undefinable age, dressed so lightly for a winter morning that it made you shiver just to look at him—neither hat nor gloves, and carrying a guitar that he was strumming all the time as though playing an accompaniment to his own words, and the women's smiles, and the clumsy capers of the puppies. From behind he could be taken for an adolescent, small, narrow in the shoulders, but his face, grayish green with cold, flaunted toothbrush mustache and black sideburns to match. The eyes looked enormous and almost round like Victoria plums, and they were as bright as the headlights of a car, and fixed upon the pups. He looked a dog lover all right, but he also looked the kind of person who could never keep money in his purse, so the old man asked cautiously: "Why should you want a dog?"

"What d'you mean why? I need somebody to stick to me, who'll go where I go." And he flashed a radiant smile at the old man.

"Why don't you take a wife?" one of the women interposed while the lad continued strumming his guitar, drawing from it sounds you could hardly call music.

"Too costly," he replied and burst into laughter, into which everybody joined except for the old man, who held the view that business was a serious matter.

"So is a dog," he murmured.

"Is it now? How much? One ruble? Two?" and gathering up in his hand the outside cloth of his coat pocket he shook it, jingling the money inside.

The tinkle of coins seemed even more distasteful to the old man, and although he had intended to charge three rubles for a pup he suddenly pronounced: "Five. Five rubles each."

The lad's round eyes went positively circular.

"Bah! Five rubles for a rat like this?"

A rat, he'd said! A rat! But the hazel irises that floated in the whites of his eyes like footballs were starry with fun.

The old man measured the slight form of the guitar player with infinite contempt and said: "You'd better learn to tell quality, son," adding that his pups were dachshunds, almost purebred, excellent hunting dogs, and selling them at five rubles was actually selling them for a song, his usual price was eight. This was what the old man said, though he'd gotten eight only once in his life, and that was when the customer had mistaken a five-ruble note for a three-ruble note, and there had been an occasion when he'd bartered a pup for four packages of Prima cigarettes — the cheapest of the cheap, but a body had to earn its keep, which applied to pups and men alike, and things and creatures bought cheaply were never valued by man, as if price could indicate value. Now the old man held forth on the beauty of Gracia, the mother-bitch, whose hair was like shiny silk, and whose legs were divinely curved, and even as he uttered her name, "Gracia," it sounded like a tender caress, as if he were reminiscing on his first love — and carried away by his own words, he swept the young man away with him, for the lad wasn't made of stone, and the frozen fingers that had been vaguely producing incoherent sounds began to play some southern and very temperamental tune, a rumba or a samba perhaps, while the cranberry women's frozen feet were stiffly stamping time, heedless of the fact that what with the puppies and the guitar player they hadn't done much business that morning, but they didn't mind because they all felt exhilarated by the old man's eloquence, and Gracia's silky fur and exquisite bow legs that were more beautiful than anything they could imagine, and by the fiery samba rhythms that pierced the seven or eight layers of clothing and flowed through their bodies and into every joint like hot rum.

"Come on! Buy him!" they urged. "Buy him! You won't find a better dog." He broke off his samba on a shrill chord, propped the guitar against the counter on which stood half-liter measuring mugs filled with scarlet cranberries as shiny as if they were varnished, surrounded by piles of berries, and he pulled out of his breast-pocket a five-ruble note that was as crisp and new as if it had been specially saved up for the occasion, and without any bargaining whatever, without even stopping to choose, he picked up the puppy closest at hand and murmured laughingly, the way one talks to a child: "Want to come with Gusts, pet?"

Then, pushing his acquisition under his coat he took his guitar and walked off out of sight with a swinging gait. The old man heaved a sigh of relief: one worry less. Inspired by his success he cried out jauntily: "Hurry up! Final bid!"

But the people had had their fun, and they began to disperse and go about their own business. The old man hitched the basket with the remaining puppies on his arm and also got moving. Again he passed sacks and barrels and counters, and about him rose and fell a hubbub of voices and a swirl of colors and faces, and toward him flowed a motley stream of warm humanity, steaming in the cold winter air. It was light, the sun had risen above the roofs and was beating down upon the glass panes of the pavilions, transforming them into sheets of blazing copper.

The old man had almost reached the canal when a girl ran full tilt into him, one of a trio of girls in trousers who were walking toward him giggling and chattering, gazing everywhere except where they were going. It may have been pure chance, but it may have been God's finger, anyway, the old man with his basket seemed just what they'd been yearning to meet. They crowded around it, greedy, impatient hands reaching for the puppies, while rosy lips curled in flashing smiles emitting steaming tender whispers of endearment as if addressing human babies. Flushed with the frost, lithe and young, dressed in similar trousers, the three seemed as identical to the old man as his three puppies, which the girls were holding in their hands and fondling. Then one of them uttered breathlessly the very words the old man was thinking: "It's fate, girls, it can't be chance! Let's buy a puppy for Alec instead of flowers! He adores dogs, doesn't he?"

There was loud approval. One single rose cost three rubles, and a calla lily was no good, except for funerals, and if they bought cyclamen they'd have to add a cake and a bottle of wine, which would be an awful lot of money, and besides it would be so bourgeois, but a dog—now wasn't that a real present, Alec would be knocked over. They chirped and twittered, forgetting to ask, in their excitement, whether the puppies were for sale and how much they cost. The old man didn't interrupt or hurry them, allowing their fervor to kindle, and knowing from experience what buyers were like— you had to know the exact time, the precise moment when they were ripe. When the moment came he cleared his throat, about to reiterate all he had been saying over and over again that morning—that the puppies were as good as purebred, and enormously valuable, and how it pained him to part with these lovely little creatures, and it was a real privilege to become the rightful owner of an animal that was so boundlessly devoted to man. But one look at the girls was enough for him to realize the futility of words: one of them had already pulled out an orange suede purse, so all he said was: "Well, take your choice! See which one you like best."

But even this was too much for them, the puppies were alike—ah, but one had a teeny-weeny white star on its chest.

"Let's have this one, with the star!" said the girl with the purse. "How much?"

"This one? Four."

"And that?"

"Five."

"Funny. Why should the prettier one be cheaper?"

"The one with the star is a bitch," said the old man, because the girls were so young, so delightfully young and pure and artless in their enthusiasm, so full of selfless joy at the prospect of buying a present that he couldn't bring himself to cheat them.

The three exchanged a glance.

"Well, girls, what do we decide?"

"I don't see why a bitch should be worse than a dog?"

"Oh come on, Alda, don't be so naive!"

"All right, let's take the expensive one!" The girl in charge of the money heaved a sigh and jingled the purse. "Aid to starving students!"

"Haven't we collected enough?"

"Don't be mean! It's only two days till we get our grant."

The old man was actually prepared to knock off a ruble or so, but these young innocents had not the faintest notion of the excitement of commercial transactions; a bit of bargaining and haggling could have enabled him to reduce the price without losing face, while they simply scraped together the full sum to a kopeck and pressed five rubles into his callused palm. The one with the purse said laughingly, "Check the money before leaving the counter!"—which the old man did not do, of course. He very much wanted to ask what the young ladies were studying, but he saw that he himself was of no consequence at all to the girls, who were deeply engrossed in the important process of cradling their puppy in a bright blue artificial leather bag. They had their own concerns and he had his, so without waiting for them he walked away and was soon back where he had started from, at the canal.

A wind had struck up, and it was chiller here than among the pavilions, but it was a tram stop where many people got off for the market and he was more likely to get rid of his dogs. The wind swished along the canal whirling and eddying the snow that had fallen overnight, here and there baring a smooth gray surface of ice, and it had swept the sky very clean as well. Swirls and wisps of snow rolled and glided across the

pavement leaving powdery traces in the crinkles of the old
man's trousers and in the dull dark fur of the pups. The pups
were scraping the wicker walls of their basket with their little
claws, trembling and whimpering faintly and blinking toward
their unknown dogs' future with weak pale baby eyes, but it
was not fear that made them whimper and shiver, but cold.

They had been there for quite a while, and it was very cold,
and no one cared to buy a dog. People would stop occasionally to fondle a pup, moved by a sudden impulse to buy a live
warm being to compensate for the stone walls of the city, but
when it came to the point they would merely shrug to express
regret and pass on. It was either a matter of sharing a flat with
other families, or of a mother-in-law, or a top floor. Maybe
they were telling the truth, and maybe they weren't, how was
he to tell, but his heart was growing heavy, and as to charging
five rubles a pup—he'd have accepted two.

At this very point a man stopped in front of him, middle-
aged, tall, rather impressive, but somehow creased and crumpled, as if he'd slept all night with his clothes on. He stopped
and looked down at the puppies in their basket with curiosity,
or perhaps with contempt, at any rate the old man didn't like
him. He couldn't have explained it—perhaps it was the man's
unkempt appearance that displeased him, perhaps the realization that he was tipsy so early in the morning, which was
something he simply couldn't stand, or perhaps because he
was standing there, hands thrust into his trouser pockets,
peering at the puppies like a rooster at two grains in a dung
heap, and this made the old man's blood boil, for he held that
life was a sacred thing.

"Anything you want?" he growled when the stranger didn't
budge and continued blinking and staring as though out to
pick a quarrel. "Never seen a dog in your life? Get along with
you, quick."

He knew full well that he had no business to tell a person
where to look or where to stand, but trade was slack, he was
getting damnably cold, and he was sick to death of all the

empty talk he'd been doing, and if you are in this state of mind you don't need much to blow up, and besides this crumpled individual didn't look as if he cared for dogs, especially if it involved spending money.

Far from moving away the man gave a hard little laugh that made the old man wrinkle his nose – the fellow reeked of drink, or perhaps it was a hangover from the night before.

"You're a touchy old blighter," he said with a hint of threat behind a drunkard's bravado. "But I don't mind your sort."

"All right, push along then and don't pick on me!" the old man growled again, unwilling to enter an argument.

"You're a funny old bird!" Now the fellow seemed genuinely surprised. "You want to sell, and you won't let me look! Who do you think is going to buy your pigs in a poke?"

"In a poke or out of a poke, you won't buy them anyway."

"What makes you think so?" the man said cockily.

"Because it's not for lice I sell them, but for money," and the old man spat on the ground.

"Why, listen to that!" The man was obviously deeply hurt. "I've got more dough than you have, I'm sure. Just wait!" He thrust a hand into his breast pocket. "How much do you want?"

And then something totally unpredictable happened. The old man suddenly knew that he did not want to sell his puppy to this man, that he'd regret it if he did, and would suffer pangs of conscience if he let that lanky good-for-nothing have it, with his insolent eyes and contemptuous mouth that spat out words like empty nutshells. To his own surprise, although he'd been prepared to let a dog go for two rubles, he found himself saying with cool arrogance: "Ten rubles! And no bargaining."

"Did I hear you say something, or did I imagine it?" The hand shot out of the breast pocket.

"You heard me," the old man said, feeling suddenly very pleased with himself, and very calm and serene.

Not so the other one—a flush of excitement covered his face, his eyes glittered, and like a card player producing his fatal trump he exclaimed: "Three! Three is my price, and not a kopeck more, and it's more than fair."

"I'm sick of you!" the old man growled and heaved a sigh, for he was sorry for the puppy, but he was also sorry to lose three rubles. "Why don't you just go your way. I wouldn't trust you with a dog of mine if you paid me twenty-five."

"Why? What's wrong with me? My hair style? My figure? Or my background perhaps?"

"A dog needs a proper master, and not a macaroni chewed at both ends."

"Why, listen to that!" Again he seemed hurt to the quick. "It's your luck that you're such an old wreck of a creature, or I'd let you have a swipe."

"Oh my God," said the old man. "Can't you leave me alone? You don't need a dog, and I don't need your money, so we're quits."

"You've got to sell me your dog!" the fellow persisted, and the old man thought that he'd experienced all sorts of things in the course of his long life, but this was the strangest thing of all. He'd always had to persuade his buyers and coax them, and rouse their pity and sympathy, but this one—why, the fellow clung to him like a leech. Truth to tell he'd be happy to be rid of one more puppy if only the chap hadn't looked so tough and mean, so utterly unfit for the lofty task of being the owner and friend of a dog, and a puppy was like a human child, it needed a firm, calm hand, and understanding, and affection. These were the old man's thoughts as he was trying to keep his eyes averted from the purse the other had produced and in which he was fumbling with long stiff fingers whipping up his own desire for the dog, wanting the puppy more every minute, though at first he had stopped to look at it out of boredom, indifferently, even contemptuously, one might say—it was resistance that had stimulated his desire, he had the disposition of a woman hunter, a heartbreaker. As if to prove the perversity of the world, he seized the old man by the coat button and, breathing alcohol right into his face and forgetting his recent anger, started assuring him at great length that the pup would have a wonderful life, he'd live on frankfurters and meat pies, because Irma worked in a café, the "Sandra," he ought to know it, best coffee in Riga, and the freshest pastries, and then followed such a vivid picture of fresh buns and crusty pies that the old man's mouth began to water, and his heart melted with a taste of approaching surrender. Everything happened as if in a dream. Without meaning to sell, the old man reached out for the green note not of his own accord but impelled by a mysterious force that pulled at his hand. When finally he found himself watching the receding figure of the tall good-for-nothing who had tucked the puppy into his coat, he couldn't believe it had happened with his conscious participation and not by a sleight of hand, or some witchcraft that was still holding him enthralled. However, there was the money in his hand, so he had to reconcile himself with reality, and folding up the three-ruble note he shoved it into his pocket.

The wind had grown icy, or so it seemed to the old man, it hit him cuttingly behind the ears and froze the remaining puppy's soft little body. Seeing it shiver all over—no more brothers to snuggle up to—the old man said: "You poor little shrimp!" And he unbuttoned his coat and pushed the dog inside it, feeling through his sweater the touch of the blunt claws and the light, quick beat of the tiny heart. The puppy continued to shiver and turned and twisted on the old man's chest. He sighed, but said nothing, for they both suffered and neither was to blame.

Eddies of powdery snow rolled over the frozen ground, trams screeched as they swerved round the bend of the rails, people hurried past, their footfalls crunching in the snow. The old man had thrust his right hand into his coat pocket, while the left was supporting the pup that had at last stopped shivering and slept inside his coat. The frost cut through the mitten, but the old man didn't dare move his stiffened fingers lest he wake the puppy—it needed a bit of sleep. The wind whirled the fine snow about the old man's legs, powdering his large black laced boots. The pup's unruffled sleep made him yearn for warmth, all his thoughts were suddenly centered on his stove, a shelf in a bathhouse, a cup of hot tea, vodka in a dewy glass, and he thought—as soon as he sold the pup he'd hurry to the store and get himself a small bottle, and then he'd go straight home and fix himself a proper grog, to make up for the long cold morning. He'd get the stove as hot as a flatiron, and then he'd drink a glass of grog—better two, it wouldn't do to get sick. Aye, that's what he'd do the moment he was rid of the pup. Such were the old man's thoughts while the wind whirled the powdery snow about his boots and swished round his ears, and the pup, snug against his chest, the tip of its black bewhiskered little muzzle peeping out from under the coat, slept its trustful sleep, blissfully unaware of the man's beautiful plans, which could be wrecked by the very fact of its unruffled sleep. Once set in motion, the man's thoughts continued to spin on and on of their own accord. Now he was thinking that the two of them, he and Gracia, were growing older and the pups were getting fewer and not so beautiful, and he wasn't at all what he used to be and had better take a philosophical view of it for he'd had a wife, and he still had his sons, and the sons had outgrown him as their sons would outgrow them in due course; that he could live with his children but didn't want to be a burden on anyone so he kept to his own flat, and he had his own pension and his garden and his Gracia and he was both master and servant, and though at this moment he was frozen stiff and trembling like a chicken in the rain, yet he could, if he chose, go home straightway, pick up his basket and go, and this was his great freedom—he could go or stay, as he pleased—it was the freedom that age had given him to make up for what it had taken away from him in the course of years—for only the young and the green saw age as the end of all.

Thinking these thoughts the old man didn't notice the boy of seven or eight who had been watching him for some time now from under a gray rabbit-skin hat that half covered an upwards-tilted face, round and rosy like a bun fresh from the oven, with two currants for eyes. Presently the boy spoke to him: "Granddad . . . I say, granddad! Where did you get that lovely dog?"

The old man looked down and said he was selling it.

"You are?!" They boy raised a red-and-white mitten and touched the little black muzzle. "He's asleep!"

The old man lifted the pup out of the dark of his bosom into broad daylight. The pup opened its eyes and gave a wide yawn. The boy broke into laughter, his brown eyes dancing.

"Look! Look! He's got teeth! And a little tongue!"

"Of course he has!" said the old man, and added: "Why not buy it? You'll have a friend. A dog is man's friend."

"Is it? Does it . . . does it cost a lot of money?"

"Well—I'll let you have it for a ruble and a half," said the old man after a moment's hesitation, but the boy's unblinking eyes remained fixed on him, and he didn't utter a sound.

"Come on, make up your mind!" said the old man, and he told the boy that he'd sold two pups at five rubles each this very morning, and he'd once had occasion to charge as much as eight, and a ruble and a half was no money at all, like selling it for a song.

"I haven't got such a lot of money," the boy said wistfully and heaved a sigh.

The old man remembered the sausage in his coat pocket, broke off a little piece and fed it to the dog.

"Granddad!"

"What is it?"

"May I look at him, just like that?"

"What do you mean—just like that?"

"I mean, if I can't pay . . ."

Now it was the old man's turn to heave a sigh. The pup was munching its sausage, pleased with its dog's life, and the two humans stood watching in silence.

"Granddad!"

"What is it?"

"Let me hold it, just for a little!"

"The boy set down his string bag, which contained an empty glass jar covered with a plastic lid, reached out for the pup, and clutched it awkwardly, laughing out loud, but the pup was uncomfortable and waggled its legs trying to reach the ground.

"How he kicks!" the boy exclaimed, clutching the pup for all he was worth, while the animal wriggled desperately to escape his grip. "He's so tiny, but look how strong he is! I can't hold him! What's his name?"

The pup had no name. So the boy tried out every dog name he knew – Dingo, and Caro, and Mars, and Jack – and when the pup failed to respond to any of them he passed over to names no dog in the world has ever been called yet – human names, and bird names – and then he invented names as long as a railway train, and others as tender as the rustle of leaves, but the pup wouldn't listen and just went on wriggling and writhing and whining.

"Don't squeeze it so hard! Hold it properly, don't squeeze!"

The old man helped the boy to slip the pup into his crooked arm. At once it quietened down and lay still, gazing into the wide world from behind the boy's coat sleeve, and only the little heart went on beating very rapidly. The boy could feel it through his red-and-white mitten, and his eyes brimmed with tenderness.

"Granddad . . ."

"Yes, what is it?"

"If I give you all the money I have . . . ?"

The old man was silent.

"And the jar, too. Please, granddad!"

"How much d'you have?" the old man growled.

The boy set down the pup, pulled off his mitten, and began to count. Seventy kopecks in the purse, eleven in the pocket — oh! and the glass jar, that was another ten. Ninety-one kopecks all in all.

Again the old man heaved a sigh.

"Oh all right! Take it."

The boy poured the coins into the old man's palm and pushed the dog into the string bag from which he had removed the jar.

"He won't escape like this!" His eyes, radiant with happiness, were glued to the pup.

"Do you have far to go?"

"Where? Home, you mean? No . . . not really . . . Through the viaduct and then a little way up. Meistaru Street. D'you know it?"

The old man didn't.

When the boy lifted the string bag the pup's little paws stuck out through the loops. The old man was about to say something but decided it wasn't worth it if the boy didn't have far to go.

"Bye-bye!" the boy said without looking up at the old man.

The old man carefully folded up the woollen shawl and put it in the empty basket. Then he added the jar. It had a green plastic lid. The memory of the boy rankled in his mind. What the hell did he want with the jar? However, he put it in the basket. His bones felt rusty with all the standing about, and his joints creaked when he got moving. The black-laced boots skidded on the trodden snow; they'd recently been thickly soled. At first his legs seemed stiff as pokers, but they loosened up by and by, the toes tingled as they came to life, and before long his whole body warmed and his thoughts grew happier and lighter. The recent experience no longer darkened his mood. He'd made thirteen rubles and ninety-one kopecks, he calculated. Barring the fare it still amounted to more than twelve rubles clear profit. Not very much, but enough to gratify some very simple human needs. A lot of things in this world acquired a different value if you looked at them a little more philosophically.

By the time the old man reached his stop it was afternoon. The pups in the basket were superseded by a sausage and a loaf of crusty new bread that lay side by side in friendly unison. A shiny metal bottle top peeped from his coat pocket. The winter sun was slanting coldly between the trees. The wind came sweeping down the white expanse of the Daugava, whipping the snow from the branches of trees. After the Riga streets that traffic and pedestrians had turned a dirty gray everything here looked sparkling white. Carefully stepping into footprints previously sunk into the snow, the old man passed the bakery where he used to work. The gate was locked, the chimney cold, there was no smoke streaming in the wind, the two-story brick building did not emit the usual fragrance of newly baked bread, everything smelled of cool wet snow—for it was Sunday. Sparrows filled the air with their chirping and twittering.

The old man lived on the bank of the Daugava. In summer, especially in the hot season, the place was alive with a hubbub of sounds—the roar of motorboats, the shrieks and squeals of bathers—but in winter it was as though a lid of ice had been lowered upon the place, from which issued now and again a sound like glass cracking. As soon as the river came into view the old man sensed the proximity of home even before he could see it, and when it finally materialized before his eyes, small and dark against the sparkling snow, with two entrances—one for his neighbors and one for himself—and two chimneys, with starling houses and snow-clad flower beds, he quickened his pace, because Gracia had been languishing indoors all this time. As he unlocked the door he could hear her shuffling about, breathing wheezily. He called to her, and her breath came quicker and louder, he could feel her impatient expectancy.

Gracia flew toward him but came to a sudden halt before

the basket and sniffed at it, pushing her black muzzle against the wickerwork.

"Come along, now!" said the old man, unpacking his purchases and pushing the basket under the steps.

Gracia trotted off to the door, impatiently begging to be let out. She was an old bitch, very gray, her belly sagging, for time had not spared her any more than it spares anybody or anything. The old man opened the door for her, then got busy with the stove. The wind had drawn all the warmth from the house, but by the time the kettle was boiling it felt quite comfortable. He put the frying pan on the range and fried up a few slices of sausage and some potatoes left over from the previous night. When everything was ready he remembered Gracia and called her from the door. She didn't appear. He stepped outside, walked round the house, and saw her. She was crouching in the snow gazing into the white distance beyond the Daugava, whimpering sadly and silently as though reliving some secret memories from her dog's life. He called to her. She started, then rose heavily and approached him, pressed herself against his legs and looked up at him questioningly.

"It's all right, all right now," said the old man, and together they returned to the warm, fragrant, steamy kitchen.

He opened the bottle and fixed himself a grog. It went down like fire — hot and strong. Gracia lay at his feet, pressing her belly against the floor, her dark glittering eyes fastened upon his face. He put a slice of fried sausage before her, but she wouldn't touch it and just lay there cooling her painfully swollen teats against the floorboards, gazing at the old man.

He made himself a second grog.

His ears were burning like fire, the wind had bitten into them good and hard. A warm, light giddiness rose to his head, all the day's events flowed through his mind, he felt a great need to talk. He could have gone out to see his next-door neighbor, if his legs hadn't felt so heavy, and his head so light, besides, he grudged him the vodka he'd have to take along, and it wouldn't be nice, anyway, if he brought a half-empty bottle – especially one that the factory hadn't provided with a stopper. So when the old man had emptied the second glass he addressed himself to Gracia. He told her about the man with the guitar who had bought her first pup, and the crazy piece of music he'd played, so wild and fiery that even the cranberry women couldn't help stamping time, it was music that sent shivers down one's spine, and it was dedicated to Gracia's first pup.

Carried away by his own story, the old man soon found himself talking about the three student girls, so young and fresh, so amazingly alike, like sisters, and how tenderly they'd placed Gracia's second pup in a bright blue bag, that sparkled like a Christmas cracker, and how they'd kept fussing over it as though it were a prince they were conveying to his royal carriage, whispering words of endearment so sweet they could melt the heart of the toughest youth, let alone that of a dog. When he recalled the third pup he saw with his mind's eye the crusty appetizing pies it would be fed on every day of its life, and as he uttered the word *pies* he could actually see them, hot and enticing, filled with the choicest meat and spiced with delicious onions, gleaming in the twilight of the room like little candles, as fragrant as violets, as heady as herbs. And finally, elated by his recollections, the old man said that no one had ever offered him anything like the price he'd received that day for the fourth pup, for people always offered no more than part of what they possessed, never all of it – but not so the boy who's bought Gracia's fourth pup – a bitch at that; he'd given him all the money he had, down to the last kopeck, and a glass jar to boot, and a man's all was a man's all, it couldn't be measured in terms of kopecks or rubles, it was the highest price in the world.

And when the old man had finished his story he saw that Gracia had picked up her slice of sausage and was munching it slowly, and, deeply moved, he said that even a dog's heart had its measure of pain, just like a man's; you could fill a glass only to the brim, for what was more would spill over. And the neighbors who heard his voice behind the wall said the old man was either drunk or crazy, he was talking to himself. Which was not true, he was neither the one nor the other, neither crazy nor drunk, nor was it to himself he'd been talking. The truth was—he was feeling happy because he hadn't lived the day in vain, he had placed his pups into good hands and not just sold them to any passerby, because man must be responsible for his dog, and this is a truth people ought to know.

JUOZAS APUTIS

The Glade with Life-Giving Water

Translated by Angus Roxburgh

EVER SINCE MORNING everyone had been sadly quiet and unwilling to speak. Only the mother had occasionally asked whether her daughter had not forgotten anything. She wouldn't be able to come home for every little thing. The father rummaged in the passage for his ax, trudged off to the woodshed, shook free the block that had embedded itself in the ground, reset it, and began chopping the young alders he had brought in the spring. A gust of wind occasionally broke through the dense green fir trees. The flowers already smelled of autumn. The sun was gleaming through the foliage of the trees, shimmering in the crowns of three oaks in the middle of the pasture. Now the father took three strokes to get through the flimsiest of the alders, while a week before he had chopped such dry saplings with a single blow. His daughter was still bending over her suitcase, checking her things, carefully turning them back with her slender fingers.

The mother, herself not quite sure why, went up to the attic, crossed over to the window, and gazed out at the rank of old fir trees; this green wall blocked almost everything from sight; all that could be seen were the branch of an oak and, farther off, at the edge of the forest, a small hill covered with trampled, blackened clover and the doleful stalks of lupins –

wild strawberries grew on this knoll, and raspberries, too, some years. From this window she had often seen her two daughters there, and her heart sank with fear every time the elder girl in her short dress stooped to pick a berry, and a passerby appeared on the path. That summer she had often seen her younger daughter throw herself into the arms of her sister, who would lift her up and whirl her round for a long time, with the younger girl's sunburned legs brushing against the lilac blossoms.

The mother sighed and was about to go back to the stairs when she suddenly caught sight of an old dress hanging on a nail: her daughter had long since grown out of it. She went over and buried her face in the dress, squeezing the thread-bare cloth in her hands. Down below the tiny window an over-ripe apple fell softly into the beetroot patch. Just under the roof ridge a speckled butterfly was fluttering in a spider's web. Father was still busy by the shed, chopping away at the logs. Then she heard him drive his ax into the block, and she knew that he was now searching his pockets for his "Prima" and matches, and as she looked through the small window she saw him setting off toward the fir wood, along the edge of the cherry orchard, and past the three oaks. There, at the road, grew a tall fir on which, before the First World War, grandfather had erected a small shrine with a little idol carved from a birch log. Everyone who walked or drove past the tree still raised his hat, although the birch idol was no longer there: some lover of antiquity had carried it off in his shining car to a distant city.

The mother stood crumpling her daughter's dress for a long time, then took it from the nail, folded it neatly, placed it under her arm, and crossed the attic, which was strewn with flax combings, to the staircase.

The younger daughter was rolling about on the grass beside the kennel, embracing the tired mongrel, who was very fond of her. The dog had long ago grown tired of rolling with the girl on the grass and, catching a moment, cast a longing glance at the forest visible beyond the clover field, but again and again the girl tumbled him onto the grass and the old dog, not wishing to offend her, began to play with her again.

Soon the elder daughter appeared outside too. She had left her room just as her mother, hiding the threadbare dress, was coming down to the hall. The little girl abandoned the now unnecessary dog and immediately scampered toward her sister.

"Are we going? Are we going?" she asked, taking her sister's hand. But her sister said nothing, and even without a reply the little girl understood that they were already on their way.

The girls' mother paced around the room, glancing with vague apprehension at the suitcase and the lilac umbrella propped against the wall, then looked out of the window at the departing girls and at the dog complaining of its lot and of its heavy chain. The daughters turned at the hay shed toward the gurgling stream; the younger girl took hold of the branches of the small alders and kept trying to put her arm round her sister's waist, but her sister did not feel like playing with her.

At the mill dam, which their father had built many years before, both girls stripped bare, and the elder dived head first from the bank, while her sister, who had not yet learned to swim well, entered the water more gingerly.

Their mother, unable to stay any longer in the room, opened the door, and the dog pinned his last hopes on her. She made her way straight to the kennel, stroked the dog's coat, which was warm after a day in the sun, glanced back and touched the part of the mongrel's neck where his hair had long ago worn away, revealing his bluish, pimply skin. Before the chain had rattled against the side of the kennel, the dog was already far away. He flung himself on the ground and rolled in the grass, then darted into the front garden, sniffed at the flowers and was about to lift his only white leg—the others were black—but changed his mind and sped off over the clover following the father's still-fresh tracks. The mother also left the yard, not for the forest, however, but for the pasture, where a cow was tethered under an oak tree. Gripped in her hands was her daughter's old dress.

In various parts of this broad forest clearing there were now four people: three adults and a child; somewhere in the forest a little dog was bounding after the scent of a wild animal; under an oak tree stood a cow; and in potato drills, in the shade of the shaws, some hens were sitting, their dusty wings spread and beaks wide open.

The elder sister dived tirelessly into the deep water, her long wet plaits hanging over her back, while the smaller girl tried to reach her, asking to be taken into the middle of the pool. But the elder girl did this only once, and even then unwillingly and without affection. Of the grown-ups living in this forest glade she alone was not lost in thoughts about the past. Having swum to the other bank, she sat on a large rock, letting her heavy, wet plaits hang down, and looked – with incomprehensible fear, as though for the first time – at her tanned breasts and at her legs, which were slightly scratched above the knees. Here too there was a scent of wild dahlias on the breeze; a strange, plaintively enticing presentiment enveloped her, as though someone not very frightening, but disquieting nonetheless, were stealing close. At that moment she seemed to sense a force that she would necessarily have to obey. This imperious force loomed somewhere in the distance, but the girl fearfully understood that it could already see her and was drawing toward her.

"You're bad!" said her little sister, this small, naked girl with scratched legs. "You always used to be good to me, but now you're not. Well just you go away then – I'll be good to myself!"

"What are you angry at?" said the older girl listlessly, forcing herself to remember her sister, who was sitting, her arms stretched out, in the water at the other bank. "I *am* good. You know I am..."

She spoke tenderly, but the vague feeling of yearning did

not leave her. She could not stay here any longer. Touching
the things of her infancy and childhood, the constantly cours-
ing and seething water and the rocks covered with slime, she
sensed that she was pushing herself away from them, breaking natural links forever, yet at the same time she was engraving these things in her memory, so that many years later she
might find strength in them in a moment of weariness.

Her father, however, was young again, like many years before, and was sitting under a large fir tree. He was a strong
man, he knew his own strength and realized that at a time like
this, on the brink of separation, it was not for a man to absorb
himself in the past—but he could not help it. Perhaps this
hour would become the foothold for a new unrealizable
dream, for new forest clearings—yet, who knows, he smiled,
who knows. There used to be dense forest here, in the middle
of which he had cleared a spacious, square glade and used the
logs for buildings, leaving only four oaks in the middle of the
clover field; he had dammed up the stream and begun to
build a mill and a bathhouse, such as no one in the neighborhood had built, on stout oak posts, where the weary traveler
could look forward to hot water. For many years the posts intended for the bathhouse jutted out of the water; something
happened to the owner—one spring day all his endeavors appeared petty and absurd to him and he grew restless, and finally with a crash the drifting ice demolished the posts of his
strange construction and bore them off. That same spring he
could not resist the call of life, and heeding the cry of the
trees and the grass and the birds he rode on horseback from
the glade that he had cleared himself in the black forest
and in the evening he returned with the young woman who
now, supporting her chin with one hand and crumpling her
daughter's old dress with the other, was standing under one
of the oaks, looking into the eyes of a chewing cow. The animal's tranquility calmed her. The woman was also immersed
in the past; she was wondering whether after this day she
would have new dreams, or that foothold that had brought a

smile to her husband's lips as he sat bareheaded under the tall fir. The mother saw only her own flesh and blood and the dress that her daughter had outgrown, and heard the words the girl had said a few days before. She had come inside, having been sitting under the oak tree, holding a linen shawl that her mother had woven, and sat down on a bench under an embroidered towel.

"You didn't stay long!"

The daughter looked out of the kitchen window.

"Wasn't it nice under the oak tree?"

"It was lovely under the oak tree, Mother. Only frightening. When the leaves rustle I can feel time passing. Right through me I can feel what time is and how it is passing."

The girl's mother started; she had experienced the same sad sensation long ago, but had not been able to express it so clearly in words. She went up to her daughter and placed her hand on her head.

The passing time rustled in the leaves of the oaks.

Now the mother squeezed her daughter's dress in her hand; the girl had outgrown it long ago. Time was passing with terrifying speed.

But her elder daughter was still sitting in the water and could not understand what was going on in this forest clearing. Trying to dispel her thoughts about the distant force that was spying on her and weighing on her, she got up from the rock, swam over to her little sister, and lifted her up in her arms, showering her with kisses. The child hurriedly blurted out words that her sister had no desire to hear: "Don't you start crying, though. We're the ones that should be crying, because you're going away."

Panting loudly, the dog came running up to the millpond, slid down the bank, and sank down greedily at the water's edge. The little girl forced him to take a swim too.

Presently, from three directions, the father, the mother, and both girls returned to the cottage. The wet dog was again rolling about on the grass, and the younger girl asked her sister: "Will you come home often? Study a bit, and then come and bathe in our pond!"

The dog was listening, and perhaps even understood a thing or two—water does refresh the brain!

The elder sister answered: "Yes, of course I'll come."

It was a joyless reply. Probably she already understood a thing or two herself: it is impossible, after all, to go away and to return just like that; never again would she be the person she used to be, neither on the knoll where strawberries grow, and sometimes raspberries, nor in the refreshing water of the pond, though this quiet glade would surely entice her more and more as the years went by, and each homecoming would be a return only to the past, to the violet clover, to the rock in the millpond and to the three oaks, because there would no longer be such things in her life.

The first to stride along the path, as was fitting, was the father, carrying his daughter's suitcase. He was followed by his elder daughter, her mother, the child, and the dog. On reaching the three oaks, the mother ran back, treading barefoot along the grass-covered path, hung her daughter's old dress on the fence, and plucked a flower from below the window; the daughter took the flower and gave her mother her umbrella. Now and again the dog would dart ahead, showing off that he also knew the way.

"There once was a secular oak here as well, but it was struck by lightning and dried up. I made a table out of it, and a footbridge across the stream. Only three remained."

"You told us about it, Father . . ."

"Over there where the clover is now, our dog was once gored by a wild boar."

"You told us, Mother . . ."

"It's all right for you, you're going away. But I've got to stay here," said the younger girl, overtaking her mother and clasping her sister's hand.

"You'll be leaving soon, too."

"Huh, that won't be for a long time."

"The time will fly – you won't even notice it."

"It just seems like that to you because you're going."

The people from the forest clearing reached the scorching road quickly. They did not have to wait long for the bus, which stopped at the curb grunting and snorting like an enormous wild boar. The father helped to carry the suitcase in, the mother gave the umbrella to her daughter and saw how the young driver stared at the girl, while her sister remained on the other side of the ditch, facing the other way and no longer looking at the bus. The bus moved off, blowing sand, which looked blue in the exhaust fumes, from the asphalt, and those who were left behind could see the girl smiling to them and holding in front of her the flower her mother had picked. The dog evidently agreed at heart with the younger sister: he leapt onto the road and, yelping angrily, tried to catch up with the bus and bite its wheel.

RITA KELLY

The Cobweb Curtain

"It can't be... Julie?"

"Yes it is. How are you?"

The coolness of it, clipped, London. Still pretty, so casual, straight cords, always could wear anything.

"Must be years, let me see..."

"About twelve I should say."

"And you haven't—"

"Changed a bit! Kate, let's not go through the clichés. Care for a drink?"

"Yes, that's an idea. I've been moping about the old town. I suppose you have noticed the changes too, even the shops."

"All plate glass, impractical, and understocked. One pharmacy after the other, I merely wanted a packet of cotton wool, and when they didn't have it they tried selling me 500 meters of the stuff, one could insulate an attic."

Still the same Julie, sprightly, yet not the same, alien almost.

"And I see they've swept the old post office away."

"And poor Larry Molloy's house beside it, car-for-hire, you remember?"

"Died, didn't he?"

"Only three months ago, and all the journeys he made to Clondelara, visitors, Christmas..."

"And late Saturday nights when my father had drunk himself out of memory and whatever miserable money he had."

"Julie, you must miss him, I didn't know how to bring it up . . ."

"Shall we try the hotel?"

"It's so awkward, impossible almost . . ."

"The hotel?"

"Sympathizing."

Along the footpath, Julie's fashionable heels pricking the stone. Not a walk, an elegant glide. Her hair is dark against the sunlit street, soft style, flowing with her footsteps. Her hair was always dark even when cut to the bone, to deal with nits, her industrious mother rubbing in pomade and paraffin oil, Kate got the whiff of it over the years, the ghost of a bare-legged little girl, now this suave young woman.

"Please, Kate, I invited you therefore I insist on buying the drinks."

"Very well then, gin and lime."

"Ice?"

"No thanks."

To reach across the years. Perhaps it is impossible. What will she drink, something rather exotic no doubt. Nice handbag too, wonder what she does. Married? Must be, and a family? Strange she bothers to come home, and the mother, God love her, well . . . hopelessly ineffectual. The jacket is becoming, she can wear it, but it's just a trifle common, superstore stuff, mustn't be a bitch, things at Scotts' were never easy.

That day by the well, overgrown now no doubt, it was a place of mossed stones, hazels, and wild strawberries. They had come to get spring water for the butter, the elastic gave in Julie's knickers and they fell about her ankles. Kate had laughed, Julie threw a whole can of water in her face and walked off leaving the pink knickers on the grass.

"Sorry for being so long, this takes time."

"A pint, I, didn't think − "

"Good for the blood, why not, besides I enjoy it."

"Of course, I just thought—"

"You know, Kate, I too must avoid the clichés, I was about to ask where you were now, and what you are doing. So silly, isn't it."

"Cheers."

"Cheers. However, let me ask how your parents are, I know that it's a relatively safe question."

"I imagine, Julie, that you know all there is to know about them. They sold the old place about eight years ago, and they're now quite comfortable—at least mother is—on the Elm Drive side of town. Quite up to date, though Dad still hankers after Clondelara, insists on pottering about, can't fully accept it you know."

"I'd say that being in town quite suits your mother. She was always, shall we say, lost in the country."

"Thanks for the understatement. You never did particularly care to, but would you like to come up and see her now?"

"Sorry, I told Mark to expect me about six."

"Mark?"

"My son. Gone five, the youngest."

"You have more then?"

"Yes, Kate, two more. They didn't come, they've slightly outgrown my mother as you might understand."

She did. Julie's mother in Clondelara, that easy way with things, excruciating really, but so likable, and the homely kitchen face having nothing in common with the fresh-air face across the lounge table.

"And your husband?"

"No, Kate, Clondelara is not his idea of happiness, and he is made to feel, well . . ."

"Out of it? It can happen, particularly if . . ."

"If he's English, no Church, abstemious, and rather vocal."

"Yet you still come back, Julie?"

"Don't we all. But don't misunderstand me, it would be less bother to write or telephone, nothing about the place draws me, I come annually for a week, it keeps my mother in touch, and as she'll neither write nor come to us, it seemed the most practical solution."

"Yes, and . . ."

"And it can't go on much longer, a few years perhaps, and then I shan't ever come. No reason."

"But Julie, how can you be so definite. And the children?"

"Quite simple really, when one nurtures no sentimental attachments. As for the children, they'll always be strangers in Clondelara, it means nothing to them, except a point on the planet where Mummy was born. It could be anywhere, and they'll find nothing of me there."

"But Julie, all your past is there, locked within the landscape, the turns and bends of the road, the furzy hills, the . . ." She stopped. She had almost said the well in the hazelwood.

"Don't be daft. The road has been flattened and steam-rolled, the corners and bends bulldozed away. Trees have been cut, lanes choked with briars and nettles. Hazel hedges ripped asunder giving on to new bungalows."

"I haven't been out there in years."

"Even your own house, Kate, I wouldn't recognize it, all shuttered up. And this morning I saw some cows in the front lawn."

"Would you like another drink?"

"No thank you, one is sufficient, and I must do something about a taxi."

"Listen, Julie, let me drive you out, I can spare the time and it will save you the bother."

"All right then. I hitched in; a Wakefield chap from way up, you know, the Attykill side, gave me a lift. I hadn't an idea who he was, and he kept insisting that I ought to know. What these people take one for."

"You don't mean that you hitched in."

"Well I'd defy you to manage mother's battered old bicycle, and the bus passes only two days a week, marvelous system. I did think of tackling the pony, but found the collar in shreds, and a draft-chain pulled off to tie a starved mongrel to the spokes."

"Your father always kept the harness, very particular about them I remember."

"Much good it has done."

"He loved dogs about the yard too."

"Dogs, yes, not curs, and he did manage to feed them."

"I know. Now that he's gone . . ."

"He too began to feel the futility of keeping the weeds from the gate."

"You're quite sure that you won't have another drink?"

"Yes, quite."

"Mind if I go to the ladies room, and then we can start. I left the car on the Square."

"And Kate, thanks for the lift."

"Not at all. My turn anyway, think of all the times you put me on the carrier of your bike and left me at the haggard-gate because I was too afraid to pass the well on my own."

"Wonder if you still are?"

There was a full-length mirror in the lavatory. "Good," she thought, the suit is still sitting properly, if I wasn't so long and skinny. The hair, I'm not sure now of the ash blonde, Julie's looks far more natural. Strange meeting her after all these years, not the same person really, I can't see her knickerless among the hazels. My mother never liked her. "Bad company, Kate," she said, "living wild with horses and dogs in that ramshackle house." Attractive house, attractive girl, beautiful skin, even today no need of makeup, I liked that house, I loved those days with Julie. So changed, elegant aloofness, hitched into town and drank a pint of Guinness. Unpredictable. I can still feel the ice-cold water full on my face. Indeterminate face, a little old half-and-half, a bit of a changeling, that is Mrs. Scott's voice, here now as in that antique kitchen, but why indeterminate? A little more eye shadow, perhaps. Why do my fingers fumble, nervous of Clondelara? Glad of the excuse to go down there again with Julie, too late for the wild strawberries, that was in June, we lay in the long grass after. God, I am afraid to go back.

She found herself reading, "Insert soiled sanitary towel and reclose the drawer firmly." "Damn," she said, and banged the door going out.

"Ready, Kate?"

"Yes. How long have you got?"

"Until Wednesday."

"I was thinking," what was she thinking anyway? "I was thinking we might go to a film, perhaps. Dinner together. There's a new place on the Woodpark Road, quite good, they do an excellent Beef Wellington."

"Thanks a lot, Kate, but I didn't come back for that kind of thing. Besides, we should very definitely run out of things to talk about."

"I see. It was just an idea. Maybe I don't agree with you, fully."

"Exhausting our topics of conversation? Well, just try it. There can't be any real contact, and you know it. Whatever we may have been to each other is long since past. And digging up all the details could do neither of us any good."

"It can help, sometimes."

"Sorry, but I'm not necromantic."

Untouchable, thought Kate, she is probably right too. Might be interesting to see more of her, but one mustn't grasp. Her tones are so final and well formed, such a change from the Clondelara cadence. We all adapt, more or less, to the new, but something drags, something to make one uneasy.

"I say, Kate, what a car. Doing all right for yourself, eh. Mother will be stupefied when she sees this thing stop at the gate. What you bet, she'll kick a few chickens from the kitchen, God between us and all harm, posh visitors and the place in a mess."

"It's nothing really, well, as cars go, Brendan ordered it for me, Easter."

"Stereo, sunroof, and sheepskin covers, the lot. A bit of all right. Did I hear you say Brendan? Some fellow this Brendan of yours."

"I didn't mean to show off. Or did I?"

"Forget it, Kate. Are you up in town for long? Or are you a lady of leisure?"

"The weekend. I come from time to time, and Brendan likes the golf course here, it's relaxing for him."

"Play yourself?"

"A little, but it doesn't mean the same to me. And the ladies' end of it can be a bore, you know, comparing nappy-rash, exam results, and adulteries."

"I can imagine. What's he do?"

"Brendan?"

"Yes."

"He's attached to the county hospital, pathology."

"I remember now, mother did have a big story for me, a doctor, a few years back."

"Six years."

"Kids?"

"None, well . . ."

"Better off maybe, sorry, Kate, that's the cliché response, forgive my asking."

"Not at all. At least you spared me the marked pause, you know, that silence while the other person wonders which of us is sterile."

"Does that still give nowadays?"

"You'd be surprised, Julie, what still gives. I haven't been on this road for so long, I had almost forgotten how narrow it is."

"Or how big your car is."

"Perhaps you're right, things go out of perspective."

"Yes, Kate, and rather quickly too. There's the letter box, remember the mail van at six p.m. and the cows had to be back in the paddock across the road before it came, speeding as always."

Mail van. Pathetic really. What creates a rhythm and a routine, anything at all to mark time. This impossible road of bushes, might be a stone round the next bend, pushed off by a full-grown lamb. Briars scrape the side of the car, how dazzling the red paint-work must seem in this tunnel of tired green. Stubble, blotched and burned, might be a harvester coming along, slowly. Cubes of straw. And Kate, there's Flynns'. Who's there now? Haven't an idea, never see them. Flynns' thresher would come into the haggard, such excitement, tumbling in the chaff and field mice scurrying from the stack, Julie's father coming to throw sheaves. Blackberries and fresh cream, the sweet tang of it, wash off all those maggots, the fear of getting a crawly thing on the tongue. Yes, and Duffys', they have cut the apple trees. Too old I suppose. Marking time. How small the fields are, cattle under trees swishing flies, swarms of midges in the quiet of the evening, brushing by one another against the setting sun. The long drawn-out decline of the sun. And Walshes'. What ever became of Helen?

"Kate, there's your old house."

Thought we could slip past it, keep talking, God, nothing, why won't she keep talking, anything.

"There it is, Kate, see what I mean? Pity, too, such a fine house, I'm sure someone would have been glad of it. Look."

Christ, the bleak blue light, the shuttered windows. Sure someone would have been glad of it, such a fine house, oh yes, nettles growing halfway up the door, the gate choked, fine house, as if nothing else mattered, what's she know about it. The front wall plundered.

"That's life, Kate. Move on."

"That's not life, that's . . ."

"Ah well, no point in moaning."

"Who's moaning?"

"You are."

"No, I'm not."

"Yes, you. Don't let's argue, it's childish."

"And if you had a can of water you'd throw it."

"You know I had quite forgotten that. Funny, wasn't it."

"Oh yes, very funny."

"Kate, you don't mean —"

"No, I don't mean anything."

There all the time, shuttered, sealing something from the light. Undisturbed for years, but spiders tenuously tying things together. A tentative opening of a door might rend the webs, making an unpleasant mess of dust, fluff, and fly bodies. A constant killing in the quiet. Damp moldering rooms, doors would creak, and a footstep ring hollow on the floor, where *Red Riding Hood* was read by the fire before mother's brisk "Time for bed." Empty echoing rooms, brittle paint and plasterwork, a trapped air smelling of decay. An empty shell.

"Kate, we're not being pursued, are we?"

Eyes fixed suddenly on the road ahead, Kate jabbed the gearshift back, and came out of the bend with a lurch.

"Julie, did you fly?"

"No, the boat still works out less expensive."

"Of course, but it can be such a bother, especially with children."

"Mark's no trouble, and he enjoys the adventure of being at sea." Letting the wind blow through his hair, and gripping the handrail, and "Mummy are there whales down there, is it really very deep?" Peering across the blue distance, there just might be a gull. The salt tang and the slap of the water, the furtive child's considering look back along the wake where Dad and Jenny and Alison remain. Then that tug at a sleeve, "Mummy look, there are gulls."

"But Julie, the plane is so fast and convenient."

"One might as well be in the Tube."

The blue light in her eyes. Kate suddenly glimpsed her, scarved, on deck, the wind billowing her skirts out from her long legs, her voice through it lively and vibrant, Mark,

Mummy. Kate felt bleak, out of it. A new realization of Julie. Living on the cheap, but liking it, somehow alive. A quiet self-reliance, hitching a lift, going her own way, grown up. Kate felt small, flushed, frustrated . . .

"Slow up, Kate, we're here. At least there's smoke."

The same smoke rising up through the beech trees. Cobweb lace on the windows, gate needs paint, the old piers are mossed and one of the caps is askew. And a huddle of out-houses tucked into the sandhill, and still the grass path and the dandelions.

"Would you like to come in, say hello to my mother, and have a cup of tea?"

"She'd be upset if I didn't. Also, I might like to meet Mark."

"He won't mind, probably up to his neck in Clondelara mud by now. It tends to attach itself to one, you know."

"Julie, you're being ironic."

"Not really, just factual."

The old dog barked, she feared that he was about to jump up at her with his friendly filthy paws. A wrinkled face had appeared at the window, the curtain slips back. Then Mrs. Scott was at the door wiping her hands in her apron, the gray hair untidily pinned back, no bottom teeth.

"Musha, I thought 'twas someone. I couldn't know who on earth was coming in with Julia. And you're heartily welcome, Lord save us but 'tis years."

"How are you, Mrs. Scott?"

"Pulling the devil by the tail, and there's no loss on yourself by the look of it."

"Mother, Kate drove me out from town."

Dazed coming in from the bright light, smell of sour milk and soap powder, and that tireless voice flowing in warmish waves over her.

"Wasn't that awful good of her, always a good-natured young one, seems no length since you were running into me here in the kitchen, day you turned the pram upside down, and the child in it, I'm sure 'twas a pure accident, and your mother in the hospital, how is she?"

A wipe of her apron on the table, she bangs a couple of buckets together and fusses a few chairs out of the way.

"She was having your little sister at the time, what's this her name was, a grown woman now, married and all I suppose. Miriam. It had always been Miriam. And you did marvelous yourself, a doctor I'm told, sure you won't have far to go for the bit of medical attention. I never heard, but did you have a family?" She was standing, brush in hand.

"No, Mother, Kate has no children. I'll put the kettle on."

"Ah well, God is good, and there's plenty of time."

The can of spring water on a table. The same old dresser with the milk jugs, and cups on hooks, can't keep the ashes off. She comes with an armful of turf and piles it on the fire. Kate's hand goes to take the tongs, so many times, the half-heard voice, the flapping flame.

"Sure they can't do enough for me, God love them. There's Julia comes home every year without fail, sends the few bob from time to time. And the little lad, what's this his name is, a cure to have a child round the house again, sticks his nose in everything, I'm sure he's up to something. Run down Julia, he was with the hens before you came, you wouldn't know what he might drink out there in the shed."

"Mother what's the oven doing? Are you baking?"

"I was just going to make a cake when I heard the car."

"But you know that there's plenty of bread in the house."

"And you kept the open-fire, Mrs. Scott?"

"Ah I did Katie, sure the kitchen wouldn't be the same without it."

"Yes, mother, you'd miss the smoke and the ashes in everything."

"Run out will you and see to the child."

The bake-oven and lid warming against the fire, just like it used to be, and she'll put the coals on the hob under it, getting the tongs again and being let put the coals on the lid. All those

days, and Julie, too, used to make a little cake from the remainder of the dough and put it on the coals. On the hearth,
watching the flames peep out through the turf, the warmth,
the rippling glint on the saucepan lids and on the delph.
Harsh March days, the fire reflected in the windowpane as if
it was out in the hedge. In the primroses. And sitting on the
hob itself, watching the smoke whirl up into the blue.

"Now that she's gone, will you tell me what in the name of
God do you think of her."

"Well, Mrs. Scott, Julie knows her own mind."

She has sat down too, in the armchair scratching the ashes
with the tongs. Hushed intimate tones.

"How right you are, Katie, did she say anything about her
man? A bit odd he is, between ourselves, not one of our kind
you know what I mean, has ideas and notions about everything, doesn't come much, oh I'd say he's very good to her
and all that. Just the way she talked about things long ago,
and she would take a Woodbine from behind the tea caddy,
and a bag of bull's-eyes, sweet and sticky. Hush now, I hear
her coming."

"Here he is. Say hello to Kate, then you may wash your
hands."

"Hello. Please Mummy who is Kate? May I go now?"

"Well isn't he the little stranger." Cool English consonants,
inquiring eyes, goes his own way. Gone.

"Well, isn't he the distant little creature, I don't know, but at
his age, honest to God but it's not natural."

"Children should not be petted, Mother."

Was Julie smiling slightly, smiling at her as she looked
across the firelit kitchen? The old woman was murmuring
about tea. She stood up, decided.

"No thanks, Mrs. Scott."

Go. She had a sudden sense of a salt breeze on a boat deck.
Her own voice, get out of this suffocating cave of a room.

"Don't fuss, Mother. We mustn't detain Kate."

Clipped and final, we mustn't detain. Dragging slattern

heels across the concrete floor, murmuring of eggs, might have the half-score, to bring back with you, God blast the same hens, wait now till I see.

"Thank you, Mrs. Scott, but I wouldn't like to leave you short."

"Plenty of eggs when we're all dead and gone. Wait now till I give them a rub of a cloth."

Rub of a cloth, dab of bread soda and a spit. Good-natured, hobbling. Hen dung trodden into the pitted concrete floor, stupid to have come, a ragged chicken drinking off the floor, some blue-gray mixture, milk and slop. Fussing about newspaper to wrap the eggs. And "Julia if you had a nice bit of a box." She had. It had held Mark's new shoes.

"Where's Mark, Julie?"

"Reading. His refuge."

Yes, his own way, his own world, shutting out the interminable voice.

"You'd want to mind his eyes, Julia, too much of that reading altogether, now if I had a bit of straw for the bottom of the box."

"Mother, for goodness' sake, Kate isn't on a bicycle."

"I'll say goodbye to you so. Mind the eggs. Julia will see you out to the gate. Lord, but I've ruined your glove with flour, wait till I get the old cloth."

"It's all right, they're an old pair anyway. Good-bye, Mrs. Scott, and . . . thank you."

"If only I'd known you were coming –"

Out into the fresh air, cool against flushed cheeks. Getting dark. There was hay down, a smell of meadowsweet. First touch of fog.

"Well, Kate, that's it."

"Yes. Mark is nicely behaved. Congratulations."

"Thanks."

"I suppose, Julie, I shan't see you before you go?"

"No. And I don't think you'll really want to."

"You don't?"

"No."

"Good-bye then. And Julie . . . I'm glad we met."

"Me too. Kate, have you forgotten?"

A pause. In the twilight Kate caught the ghost of a smile. A clasp across the void, quick and eager, and cool impression on the lips. Go, or the moment will have spent itself. Break.

She stopped the car at the mouth of a laneway. Taking the box with her she strode along between the hazels, wisps of fog hung in the leaves, there were the beginnings of nuts in their pale green frills. She found the well in a thicket of briar and blackthorn, a cow-track torn through it to a glint of black water.

I'll keep the box, she thought. Nice child. One by one she dropped in the whole half-score, light in her hand they went down like stones.

Lebanon / England

HANAN AL SHAYKH

The Women's Swimming Pool

Translated by Denys Johnson-Davies

I AM IN the tent for threading the tobacco amidst the mounds of tobacco plants and the skewers. Cross-legged, I breathe in the green odor, threading one leaf after another. I find myself dreaming and growing thirsty and dreaming. I open the magazine: I devour the words and surreptitiously gaze at the pictures. Exasperated at being in the tent, my exasperation then turns to sadness.

Thirsty, I rise to my feet. I hear Abu Ghalib say, "Where are you off to, little lady?" I make my way to my grandmother, saying, "I'm thirsty." I go out. I make my way to the cistern, stumbling in the sandy ground. I see the greenish blue waters. I stretch out my hand to its still surface, hot from the harsh sun. I stretch out my hand and wipe it across my brow and face and neck, across my chest. Before being able to savor its relative coldness, I hear my name and see my grandmother standing in her black dress at the doorway of the tent. Aloud I express the wish that someone else had called to me. We have become like an orange and its navel: my grandmother has welded me so close to her that the village girls no longer dare to make friends with me, perhaps for fear of rupturing this close union.

I return to the tent, growing thirsty and dreaming, with the sea ever in my mind. What were its waters like? What color would they be now? If only this week would pass in a flash for I had at last persuaded my grandmother to go down to Beirut and the sea, after my friend Sumayya had sworn that the swimming pool she'd been to had been for women only.

My grandmother sat on the edge of a jagged slab of stone, leaning on my arm. Her hand was hot and rough. She sighed as she chased away a fly.

What is my grandmother gazing at? There was nothing in front of us but the asphalt road, which, despite the sun's rays, gave off no light, and the white marble tombs that stretched along the high mountainside, while the houses of Upper Nabatieh looked like deserted Crusader castles, their alleyways empty, their windows of iron. Our house likewise seemed to be groaning in its solitude, shaded by the fig tree. The washing line stirs with the wind above the tomb of my grandfather, the celebrated religious scholar, in the courtyard of the house. What is my grandmother staring at? Or does someone who is waiting not stare?

Turning her face toward me, she said, "Child, what will we do if the bus doesn't come?" Her face, engraved in my mind, seemed overcast, also her half-crossed eyes and the blue tattoo mark on her chin. I didn't answer her for fear I'd cry if I talked. This time I averted my gaze from the white tombs; moving my foot away from my grandmother's leg clothed in thick black stockings, I began to walk about, my gaze directed to the other side where lay the extensive fields of green tobacco, their leaves glinting under the sun, leaves that were imprinted on my brain, and with the marks of them still showing on my hands, towering and gently swaying.

My gaze reached out behind the thousands of plants, then beyond them, moving away till it arrived at the tent where the tobacco was threaded. I came up close to my grandmother, who was still sitting in her place, still gazing in front of her. As I drew close to her, I heard her give a sigh. A sprinkling of sweat lay on the pouches under her eyes. "Child, what do you

want with the sea? Don't you know that the sea puts a spell on
people?" I didn't answer her: I was so worried that the morning would pass, that noonday would pass and that I wouldn't
see the green bus come to a stop by the stone my grandmother sat on and take us with it to the sea, to Beirut. Again I
heard my grandmother mumbling, "That devil Sumayya..."
I pleaded with her to stop, and my thoughts rose up and left
the stone upon which my grandmother sat, the rough road,
left everything. I went back to my dreams, to the sea.

The sea had remained my preoccupation ever since I had
seen it for the first time inside a colored ball; with its blue
color it was like a magic lantern, wide open, the surface of its
water unrippled unless you tilted the piece of glass, with its
small shells and white specks like snow. When I first became
aware of things, it was this ball, which I had found in the parlor, that was the sole thing that animated and amused me.
The more I gazed at it the more cold I could feel its waters,
the more they invited me to bathe myself in them; they knew
that I had been born amidst dust and mud and the stench of
tobacco.

If only the green bus would come along – and I shifted my
bag from one hand to the other. I heard my grandmother
wail, "Child, bring up a stone and sit down. Put down the bag
and don't worry." My distress increased and I was no longer
able to stop it turning into tears that flowed freely down my
face, veiling it from the road. I stretched up to wipe them
with my sleeve: in this heat I still had to wear that dress with
long sleeves, that head-covering over my plaits, despite the
hot wind that set the tobacco plants and the sparse poplars
swaying. Thank God I had resisted her and refused to wear
my stockings. I gave a deep sigh as I heard the bus's horn
from afar. Fearful and anxious, I shouted at my grandmother
as I helped her to her feet, turning round to make sure that
my bag was still in my hand and my grandmother's hand in
the other. The bus came to a stop and the conductor helped
my grandmother on. When I saw myself alongside her and

the stone on its own, I tightened my grip on my bag, in which lay Sumayya's bathing costume, a sleeveless dress, and my money.

I noticed as the bus slowly made its way along the road that my anxiety was still there, that it was in fact increasing. Why didn't the bus pass by all these trees and fallow land like lightning? Why was it crawling along? My anxiety was still there and increased till it predominated over my other sensations, such as nausea and curiosity.

How would we find our way to the sea? Would we see it as soon as we arrived in Beirut? Was it at the other end of it? Would the bus stop in the district of Zeytouna, at the door of the women's swimming pool? Why, I wondered, was it called Zeytouna?* Were there olive trees there? I leaned toward my grandmother with her silent face and long nose, which almost met up with her mouth. Thinking that I wanted a piece of cane sugar, she put her hand to her bosom to take out a small twist of cloth. Impatiently I asked her if she was sure that Maryam al-Taweela knew Zeytouna, to which she answered, her mouth sucking at the cane sugar and making a noise with her tongue, "God will look after everything." Then she broke the silence by saying, "All this trouble is that devil Sumayya's fault – it was she who told you she'd seen with her own eyes the swimming pool just for women and not for men."

"Yes, Grandma," I answered her.

She said, "Swear by your mother's grave."

I thought to myself absentmindedly, Why only my mother's grave? What about my father's? Or did she acknowledge only her daughter's death? "By my mother's grave, it's for women."

She inclined her head and still munching the cane sugar and making a noise with her tongue, she said, "If any man were to see you, you'd be done for, and so would your mother and father and your grandfather, the religious scholar – and

*The word means "olive tree" in Arabic.

I'd be done for more than anyone because it's I who agreed to you and helped you."

I would have liked to say to her, They've all gone, they've all died, so what do we have to be afraid of? But I knew what she meant: that she was frightened they wouldn't go to heaven.

I began to sweat and my heart again contracted as Beirut came into view with its lofty buildings, car horns, the bared arms of the women, the girls' hair, the tight trousers they were wearing. People were sitting on chairs in the middle of the pavement eating and drinking; the trams; the roasting chickens revolving on spits. Ah, these dresses for sale in the windows, would anyone be found actually to wear them? I see a Japanese man, the first ever member of the yellow races outside of books; the Martyrs' monument, Riad Solh Square. I was wringing wet with sweat and my heart pounded – it was as though I regretted having come to Beirut, perhaps because I was accompanied by my grandmother. It was soon all too evident that we were outsiders to the capital. We began walking after my grandmother had asked the bus driver the whereabouts of the district of Khandak al-Ghamik where Maryam al-Taweela lived. Once again my body absorbed all the sweat and allowed my heart to flee its cage. I find myself treading on a pavement on which for long years I have dreamed of walking; I hear sounds that have been engraved on my imagination, and everything I see I have seen in daydreams at school or in the tobacco-threading tent. Perhaps I shouldn't say that I was regretting it, for after this I would never forget Beirut. We begin walking and losing our way in a Beirut that never ends, leads nowhere. We begin asking and walking and losing our way, and my going to the sea seems an impossibility; the sea is fleeing from me. My grandmother comes to a stop and leans against a lamppost, or against the litter bin attached to it, and against my shoulders, and puffs and blows. I have the feeling that we shall never find Maryam al-Taweela's

house. A man we had stopped to ask the way walks with us.
When we knock at the door and no one opens to us, I become
convinced that my bathing in the sea is no longer possible.
The sweat again pours off me, my throat contracts. A woman's voice brings me back to my senses as I drown in a lake
of anxiety, sadness, and fear; then it drowns me once again. It
was not Maryam al-Taweela but her neighbor who is asking
us to wait at her place. We go down the steps to the neighbor's
outdoor stone bench, and my grandmother sits down by the
door but gets to her feet again when the woman entreats her
to sit in the cane chair. Then she asks to be excused while she
finishes washing down the steps. While she is cursing the heat
of Beirut in the summer, I notice the tin containers lined up
side by side containing red and green peppers. We have a
long wait, and I begin to weep inwardly as I stare at the containers.

I wouldn't be seeing the sea today, perhaps not for years,
but the thought of its waters would not leave me, would not
be erased from my dreams. I must persuade my grandmother
to come to Beirut with Sumayya. Perhaps I should not have
mentioned the swimming pool in front of her. I wouldn't be
seeing the sea today – and once again I sank back into a lake
of doubt and fear and sadness. A woman's voice again
brought me back to my senses: it was Maryam al-Taweela,
who had stretched out her long neck and had kissed me,
while she asked my grandmother, "She's the child of your late
daughter, isn't she?" – and she swore by the Imam* that we
must have lunch with her, doing so before we had protested,
feeling perhaps that I would do so. When she stood up and
took the Primus stove from under her bed and brought out
potatoes and tomatoes and bits of meat, I had a feeling of
nausea, then of frustration. I nudged my grandmother, who
leaned over and whispered, "What is it, dear?" at which

*This refers to Ali ibu Abi Talib, cousin and son-in-law of the Prophet, and is
an indication that the characters in the story are Shi'ite Muslims.

Maryam al-Taweela turned and asked, "What's your grand-
daughter want – to go to the bathroom?" My mouth went
quite dry and my tears were all stored up waiting for a signal
from my heartbeats to descend. My grandmother said with
embarrassment, "She wants to go to the sea, to the women's
swimming pool – that devil Sumayya put it into her head." To
my amazement Maryam al-Taweela said loudly, "And why
not? Right now Ali Mousa, our neighbor, will be coming and
he'll take you, he's got a car" – and Maryam al-Taweela began
peeling the potatoes at a low table in the middle of the room
and my grandmother asked, "Where's Ali Mousa from?
Where does he live?"

I can't wait, I shan't eat, I shan't drink. I want to go now,
now. I remained seated, crying inwardly because I was born
in the South, because there's no escape for me from the
South, and I go on rubbing my fingers and gnawing at my
nails. Again I begin to sweat: I shan't eat, I shan't drink, I
shan't reply to Maryam al-Taweela. It was as though I were
taking vengeance on my grandmother for some wrong she
did not know about. My patience vanished. I stood up and
said to my grandmother before I should burst out sobbing,
"Come along, Grandma, get up and let's go." I helped her to
her feet and Maryam al-Taweela asked in bewilderment what
had suddenly come over me. I went on dragging my grandmother out to the street so that I might stop the first taxi.

Only moments passed before the driver shut off his engine
and said, "Zeytouna." I looked about me but saw no sea. As I
gave him a lira I asked him, "Where's the women's swimming
pool?" He shrugged his shoulders. We got out of the car with
difficulty, as was always the case with my grandmother. To
my astonishment the driver returned, stretching out his head
in concern at us. "Jump in," he said, and we got in. He took us
round and round, stopping once at a petrol station and then
by a newspaper seller, asking about the women's swimming
pool and nobody knowing where it was. Once again he
dropped us in the middle of Zeytouna Street.

Then, behind the hotels and the beautiful buildings and the date palms, I saw the sea. It was like a blue line of quicksilver: it was as though pieces of silver paper were resting on it. The sea that was in front of me was more beautiful than it had been in the glass ball. I didn't know how to get close to it, how to touch it. Cement lay between us. We began enquiring about the whereabouts of the swimming pool, but no one knew. The sea remains without waves, a blue line. I feel frustrated. Perhaps this swimming pool is some secret known only to the girls of the South. I began asking every person I saw. I tried to choke back my tears; I let go of my grandmother's hand as though wishing to reproach her, to punish her for having insisted on accompanying me instead of Sumayya. Poor me. Poor Grandma. Poor Beirut. Had my dreams come to an end in the middle of the street? I clasp my bag and my grandmother's hand, with the sea in front of me, separating her from me. My stubbornness and vexation impel me to ask and go on asking. I approached a man leaning against a bus and to my surprise he pointed to an opening between two shops. I hurried back to my grandmother, who was supporting herself against a lamppost, to tell her I'd found it. When I saw with what difficulty she attempted to walk, I asked her to wait for me while I made sure. I went through the opening but didn't see the sea. All I saw was a fat woman with bare shoulders sitting behind a table. Hesitating, I stood and looked at her, not daring to step forward. My enthusiasm had vanished, taking with it my courage.

"Yes," said the woman.

I came forward and asked her, "Is the women's swimming pool here?"

She nodded her head and said, "The entrance fee is a lira."

I asked her if it was possible for my grandmother to wait for me here and she stared at me and said, "Of course." There was contempt in the way she looked at me—was it my southern accent or my long-sleeved dress? I had disregarded my grandmother and had taken off my headshawl and hidden it in my bag. I handed her a lira and could hear the sounds of women and children – and still I did not see the sea. At the end of the portico were steps that I was certain led to the roofed-in sea. The important thing was that I'd arrived, that I would be tasting the salty spray of its waters. I wouldn't be seeing the waves; never mind, I'd be bathing in its waters.

I found myself saying to the woman, or rather to myself because no sound issued from my throat, "I'll bring my grandmother." Going out through the opening and still clasping my bag to my chest, I saw my grandmother standing and looking up at the sky. I called to her but she was reciting to herself under her breath as she continued to look upwards: she was praying, right there in the street, praying on the pavement at the door of the swimming pool. She had spread out a paper bag and had stretched out her hands to the sky. I walked off in another direction and stopped looking at her. I would have liked to persuade myself that she had nothing to do with me, that I didn't know her. How, though? She's my grandmother, whom I've dragged with my entreaties from the tobacco-threading tent, from the jagged slab of stone, from the winds of the South; I have crammed her into the bus and been lost with her in the streets as we searched for Maryam al-Taweela's house. And now here were the two of us standing at the door of the swimming pool and she, having heard the call to prayers, had prostrated herself in prayer. She was destroying what lay in my bag, blocking the road between me and the sea. I felt sorry for her, for her knees that knelt on the cruelly hard pavement, for her tattooed hands that lay on the dirt. I looked at her again and saw the passersby staring at her. For the first time her black dress looked shabby to me. I felt how far removed we were from these passersby, from this street, this city, this sea. I approached her and she again put her weight on my hand.

HALLDÓR LAXNESS

A Place of Safety

Translated by Alan Boucher

SOMETIMES earlier I have mentioned an old woman I once knew, who had lived all her married life beyond the mountains to the east. She bore her husband six children, but only one daughter survived. These people were related to me.

Among the children of this woman there were three Gudruns. Gudrun the First was born about haymaking time in the first year of marriage. She died just over three years old. That was in the early winter. A year later, also at haymaking time, Gudrun the Second was born. When she was fourteen the pastor entered her in the records as "farmer's daughter of that property." These were big words in those days. The words are the girl's only memorial. She died in the year in which she was accorded the title in the church register. Gudrun the Third smiled on the world for only a short while, for she first saw the light of day about lamb-weaning time a year later, and died the following Christmas. It's strange that the woman should have stuck so persistently to the name Gudrun in her dealings with the Lord, who giveth and taketh away and never changeth. The Gudrun after whom she christened her daughters must have made a fairly strong impression on her mind. In the end the woman gave up the unequal struggle, for in the spring, about Eastertide, her husband was drowned. After that there were no further Gudruns.

She was perhaps a woman of not more than average intelligence. Nevertheless she was intelligent enough not to indulge in philosophy. Although I knew her pretty well, having to a large extent grown up at her knee, never once did I hear her utter a word of complaint. She knew the Hymns of the Passion by heart, but would recite them with rather an odd intonation, as though they were Latin. From the time I first remember her she looked so frail that it seemed more than probable that a little wind could blow her away like a straw; yet she stood up to more winds than many a strong man and lived to be two years past ninety. Then, after waking up one morning, she went to sleep again, and was gone.

Did I say she was no philosopher? It is true. Maybe I was not much of a philosopher myself. On the one occasion when I ought to have asked a question, I did not. I was scarcely over ten at the time. I was reading the new Bible when this woman walked by. She was no reader, but she always wanted to know what I was reading. I don't remember her ever asking me to read anything aloud, except Benedikt Gröndal's satire on the Battle of Solferino. And though she was not in the habit of laughing, I only had to read for a short while from this work and without fail she would be seized by a fit of laughter, and would tell me to put the book down.

"What are you reading now, little Dori?" asked the woman.

"It's the Bible," I said.

"Is that so," said the woman.

When thoughtful she would often poke her forefinger between her gums. As she walked away I heard her mumbling to herself, "Not everything in that Bible there is true. Oh no."

What did the woman mean? Surely not that the God who had inspired the Bible wasn't true? Or that the world he had created was a fake? Not all true, but perhaps some of it! In other words, better believe too little than too much. Did she take the view that the Almighty had rebuked her for the sin of believing too much when she had the three Gudruns in the hope that one, perhaps, would be allowed to live? Be that as it may, here sat little Dori, so there couldn't be any harm in believing a bit, could there? It was a great pity that I didn't ask.

Our dog was just called Rover—we were probably lacking in imagination where dogs' names were concerned. Besides, he was doubtless a very ordinary dog. However, we were good friends and I would cuddle and make a fuss of him when he curled up to sleep in the mornings out in the field where everyone was mowing and raking. I believed this dog to be my special friend, though he considered himself bound by equal obligations to the shepherd; as demonstrated by the fact that if I and the shepherd both called Rover, he would go with the shepherd, while if the hired man called against the shepherd, he followed the hired man. I interpreted this as showing that the dog had a clear conception of his duties toward society.

"Ai, don't you be making the sign of the cross over the poor tyke, my pet," the old woman said.

She adopted a tolerant and apologetic tone about everyone and everything, even bad weather. When I went abroad for the first time she asked me to do something for her. "If you should ever happen to meet some wretch of a woman as good-for-nothing as I am, then remember me to her."

I thought this rather a poor kind of message to be bearing out into the world. In later years, though, the humility, goodwill, and uncomplaining acceptance implicit in those few words amaze me.

When referring to animals she always followed a strict traditional order of rank. There was no confusion here. She said you should never pray for a dog, nor even speak to or of one in terms of praise. It should not be called animal, and preferably not creature, but beast, tyke, or cur. On the other hand, titles such as scamp, scallywag, scapegrace, ragamuffin, and imp of darkness were reserved for the cat. It was unthinkable that this woman should ever kick an animal. Once she forbade me to stroke the cat the wrong way. But I never saw her stroke it the right way, nor heard her speak affectionately to the imp of darkness. And yet, throughout the whole of my childhood I can remember no time when the cat regarded any place other than this old woman's bed as its rightful and undisputed sleeping place.

Though she seldom referred to Rover by terms other than tyke or cur, she always kept the bone from her piece of meat for him, as well as the twisted skin of her dried fish, and the crusts of rye bread that she couldn't bite. She would wrap these titbits in a rag to keep in her apron pocket, in case she happened to go outside. It wasn't one of her duties to feed the dog, though; he had plenty without this. But no sooner was the woman out of the door than he would forget me, his special friend, and begin jumping up at her with a joy and trust that indicated his low opinion of others for the time being. She never made any display of affection, but would pull the scraps out of her pocket and throw them to him with a "there now, and shame upon you!"

May I add, in parenthesis, that our cat was the dog's mortal enemy. Their antagonism seemed to derive from beyond this world. No logic ruled their dealings with each other; only tooth and claw and no quarter given. Sometimes they would give each other a wide berth to spare people the embarrassment of their relationship. This courtesy did not hold good, however, when they met out of doors. I sometimes think that the old woman would have been heartily relieved had both cat and dog been hanged.

I have seldom seen an expression more ceremonious than that assumed by Rover when we went with the old woman out on the moors on a bright spring day to look for sheep droppings. They lie there like glossy artifacts of varnished hardwood glittering in the sunshine, and make excellent fuel. She would carry them home in her apron. All the birds had come. We would also go on still, sun-bright autumn days to gather

sweet vernal grass in the hollow at the bottom of the homefield where three streams meet. The fragrance of the grass is
there to this day; you can smell it in midwinter too. We gathered it in small bundles to lay in her best jacket; the one she
was buried in.

"It's fun when the three of us are out in the sunshine picking," I say.

"There are only two of us, Dori dear," says the old woman.

"One, two, three," I count.

"You don't count a dog," she says.

"He's a creature, though," I say.

"Well that's something I've never heard," says the old
woman. "In the east country we called the cow a creature, and
a blessed creature, what's more. A dog is just a beast."

Somehow I didn't find this altogether a democratic way of
thinking, but I let it pass, knowing that this old woman was
not in the habit of saying things lightly. The dog rolled in the
grass, growling with contentment over our expedition. I still
feel that these expeditions were among the greatest I have
made, and the only ones I am likely to recall when I am a
sightless centenarian, sitting in an armchair by the window.

I don't know whether it has always been so in Iceland, but
in no place I knew of were dogs allowed indoors. Maybe this
dates back no earlier than the war against the echinococcus
tapeworm in sheep. Rover never ventured farther than the
lean-to by the cellar door. His sack was kept here. Few dogs
knew better than he the limits by which a dog's rights were defined. Inside the lean-to there was a large lobby where the
workpeople would hang their wet clothes and implements.
Then there was a door on a weighted string that opened a few
inches when touched from the outside. Beyond this were the
steps that led up to the kitchen. The kitchen itself opened
onto the women's parlor, which did double duty as bedroom
and wool workroom. The old woman's bed was in the far corner of the parlor, under the window. Here she would sit by
herself all the long summer day while the others were in the

fields. She would card wool, spin yarn, and knit, and I would go there to tell her the news from the world outside.

One day when the homefield was being mowed I was out with the others, while the dog lay asleep in the new-mown hay. Then came the thunder. I suppose I must have been about seven years old. It was my first thunderstorm, and it gave me a shock. I had never realized that such things existed. A moment earlier the sun was shining out of a clear sky. I had covered the dog with hay and was turning somersaults in it myself. Suddenly the sun went in. A rapidly rising warm current had piled up a bank of blue-black cloud. Now there was a breath of cold air. A fiery image appeared in the cloud. Storm lights flickered high above the fells. Then came the clap of thunder.

It rumbled from one mountain and another replied.

"The mountains tremble like a leaf," said the poetically minded hired woman.

"It must be the end of the world coming," said another, inclining to melancholy, and she gave me a look as though it were all for my benefit.

I stood there in the field, terrified. Everyone continued mowing and raking for a while, as if nothing had happened – even the girl who had predicted doomsday. I wasn't sure whether I should burst into tears or try to pluck up my courage. Nor did I know where to flee for refuge. The next moment, in mounting rolls of thunder, the ugly blue-black cloud began to empty itself on us. Still no one seemed to take any notice – except the dog. Standing up, tail between his legs, he lifted his nose to heaven and howled dolefully. The downpour was so heavy that in a few seconds everyone was wet to the skin. Nobody worried in the least either about me or the dog. And there being no comfort to be found in any quarter, and no abatement of the thunder and lightning, the animal was reduced to its own resources and fled for dear life to the house. The poor beast drew in its tail as though someone was after it with a stick. I had burst into tears.

A shout was given, to down tools and go inside until the shower had passed over. The thunderstorm went on for a while without a pause.

"Where is Rover?"

Grown-up folk don't ask about animals, but the fear of a child and a dog are akin, and I was still crying when I enquired after my comrade in terror.

"Well I can't really say," answered the old woman, and she went on knitting.

The cat was not lying on her bed as usual, but had established itself on top of the cupboard, where it sat with arched back and baleful eyes. There were wet footmarks on the floor.

The woman added, "I suppose there couldn't be a bundle of misery hiding under my bed?"

I peeped under the bed and saw a glitter as of two green lights in the gloom.

"I saw eyes." I said.

"Bless me if dogs have eyes, my lamb," said the old woman. "They are called gleamers."

The rain stopped later that afternoon and the sun came out again, throwing its beams across the floor at the feet of this old woman. The dog crawled guiltily from under the bed. This dog had broken the dogs' moral code, out of fear. He had crossed the threshold from the lean-to, pushing the spring-door open with his muzzle – a thing he had never done before. He had then run up the steps into the kitchen, where he knew very well a dog must never go. Finally he had nosed his way forward into the women's parlor to the old woman. No wonder he looked guilty when he crawled out from under her bed: no creature on earth has so clear a sense of sin as a dog. He shook himself, and I felt the spray on my face, for he was still wet.

"Out with you, rascal," said the old woman.

At this the dog slunk out and settled down to nip his coat in the sunshine of the yard. He had forgotten his fear and didn't remember it until the next thunderstorm a year later, when he took refuge in the same place.

Why hadn't that dog run to the shepherd when doomsday was at hand? – a great mutual esteem existed between them. Or to the hired man whom he always seemed to respect the more highly of the two when they were at odds? And yes, why not to me, his trusty friend, who had sung to him and made a fuss of him and put him to sleep?

Why was this the one place of safety for a frightened creature here on earth?

Bird on the Fence-Post

THE RIVER runs with a gentle murmur by the homefield fence.

When the bitch barked at the visitors riding along the track to the house, the bird on the fence-post was not unduly concerned, but continued to preen itself. The men left their horses in the homefield, which had not been mown that summer, and went into the house without knocking. When they said "Good-day" in the doorway there was no reply. The bitch continued to bark in the yard outside, after the visitors had gone in.

From a poor bunk in one corner of the room there came a queer voice, flat and colorless as in a long-distance telephone call with a bad connection:

"Who is it?"

"It's us, the people you sent for, Knut old fellow: the parish officer, the chairman of the parish council, and myself – your pastor."

They approached and stretched out their hands in greeting, but the old man did not look at them, and there were no handshakes. He was very wasted: there seemed to be scarcely anything under the blanket. The fingers of his thin, bony hands were disjointed from a lifetime acquaintance with primitive implements, but the knuckles were white from long lying abed. The complexion of the gaunt face was transparent and the beard like grass stubble growing straight upwards as he lay there on his back.

"Well, my poor fellow, how is it going with you?" they asked.

"Well enough," said the old man; "all going the right road. I inch along from day to day. Maybe I'll die tonight. But I'm no more a poor fellow than any one of you, for all that."

"Have you everything you need?"

"I've old Bridie, and she brings me water and that sort of thing. Bridie, don't let the bitch go on howling out there in the yard. She might stampede their horses."

Behind the cooking-oven a door was half opened onto a small cupboard of a room, from which a rather surly answer was heard: "Why shouldn't she howl, I'd like to know? Why shouldn't the creature howl?"

"Are you taking a little nourishment, Knut?" they asked.

"I take what I earn," he said.

"Would you care for a whiff of tobacco?" said one of the visitors, taking out his snuffbox.

"No," said the old man. "The only thing I regret in my past life is not to have used tobacco, and plenty of it at that."

"Well, you've always been known as Hard-Knut," said the snuff-taker.

"Well, now," said the pastor, "is there anything we can do for you?"

"No," said Hard-Knut. "But I thought I'd maybe make my will."

"Huh, imagines he's going to make his will, that one!" came the mutter from the cupboard-room.

"Do you think you'll have much to dispose of after funeral expenses have been paid, old chap?" said the chairman of the parish council.

"I never depended on anyone" said the old man. "To the best of my knowledge the cottage is accounted mine, according to your law."

"Accounted and accounted," they said; "that may be."

The parish officer added, "I wonder whether the cottage will do more than meet the dues that haven't been paid for many years; even the fire insurance premiums you never completed, to say nothing of the parish rates."

"I never asked you for anything. Nor will I put up with any extortion on your part. I built my shack with my own hands, and I can burn it when I want to. The first thing in my will shall be that the shack is to be set fire to when they carry me out."

They looked at one another and the pastor noted something down. Then one of them said, "It can't be of much capital value, the old cottage, and might as well be written off on that account. The smallholding will answer, though the building be burned. That's how it is, my dear Knut: society must have its due."

"I moved up here beyond the hills to be rid of folk. If you're going to take the land for fire insurance or something of that sort, it's your business. But I demand that it be put down in the will that I declare any man taking possession of the land a thief."

The pastor continued to write in his notebook, but the others asked, "Then who's to have the land after you?"

"My land is land that belongs to no one, and shall belong to no one. That is my last will and testament."

"You had children in another district, Knut. What are they going to say?" asked the parish authorities.

"That's no concern of mine," said the old man. "When children stop being children, they're just like any other strangers."

"Isn't it nearer the truth," said the pastor, "that when children stop being children, they become our best friends?"

"I've never cared about friends," said the old man. "I always wanted to be an outlaw."

"The outlaw hardly ever existed who didn't have some dealings with people, even if it was only to steal their sheep in the fells—which, I'm glad to say, you've never been guilty of."

"No, it's true, I've been a useless outlaw," said the old man.

"Moreover," added the pastor, "if only for the reason that man is endowed with speech, he is thereby a partaker in human society through words and ideas—even if he only talks to himself. The consequences of this association are inescapable."

"I can't help being able to speak," said the old man. "I make no secret of the fact that I consider human speech a curse in the world. That's why I cut myself off."

"All the same, you talk, my dear Knut!"

"Yes, it was a great disaster for the human being when he began to form words—instead of singing. When a human being spoke the first word, some time long ago, that was the beginning of lies."

"But the understanding between two souls; the love between man and woman; where would man be without that? I believe that he who denies that has ceased to be a man; even an outlaw."

"I don't believe in any blasted old wives' tales," said the old man. "I refuse to listen to people's nonsense. It's a plague to me to have dealings with another man. I want to be alone."

"Human intercourse—that's world history, after all, Knut," said the pastor.

"I don't believe in any world history," said the old man. "It's just a folktale. Anything that can be said with words makes me suspect the worst. I listen to the river flowing."

"Then, Knut, what do you believe in?"

"The bird perched on the fence-post there bobs and twitters, and that tells me enough, my lads," said the old man. "That bird knows all that needs to be known about the world.

And it's the greatest fountain of stories in the land. I believe in the beings that have turned into birds. Maybe the time will come when men will turn into birds. But there's not much prospect of that at present."

"Now the end of the road is near, and the Christian Church presents the soul with what it has to offer—what of that?" asked the pastor.

"I managed things so that I wouldn't have to mix with other folk," said old Knut. "So I reckon I've been in heaven these few years I've hung on here. But the day comes when a man wants to be rid of the birds and heaven, God and all the angels, and that day has come for me now. It's a good day, too."

One of the visitors now put in, "At last here's one who's not scared of dropping off."

"What a dreadfully dreary life yours must have been, poor fellow," said another with a shudder.

"I don't know about that, my lad," said the old man. "Whoever hears the river flowing won't gain much from listening to you. And it needs no more than a single dry day to make up for a whole summer of rain. The bird sits on the fence-post and chirps endlessly, night and day, for two and a half months of summer. The rest of the year is an echo of the summer. A day is measured off in hours and watches, but of all the hours the happiest is when a weary man falls asleep—though it's one that can't be measured; yes, one that a man will never really know. What has the pastor written down? Has he written about the land and the house? I'm getting sleepy."

"Doesn't it seem to you a bit pointless, my dear Knut," said the pastor, "to be having anything put in writing about this patch of land and this shack that you are leaving and care nothing about? Does it matter on which side of the hills they lie? Don't you think you'd do better to use the short time that's left to turn your thoughts to the happy land and the everlasting mansions?"

"It may well be that this world is nothing but a confounded

rubbish heap," said the ancient. "However, I've got used to treating it as a fact. That's why I feel better if I tell you my wishes than I would if I just slipped off without a word. I have seventeen ewes – "

The pastor could not restrain himself from interrupting: "My dearest Knut, as a priest I make no apologies for my desire to arouse even a trace of feeling for sound doctrine in you at a moment like this. I am sure it would ease the burden for you, and for us all."

Hard-Knut: "When I was young I read a large number of books. I believed in seven doctrines. Facts killed them all in the order in which I adopted them, I am a heretic of seven faiths. Now you come along with the eighth. Facts refute all doctrines. How weary I am with people's talk. And I haven't opened a book for more than fifty years. Wouldn't it be better for us to make a note of what I want done with those seventeen wretched ewes of mine?"

The pastor cleared his throat and swallowed several times while rallying his resources. Then he tried once more.

"Don't you find security in accepting the doctrine that others believe all round you?"

"I believe in the world apart from doctrines, so there!" said the old man. "I always tried to be on my own, to be rid of having to accept all the nonsense that men must endure in society."

"But then you have also missed Christmas," said the pastor.

"After the bird on the fence-post has sung, night and day, for two and a half months, it stops and begins to listen. The holiday is not over. Autumn is now far advanced, and still it sits on the fence-post and listens to the echo of its past song. Who knows whether that may not be even more of a fact than the song itself? I'm listening too, lads, though I've crawled into my hole."

"Some good doctrines seem to be inborn in all men," said the shepherd of souls. "And there are institutions that have never failed mankind, from time immemorial. For example,

the cow, which has sometimes been called the foster mother
of man. She continues to provide us with milk from generation to generation in the simple way with which we are familiar, and to low a little the while, whatever leaps forward
science and philosophy may make. Or, for instance, take the
church, which some call the kingdom of God on earth: human knowledge advances by leaps and bounds, but the same
hymns continue to be sung as were when we were little."

"I've never owned a cow," said the old man. "Cow's milk is
for calves. Milk makes my gorge rise, even when it's given to
babies. On the other hand, these seventeen ewes which I
couldn't avoid owning: when they come back from the mountain I want them slaughtered for the benefit of old Bridie,
who has hung on here in the hut with me longest of all—
please put that down."

The pastor saw no alternative but to go on writing. Then a
mumble was heard from inside the open door:

"What should the likes of me be doing owning things? Has
anyone ever heard such nonsense! Enough if they get something here in the parish. I lack nothing."

But this mumble received no answer. Hard-Knut closed the
matter by saying, "I'll try and scribble my name under it before I go."

It can be quite a difficult task to compose a will of this kind.
They had to tear up their attempts two or three times before
getting this short text on paper, and still they were not satis-
fied. Then they read what they had written. There was something to the effect that the poor, dilapidated farm buildings
of the testator be razed to the ground upon his decease, but
his land disposed of by the authorities according to the law.
Livestock earmarked the testator's property, still on the
mountain pastures at the time of compiling the present document, viz. at the Eve of Winter, before All Saints' Day—the
aforesaid stock be assigned to the testator's housekeeper—
"What sort of housekeeper am I supposed to be?" was

mumbled invisibly behind the door; "not much of a house-keeper I'd say...not even a housemaid; good-for-nothing creature that I've always been...a miserable wretch and a slut..."

"Bridie?" they said, and looked questioningly at one another. "Well, what exactly is her name, the old woman?"

Then came the mutter from the cupboard-room: "Pah, what d'you suppose my name is? Not much of a name, I'd say: Brightmay Jonsdottir, drat it. It's a disgrace to be putting such a name down on paper...."

They now read the document carefully to the testator, and he said it will do. Then they raised this shrunken sage in his bed and supported his shoulders while he signed it.

"I haven't held a pen in my hand for fifty or sixty odd years," he remarked apologetically.

It was good enough, they said. When they had arranged him in the bunk again he turned his face to the wall and said no more. He made no attempt to give them his hand when they took their leave of him.

"We bid you good-bye, all the same; and moreover I give you God's blessing on your journey, my dear Knut, whether you will or no," said the pastor. The chairman of the parish council and parish officer stood up and agreed with some embarrassment: "We say the same."

The bitch had long stopped barking, and lay with head on paws on the doorstep, gazing portentously into the house. She did not stir even when they stepped over her; was no longer really concerned about these men, for all the fuss she had made on their arrival. Perhaps in some way she was disappointed with the visit. They walked to their horses, which stood grazing in the unmown homefield: the parish authorities in front and the pastor behind, bent and maybe a little subdued.

"There's a hard devil of a man for you," said the parish officer in a low voice.

"If there were many like that, the parish wouldn't last long," said the chairman. "The country and nation would be finished."

"Yes, it's a deliverance when men of his kind breathe their last," said the parish officer.

They mounted their horses and rode slowly down the track, as if to show that they were not afraid.

Then behind them they heard a piercing wail, as of some strange animal, and they turned. An aged woman was tottering after them on unsteady legs and doing her utmost to make herself heard. It was Brightmay Jonsdottir. They drew up and asked what was the matter.

The woman replied that Knut wanted the pastor to come back quickly and hear a word or two he had to say.

They nodded to one another in tacit understanding and the pastor's face softened. As he turned back confidently toward the house he said to his companions:

"I have gone on hoping and hoping to the very last. Now, at the eleventh hour, it seems to have happened. Thank God it can never be too late. Perhaps I shall call you."

"Well now," said the parish officer, when the two laymen were alone in the field, "it's something that the old devil had second thoughts at the end."

"Yes," said the chairman, "sooner or later these atheists and haters of mankind always give in and repent."

"As it happens I brought my hymnbook with me, to be on the safe side; just in case the old man wanted something sung for him after all," said the parish officer. "What do you think we should sing if he does?"

"We've quite a few beautiful old hymns," said the chairman.

They turned the pages of the hymnbook back and forth for a time, finding each hymn better than the one before. In the end they agreed to let the pastor decide whether they should sing "I Live and Know" or "Abide with Me" if he called them back.

They still had the hymnbook open between them when the

pastor reappeared from the cottage. They saw at once that he was neither so light-footed nor so confident as he had been when he went inside a short while before.

"What happened?" they asked.

"Oh, nothing special," replied the pastor dully.

"Was his heart softened?" they asked.

"There wasn't much sign of that," said the pastor.

"What did he say?" they asked.

"It was nothing important," said the pastor, and he tightened the girths of his saddle two holes before mounting again. "He asked me to take care of his dog for him, so that she didn't turn stray when he was dead."

The parish officer and the chairman of the parish council put away the hymnbook in silence.

The river continued to flow at the bottom of the homefield.

As they rode through the gate the bird was still sitting on the fence-post, listening to the echo of the song it had chirped in summer.

ANGEL LERTXUNDI

This Cold Earth Is Not Santo Domingo

Translated by Michael E. Morris

BY THE TIME they buried me, the tired wrinkles on their faces, their imperceptible, deliberately shed tears, and their soft fleeting sighs had disappeared.

If you had been there you would have seen how Enkarni played with her skirt while the priest prayed. It was as if she wanted to protect it from a nonexistent south wind, or free it from an attack out of nowhere, looking for a reason to stare at my husband, everything in its place and hidden loves revealed, in public, among the continuous darting of teary eyes, waiting, seeking, looking, and praying, amen! all their mouths opened, and I noticed a gold tooth in Enkarni's.

"Amen!" As if saying that small word required showing the gold tooth, she went to my husband and took his hand in hers, who knows what she said to him, "I'm sorry" or "I'm glad," naturally I was in no position to do more than read gestures, furthermore, in situations like that people speak in whispers, not because we will hear them of course, an unexpected flapping of wings and a lapwing flutters by and circles the group, surprise and indecision on the bowed faces of the people, Enkarni's breast heaves as if she were startled by the bursting of an invisible balloon, and only when the bird disappears in the purple sky does she release my husband's hand,

but he pays no attention to her, his gaze is directed at Jose,
even though he has to crane his neck to see him, as if watching a soccer match from the cheapest seats, but Jose does not
acknowledge him, doesn't look at him, he was standing dis-
creetly in back of the crowd, not like that slut Enkarni, it's
easy to see the difference, like when Jose said "you must take
your wife to Santo Domingo," my husband ignored him, he
aimed a glare as sharp as an acupuncture needle at him and
replied stingingly, "Who asked you to bring a candle to this
wake?" and actually my husband had no right to respond that
way, Jose had offered me not only the candle but the fire to
light it with, offered it, gave it, and tested it, of course my husband never knew what happened, but he always suspected
something, otherwise why would he be craning his neck to get
a look at Jose, but Jose was at the back of the group, and it
wasn't polite for my husband to spend the whole ceremony
straining for a look at him.

It must have been about ten years ago when my husband
first began looking ridiculous to me, he would kiss me, with
his bristly mustache, "do you like it?" and I had to say yes,
what else could I do, but it scratched me and even disgusted
me, especially after he ate, then I realized what was happening after I noticed how the phone bills were going up, the secret calls, I told him either the mustache goes or I do, he gave
in, he thought he fooled me, both the mustache and the telephone at the same time, but one thing was certain, two years
after I found out about Enkarni I took up with Jose, on my
own initiative, on purpose, not for physical satisfaction at all, I
was used to doing without, it was a game, a desire to do the
same to my husband, and I'm sure I won, although speaking
in this way from such a place certainly has its share of irony,
to hell with that slut Enkarni, and I'm not saying that now because my husband didn't take me to Santo Domingo, not at
all, my reasons started long before, almost right after we were
married, my husband knew about my lung problem as well as
I did, but he insisted on buying a house by the sea, and I had

to breathe all the sea winds from Galicia and from the North, take them into my lungs and make them a part of me, until every breath felt like a rope tightening around my chest.

My blasted husband choked the life out of me by failing in his duty, my eyes were often wet with tears of hopelessness, a lot of time can pass before you're aware of it, until one day you look at yourself in the mirror and don't recognize what you see, who the hell are you? the answer frightens you, there are dark puffy bags under your eyes, and that night for the first time your heart wins the battle against sleep, I decided to quit wasting my time, and I left the shabby hotel that was my life and went out into the world, I had no one but Jose, I myself had closed the door to any possibility between us, when you're young words like *adultery* pierce your heart like a knife, and later when you learn what they mean, you realize that the knife is still there, at first our relationship was superficial, I could not overcome my anxiety, poor Jose went away without a harsh word, I suffered a lot, I think he suffered, too, and when I saw in the mirror that I had no one but Jose, I went out after calling him on the phone, and he said,

"Daydreaming?"

I was waiting for him in front of a store window, watching people who meant nothing to me pass by in the glass, and he said again,

"Are you daydreaming?"

And I said, "It's something to do. How are you?"

We hadn't seen each other in two years, his expression was more somber, but as for the rest he looked as handsome as ever, his powerful shoulders could protect my dreams, my desire to live, and Jose said,

"Let's catch up on the last two years over a cup of coffee."

"Is there anything worth telling?"

A sympathetic smile.

"Have things been that bad for you?"

"Just life in general."

"You moved again, didn't you?"

We were sitting in a bar and I answered him, and as I did so, I began to cough, my lungs rebelled violently, Jose seized my elbows, two years before it might have been out of desire, out of a need to satisfy my sensuality, but Jose put his arm around my shoulders and I felt something stronger than compassion in the weight of his arm.

"What's wrong? You're not well."

Two years without seeing each other, without exploring each other's desire, and we had to meet like that, I was angry with myself, but it was useless, my cough grew drier and drier, he ordered me a chamomile tea, and said,

"You're not at all well."

He asked me about my husband and I asked him not to mention him, but Jose was adamant:

"Yes, I must speak to your husband."

He went to a telephone, I begged him not to do it, he ignored me, dialed the number I reluctantly gave him, and said,

"Think what you want, but come as soon as possible. Your wife is not at all well."

I could not stop coughing, it was impossible to breathe, my life, my world, the bar were all suffocating in the short passage between my throat and my lungs, I don't remember anything, twenty days between white sheets in a hospital, my husband didn't tell anyone where he took me and I had no visits but his, as brief as they were boring, twenty days and he took me home again, to the seaside, to breathe in and swallow all the winds from Galicia, from the North, and all points on the compass. Jose was brave enough to come to the house and say,

"You have to take her to Santo Domingo."

My husband seized his arm and dragged him to the door.

"Who asked you to bring a candle to this wake?"

I don't know if my husband said these words or if I imagined them, it's been three long months since then, and now here, this is the first time I've seen Jose since, there at the back of the crowd, I don't need to stretch my neck, "Let's catch up on the last two years over a cup of coffee," but we couldn't have that cup of coffee, Jose, I asked you if there was anything worth telling, and of course there was, but when Enkarni saves her ridiculous skirt from the attack of an invisible wind, my husband will look at her, the priest will toss a handful of dirt on me, and it'll be over, I'll never breathe the sea air again, Jose, and as sure as there's a God, this cold earth is not Santo Domingo!

Basque

KOLDO IZAGIRRE

from *They Deserved Euzkadi*

Translated by Michael E. Morris

HE HAD day-shirt duty on Tuesdays and had to be there.
News came that in Hernani they had been closed down since
morning; they called Ereinotzu, but nobody knew anything
there, it was possible that some had, they said. It wasn't yet
nine o'clock when they heard the music. "Here they are!" said
the foreman, "The Marseillaise!" and they went out to the
bridge. Down the road came a brass band, a group of workers
marching along behind. It looked like Holy Week, like when
Hernani residents made a mock procession with whores up to
the cider tavern of Ergobia, a flayed lamb carried on two
boards, sausages hanging from sticks, and long loaves of
bread for candles. They carried the Spanish tricolor flag.
*"Muera el rey!"** a woman yelled over and over again.

They paraded past the station toward the cider taverns.
They were at the door. *"Viva la república obrera!"*** they
shouted with fists raised. The manager closed up. The tram
to San Sebastián left, full of people.

Basque farmers watched them with suspicion. "The Republic!" Hernani residents shouted at them, "The Republic!"

*"Death to the King!"
**"Long live the workers' republic!"

They didn't need to knock on many doors. The taverns in Pagua, Otaño, Garratxena, Gurutzeta, and Oiharbide were soon filled with shouting. The Republic's proud flag stood on a pile of ferns.

They asked for silence, they couldn't hear him very well, and they asked him to start over. Then they lifted Indalecio Prieto onto a table, under the light bulb, a glass in his hand. When all the murmuring stopped, he repeated, "Workers! Before laws were made, kings ruled!" He waited for his audience to quiet down. He waved his arms clumsily, "And that's why they say there's no law that can dethrone a king!" The audience thought he would smash his glass against a cask. "Listen!" he said to them, holding it against his ear instead. The beads of sweat on Prieto's face looked like wax dripping from an Easter candle in the Hernani church. "Listen!" and as even the sloshing in the cask quieted, he murmured, *"Esa campana que se oye es la campana del Kremlin!"** and leaned toward the surprised faces of his audience. "Viva Rusia!" he shouted, and straightened so suddenly he struck the light bulb.

Neither on the job, where he extended the railroad from the dock, nor at home, where bread dipped in wine was his favorite dessert, did he speak a word. He was a man accustomed to hardship, he had become a total homebody. His words came like water from an eyedropper. He had been a sheepherder in the Pampas. Claudia had remained in Buenos Aires, working as a maid. Once every three months they went to Santa Rosa. He would learn to drink *mate*. Some Indians were raffling off a mare at the fair, and he got lucky. He was happily leading it back to the ranch when it reared up, he couldn't handle it, surprised by a snake or something, and it ran off, dragging its bridle rope in the dust. Later he would see the

*"That bell that you hear is the bell of the Kremlin!"

Indians raffling off another horse, and it seemed to him it was the same one that ran away from him.

He had spent twelve years in America and six months in Amara. He paid for his return passage by working as a stoker on the steamship. He was a grateful man, a docile man, but he carried his head down in silence, stubborn, without murmuring so much as the blessing before a meal, and every Sunday when Maria hinted at breakfast that he should go to mass, he would get up from the table and go out into the garden. On the Sunday after his arrival, Father Matthew gave a sermon about the prodigal son, "Our brother, whom we thought dead, has come home, he who was lost has come back to life, and has appeared among us!" but Inazio Errazkin "wouldn't look to the church to see what time it was!"

Since the night before, the town had been buzzing with the news that they were going to mobilize, and he headed for downtown San Sebastián. Soldiers were on patrol, people hurried by. In San Ignacio station a tram lay on its side like a cow struck down by dysentery. He heard they stopped Luzuriaga at gunpoint, in Pasaia, that they were ordering home Galicians detained on the picket lines. He heard they wanted to sack San Sebastián. Few shops and bars were open. The incident at Trintxerpe was ghastly.

In Ategorrieta there were people at the windows. He headed out, ahead of time, fearful, the neighing of horses and the sound of their hooves, a dozen horse soldiers and a foot patrol. He passed by without even looking, careful not to quicken his pace, tense. "Halt!" He stopped, not knowing if he should turn around. The trees on Miracruz Street were as tense as he was. *"Arriba las manos!"* * said the voice of a pair of hands that pressed a gun to his back, "What have you got there?" said the voice insolently, ready to fire. "Drop it!" The

*"Put your hands up!"

lunch pail struck the sidewalk with the clunk of any empty container. Nervous hands loaded a bullet into the chamber, and a rough voice said, "Open it!" He bent down slowly, untied the knot. The rifle pressed against the nape of his neck. "Keep going!" They laughed at him, they wouldn't fire yet, "He's pissed his pants!" he was so afraid. Yelling was heard. He turned his head to look.

They came from Bidebieta, women and children in front, bold, fearless, they had broken through the police cordon and were coming down the street. They filled the street from one side to the other, Trintxerpe must have been emptied when they came. "We don't need spectators," said Zabaleta, taking his arm. "But the mounted police are in Ategorrieta!" he announced in surprise, but Zabaleta did not release his arm. "Individually we are nothing; united we are the people!" They moved up the street, and before he knew it, he was surrounded by bodies and shouting.

The captain moved to his troops, the union leader to the demonstrators. *"Dice que teñen ordes de non deixarnos pasar!"** The captain spoke to the guards as well. No one moved. "Forward!" cried a woman, turning to the crowd. *"A república é nosa, non deles!"*** They advanced slowly, silently. There were people at the windows in Ategorrieta. A trumpet sounded. They were twenty meters from the Guardia Civil. The trumpet sounded, then a volley of shots, nobody moved. "Forward!" cried the union leader. The guards had shot into the air. They moved toward the guns to the sounds of shouting and hooves striking pavement, the guns were now pointed at the people. When the trumpet sounded again, they fired the guns, the shouts became wailing, children before smoking guns, between stamping horses, brains spattered on trees like spit. "They belonged to someone, too!" Fleeing horses fright-

---

*"He says he has orders not to let us pass."
**"The republic is ours, not theirs."

ened the people, he saw it, they trampled the fallen. One man escaped by scrambling up Mount Ulia, his empty sleeve flapping in the wind like an old flag. Hunched behind a tree, he saw the open door. The captain ordered the wounded to be placed in the truck, the weeping women came looking for their husbands. The door was open, he reached it in a breath. It would be better to go upstairs, an old woman stopped him on the first landing. "Assassins, that's what they are, those wild pigs!" The Guardia Civil in the street asked for mattresses to transport the wounded. Someone groaned in the doorway, they went down, he was leaning on the bannister, cursing, at the end of a trail of blood that led from the doorway. Afraid they would follow the trail of blood, the old woman went looking for the door key. He undid the napkin that wrapped his lunch box, the man's leg was badly injured, he didn't tie it too tightly. When the old lady locked the door, she murmured "I want nothing to do with those pigs!" but the man cut her off in mid sentence with a pistol he pulled from his belt, *"Abóa, gárdeme iste cachafullo!"** The old woman took it silently and told them to go upstairs. He squatted to retrieve his lunch box, then stayed there, staring at the tiny hole in the bottom of it.

There was an old saying that the people of Goizueta never fail. People at headquarters had warned them that after three days of rain the water would roar down the Urumea river. The stars moved in a crazy pattern, the rumbling of those black clouds would bring nothing good. The hurricane hit "on the day of Corpus Christi!"

Torrents of water came down Mount Jaizkibel, uprooting trees, covering bridges, giant spools and pine logs from the Rentería paper mill filling the canal along with wood from the sawmill, like dead porpoises floating belly up. "Such a river,

*"Keep this for me, old woman."

and no water in the house!" The ground began to open up and the people were afraid (many thought it was punishment from God), many cattle must have been lost.

On Saturday the assistant mayor came to their house to tell them they had to leave, everyone living on the side of the mountain had to move to high ground as soon as possible. They gathered a few clothes in the dark, they took some tools and that little winding motor. They weren't angry with the assistant mayor's order, "It's no use trying to hold back flood waters!" in the cellar the water was knee deep and it rushed down the slope of the garden clear to the chicken coop. In the schools they had placed mattresses for the evacuees. They turned the dog loose. Their sister told them to wait, she'd be back soon, and turned back to the house, she couldn't get her wooden shoes out of the mud, she went on with a sack, on to the chicken coop and barely made it inside before the wall collapsed destroying the cages, and the roof collapsed like a rock slide loosened by a blast.

Basque

LAURA MINTEGI

Mole Hole

Translated by Michael E. Morris

Raising her golden scepter, the queen ordered the brave young captive mouse brought before her, and the princess's heart beat so fast it seemed it would leap from her chest. The throne room was filled with silence. When the guards tossed the young prince at the queen's feet, a long "ooooh!" rose from the throats of all the mice. The prince was so handsome and graceful!

But he was a prisoner of the cruel war and, moreover, the son of the enemy king. The princess did not understand about armies or war. She didn't know why the mouse she loved had been thrown to the ground, and her eyes filled with tears.

No, this is no good. The prince should appear proud and haughty so that the court that captured him will be aware of the insult they've done him. Furthermore, when his father's army comes looking for him, he will legally take command and he must maintain his image as a leader at all times. Later will come the explanation of how they get married, and of how the two kingdoms were always attacking each other, and of how they are joined through marriage. Finally, the fruit of their union, a son, shall combine his mother's beauty with his father's daring.

Perhaps the story should take off from there. But what time is it? No wonder I was hungry! What do we have for lunch today? Leeks, potatoes, and fish! Fish makes everything better! Bread is not as black as it used to be, and I drink a glass of wine every day at lunchtime. Karmen, what kind of fish do you have there? Mackerel! Not bad. This morning I gave the story a big boost, but I won't write anything in the afternoon. I want to finish the illustration of the prince before the queen's court, his clothes torn and bloodied . . . the throne room is full of subjects . . . Who's knocking on the door? Go, go up! Shut the door and fasten the padlock!

The door is closed. On the wooden staircase in the light of a low-watt bulb, the cellar is left in a fog of darkness. Under the light of a folding lamp, the shine of a nearly bald head, and the silhouette of a receding chin and strong nose is visible against the darkness of the wall. On the table, pens and paper, a blue inkwell, black pencils and colored pencils, and a bunch of illustrated children's stories. In the corner, a bed eighty centimeters wide, and on it, clean sheets and a feather pillow in a pillowcase with the hand-embroidered initials "I. M." Over this, a white crocheted bedspread.

In the middle of the room, a dark table, flanked by two folding chairs and a small table lamp. Behind a blue-flowered cloth that served as a curtain were a sink, toilet, half bathtub, and small mirror with the silver backing showing at the corners. On a shelf under the mirror, a shaving kit, including an old brush, a comb and a toothbrush, soap, and lastly, fingernail clippers.

At both sides of the curtain a long white cloth was hanging as if to dry. To the right of the stairs, an armoire with a center door higher than its two side ones.

Footsteps are heard on the floor above. Who can it be? They hadn't had any unknown visitors in a long time and the ones they knew notified them ahead of time: Karmen's sister on Thursdays and Saturdays, to knit or have a snack; and her daughter, when it was necessary to help with the housework or to go to the city to do some shopping.

They hardly had any friends. Since '36, they had lost track of everyone; that was the best that could be said. The fate of others was known well enough. Dead in Madrid and Ebro-Santander. Nineteen-thirty-seven was the hardest, when the final decision had to be made. The town was searched, the whole city council was shot, and all the young men dead, imprisoned, fled to the mountains, or God knows where. (He would certainly know their whereabouts.)

That wasn't the worst of it, no. Lost, we lost. No help from outside and inside a lack of organization, guns, leadership. We were born to lose. We had the onus of their victory sign engraved on our foreheads from the first day. The horns were lowered and the summit unreachable. On the front lines when the Black Lady called us to the kingdom of darkness with winking and trickery, we knew there was no victory sign in the trenches.

But who could be upstairs? Who is with Karmen? Those years, stained with the blood of youth, are revived for me in nightmares.

Karmen isn't coming, and I hear nothing upstairs.

Those years, soiled with poverty and decay. Denunciations everywhere, and our women displayed on ox carts, their bare heads covered with tar. Karmen, the mayor's wife. Karmen on the ox cart, under the evil red eye of the denouncer. Days filled with filthy insults and humiliation. And her prince, in the mountains; a prince without a kingdom, a leader without an army.

I haven't heard anything upstairs in a long time.

But every dragon has its prince, and every prince his princess, and they have a white, winged horse that flies over problems and enemies to the kingdom of happiness. Without warning the prince's invincible sword blinds their enemies with reflected sunshine and the light of truth. That very sword will free the princess, seated silently in the court on her velvet throne, watching everyone, all of them gaping at her beauty.

Surely it's the neighbors. When the hell will that couple leave us in peace? When Karmen is out, they hear the faucet running; Karmen must have mice, because on many evenings they hear squeaking noises coming from the house; whenever she likes she should come to their house for a visit because living alone is not good for a woman. . . .

Being alone, noises, faucets, neighborhood enemies. Such things do not exist in the kingdom of light. Neither do ration books. There is no black bread and no hunger. There's no fear either.

Fear, fear of noises. Fear of unusual silences. Barely visible behind the fog, the sun fell lower and lower, as if to keep the short winter days from lasting too long. A few street lamps lit up, and the gray humanity coming home from work formed a silent river whose water never changes. The capricious border between day and night danced about. Light and dark were friends, walking hand in hand. . . .

In the cellar, the latter predominated. The dark cellar had not known sunlight since 1939. Since that time the brick-covered windows had not fulfilled their function of allowing light and fresh air to enter.

After throwing out all the old trash, we furnished this cellar, a place we wanted to make livable down through the years. A mole cellar. A mole hole.

On the floor in one corner are piled paper and documents on official letterhead. Next to that, letter files and municipal archive cards. On the other side, brightly colored pictures and sketches, white horses and fire-breathing dragons next to princesses dressed in gold cloth. Next to these, brave and loyal mouse princes, facing danger, not knowing the meaning of the word *fear*.

Karmen hurried down to the cellar. She was carrying dessert and coffee. Someone who wanted to sell her an automatic vacuum cleaner kept her at the door for twenty minutes. When the salesman left, her sister arrived, out of breath. She had a newspaper under her arm: because the first of October was approaching, the generalissimo had decided to grant an open amnesty, and many political prisoners would be freed: communists, reds, republicans, and anarchists.

The autocracy was loosening a bit, and upon hearing the news, many narrow-muzzled mustachioed mole leaders poked their blind eyes and earless heads into the light.

Karmen didn't have too much faith in it, but she had dreams of ending her double life, and this article gave them renewed strength. She tried to make the shiny-domed inhabitant of the cellar believe the good news.

Go out. To go out, after spending his adult life forgetting what sunshine is like. Into the world of real light. Go out. How can I go out into a world where dragons take on the appearance of men? Into a world without the blue-eyed, red-lipped princess? Verified, revealed to reality, and taken away from me; it would defile my dreams!

In the days that followed, after a long period of idleness, he engaged in furious bursts of activity that Karmen knew nothing about.

I will place wings behind the white horse's ribs. They must be long and finer at the tips, thrown back so they don't strike the hind legs. Long and ethereal, like the deeds he must achieve. I shall create long-legged, slender-bellied horses, like those El Greco would draw. This princess has very large feet. They must be finer, in the Japanese fashion. I'll shorten them a bit.

I don't think it's appropriate to have a dark princess. Her hair should be golden, to reflect the sunlight.

Karmen returned the cold, untouched dishes to the kitchen. Her husband wasn't tasting, or even smelling, the food. The daily newspapers, unopened, were piling up in the space under the stairs.

The cellar had taken on the unpleasant odor of a closed,

stuffy space. Karmen, the good wife, preached useless sermons at him. The subject of amnesty was neither forbidden nor welcome; it was just ignored. The ghost of the imaginary princess filled every nook and cranny of the cellar, her light conquering the dark.

Karmen brought dinner. He wasn't there. Her question brought forth no answer from behind the curtain that concealed the toilet. He wasn't under the stairs, or under the bed either.

Beside the table, moving toward the circle of light defined by the folding lamp, she saw a reddish-brown mouse about twenty-five centimeters long, very proud and arrogant, with blind eyes and no ears.

A crown sparkled on its head, and next to its right front leg, a pencil hung like a sword.

The mole became a mouse, became a mole in the cellar.

Catalonia

MONTSERRAT ROIG

from *The Everyday Opera*

Translated by J. M. Sobrer

MARI CRUZ:* Ivonne had green eyes, bottle green, sparkling, and her hair, worn up, had a sheen the color of corncobs. Her hair was always poorly combed, the discolored bangs falling on her forehead. The day she showed me the ashes in the flask, the veins in her neck bulged as if they were about to burst. She goaded me with her gaze. I felt she wanted to turn me into a thousand pieces, smaller than her father's ashes. Me, like a scarecrow, with my palm extended, not knowing what to do. I was afraid I might scatter the ashes, the ashes that were perhaps her father's. I didn't quite understand why she called me that, fascist pig.

A few days later I asked the "poet of the phalluses" why his wife had insulted me. He explained to me that Ivonne was a little confused since she had learned all that had happened to her family, that at first they told her only that they had disappeared in a concentration camp during the German war, but that, little by little, she learned the details, and that those de-

*Mari Cruz is a young Andalusian woman trying to survive as a maid in Barcelona. She cleans house for Senyora Miralpeix, whose boarder, Senyor Duc, she falls in love with. She also acts as maid/companion to Senyora Altafulla, and previously worked for "*el poeta dels phallus*" and his wife, Ivonne.

tails were hard to accept, because no one can take lightly that her grandmother has been converted into a bar of soap. And that her father is now only a pile of ashes. And that, according to Ivonne, we were all responsible. He too believed this, that those of us who had done nothing to kill Franco when it was high time to do so were a bunch of fascists, and also a bunch of pigs. But it didn't worry me much, to be called fascist pig by Ivonne, and that the poet of the phalluses would believe it too, because when Franco died I was only twelve, and at school they barely made a comment. And fascists are these gentlemen who appear once in a while in the newspapers, dressed in black, shouting a lot and brandishing pistols. I thought it was truly a pity for a woman to go berserk and go around with her father's ashes in a little flask.

Because I have never had a father. I do not know what he looked like, I have no pictures of him, no letter from him; I do not know his name, I cannot hope to gather his ashes in a little flask. My mother is from a village lost in the geography of Spain; no one lives there anymore, or at most a few old folks and a couple of children. My mother always says that she has sponged it off clean, that the house where she was born has faded in her memory, and the animals they had, and the land dying of drought. She claims it's better that way, that if you want to start a new life you can't drag along the sorrows of all that you left behind. That her village is static in the past, in a corner of Castile. Only barren land, a few ruins that used to be houses, Mother says, and the wind whistling at night as a vigil to the dead left alone in the graveyard. My mother taught me to have no memories. Because my mother is very different from Senyora Altafulla, who was chock-full of memories, and from Senyor Duc, who had them but who did not want to share them with me.

One day, when I was three, mother told me that she was fed up with so much poverty and that we would go to Barcelona. Our grandparents were dead and she had only two sisters, Aunt Florentina, who had married an Asturian, and Aunt

Angels, who was a hooker but my mother said she was a good person. Aunt Angels had come to Barcelona as a young woman, to be a maid in a house in the upper part of the city. The brother of the lady of the house went after her because my aunt had been a very good-looking woman. My mother would explain to me sometimes that the train ride had been as long as Moses' stay in the desert, and that she mostly wanted to piss, she was so nervous. All I remember is that the moon followed the train and that, from time to time, it would hide behind some shreds of cloud. When it came out again, it winked.

I will go quickly over what happened later because it is not very important for this story. My mother became a maid and she locked me up in a school run by nuns in the neighborhood called Gracia. For ten years I did not leave the place at all, not even in summers, my mother had no vacations, and even if she had had them, well, we would not have known where to go, the two of us alone. She came to see me one Sunday every month. Once in a while the aunties came, the one from Asturias, and the whore, with makeup, looking like an Easter cake, with her tall hairdo that seemed to have no end. Aunt Angels smelled of lavender and gave me candy. Aunt Florentina looked like Ivonne, she was very tall and had a parrot nose; from my height I could see only her nose because she barely had breasts. Aunt Florentina looked at me and said, poor little one, what a pity, and she told me that I had to do like her, I had to preserve myself in order to find a good husband, that then I could go through life with my head very high and I would not end up like others who, because of their carelessness, had "lost cattle and bells, if you know what I mean." I did not understand very well. Later I gathered that she was referring to my mother, who had me by a man whose name nobody even knew. When my aunt told me that, told me not to end up like others, and that I should "keep my thing" for my future husband, my mother always burst out crying, no one could stop her. Aunt Angels looked furious and told Aunt Florentina to stick her tongue where she could fit it; Aunt Florentina told her to keep quiet; and as the two of them started shouting at each other, my mother would blow her nose and wipe her tears, which were unstoppable. Then I knew that the drama would last the whole Sunday afternoon and I let my thoughts fly. Because when my mother cried, her face became like a tomato, as if they had slapped it, and she would blow and blow her nose. My aunt who was a whore would give her one Kleenex after another, but my mother tore them all up, saying that she was not used to blowing her nose with a paper handkerchief, and a whole bunch of shreds always stuck to her fingers.

Auntie Florentina was the one with authority in the family. She had as much authority as the old woman, Senyora Altafulla, though I must admit that it was a different kind, perhaps because she was more elegant, I don't know. Aunt Florentina was very proud of how things had been for her, in life, mostly because she had a husband who brought home the cash and she did not have to clean up other people's houses, like my mother. Her husband, Uncle Baldomeru, had gone to Argentina to strike it rich. He came back poorer than a church mouse and Aunt Florentina was very angry at him, said he was lazy. Then she sent him to Switzerland, and there things went very well, Auntie says, because there her husband couldn't bum around or have bad women or drink, like he did in Argentina, and he took to working and working so he could come back sooner. He slaved like a mule until he had enough saved. In a few years, with the savings, Aunt Florentina decided it was time to go back to Asturias. Uncle Baldomeru never forgave her for having made him sweat it out so much and thought, I'll get even. Aunt Florentina told her husband, you could be a barber, and they opened a barbershop. And he told Auntie, you ought to open up a notions store. Next to the barbershop they set up one of those stores that sells everything, from pins to writing pads, thumbtacks, and toilet water. Uncle became fat, his belly grew round like a ball about to burst, because barbershops are a bad business now that men shave at home with electric shavers, and Auntie became so skinny that, as I said, you could see only her parrot nose. She looked like one of those old parchments, dry like a bone, and that was because her dime store was going very well. One day Aunt Angels whispered in my ear that Uncle Baldomeru had never seen his wife naked and that she was always saying her rosary when they were doing it. My aunt the whore added that with a woman like that a man must be unhappy no matter how you cut it.

Most of the girls in the school had no known father, and the nuns kept saying to us that we had to pray so that the souls of our mothers would not be condemned and go to hell, where they would burn for all eternity. Our mothers, they said, were sheep that had been thrown to sin and vice, and we were the branches thereof, and we could as easily be saved as damned. But that Our Lord God had not abandoned us, and that was why we were in the school now, to be protected from all the evil in the world. And that once outside it would be very hard for us to preserve ourselves intact.

There were a few who did have one, a father, and every Sunday, during visiting hours, the girls without a father had to stand in line to be kissed by the fathers. There were fights; we slapped one another and scratched to be first in line, because we knew that the first kisses were warmer, they were bigger and the hugs tighter, and that the last ones would be the kisses of a tired father. The girls who had fathers were our bosses and during the week we had to obey them in everything, from giving them the candy we had received to making up their beds, unseen by the nuns. They even started a father-kisses business, selling them for so much a unit. To get the first place in line was much more expensive, and at times we fatherless girls would sell the numbers among ourselves. A first kiss from a father, for example, would cost about fifteen pieces of candy, and then you still had to copy the homework of the bossy girl. Once I spent a whole week scrubbing the altar of the Immaculate in order to earn the kiss of a very hand-some father who, besides, stroked my cheek. Later the daughter of that father told me that wasn't enough, scrubbing the altar of the Immaculate for her, and that I had to give her the marron glacé that my aunt the whore would bring me. I got angry at her, I told her that it was not fair, that deals are deals, but there was nothing I could do. So I gave her the marron glacé in exchange for the first kiss of the father who, besides, caressed my cheek, which was like a tip. After a while I realized that Senyor Duc looked a lot like this father and the first time he kissed me I felt in my mouth the taste of the mar-ron glacé.

Ivonne, after showing me the flask with the ashes, took to thinking that I was going to bed with her husband, and she followed me the whole day long. And the poet of the phal-luses, all he ever did was explain to me the poem he intended to write, in which he would describe how the creation of the world had really happened, where we women come from, and men, and he would prove that all this theory of Darwin's was idiotic. He told me Darwin was a sage who had discovered that the earth was millions and millions of years old and that we the species had evolved from pure matter to become what we were, men. That is to say, rational beings. But it's poetry that says what we imagine as truthful, what science does not dare admit, and for this reason he intended to write a poem in which he would explain the whole truth about creation. As I was dusting with the feather brush he followed me and ex-plained that we all proceeded from an enormous phallus that God had planted one day, at six in the morning, in the middle of the earth, a phallus that was made out of bark, covered with sea algae as if these were branches, and that's why the Bible spoke of the Tree of Good and Evil. But God got it wrong: instead of planting it in the middle of a garden He planted it in the desert, and Eve, who had sprouted as a woman from some of the algae, was dying of thirst and spent a whole moonless night embracing the phallus. She began to lick it, to see if there was moisture in the bark, but little by little she fell in love with it and ended up eating the phallus. Then she was satiated. She was so happy that she did not realize until nine months later that she was pregnant, not by a man but by a phallus. According to the poet the phallus is the beginning of all created things, and that is why Eve felt a deep desire to swallow it in order to survive. And so the first child she gave birth to, a male, had a penis in remembrance of that phallus made of bark and sea algae. While he explained all of this, the poet had me caress an enormous white marble phallus, with purple veins, just like his own, he said, at once slippery and cold. Ivonne heard his mumblings and she started to scream hysterically; I grabbed the feather brush and went to dust the dining room paintings. For, to tell the truth, I couldn't care less about the history of the first phallus, creator of all things that have a soul.

That is how Ivonne started disliking me and chasing me through the house, you must clean real well, you must fix dinner, you forgot to buy butter.... Whew, I had had it up to here. She howled at me, her eyes ablaze, what you want—you—is to go to bed with my husband, how funny, she said, you'll see what a surprise, because his is smaller than a sparrow's beak.

I decided to go back. I was up to my eyebrows with Ivonne and with her husband's phalluses. I would look for work in Barcelona; the Paris adventure was over. All in all, young people want to have an adventure in Paris. Now that my mother had moved in with Heraclio, I could organize my life with no problem. Besides, in my *chambre de bonne* I just shivered with cold. Every morning I had to stand in line in that frozen corridor to wash myself after a very quiet Moroccan and a chubby Valencian who kept saying "What a *rigolade!*" and spied on me through the keyhole while I was in the toilet. I was fed up with having to crouch in order to piss and not splash my legs, and with having to wipe myself with pages from magazines because I always forgot the toilet paper in my *chambre.* Because if I went back to get the paper, I would lose my place and would have to stand in line all over again.

The Dutchman tore me away from my thoughts by offering me another marron glacé. Then he told me he felt very lonely and I thought, here we go, please don't explain your life to me, he saw clearly that only women would understand him, because we knew how to listen. He asked for my address in Barcelona and I told him I had no home. What a pity, he said, what a pity, he repeated. He spoke, waving his fishy hands about and nodding as if he felt very sorry.

Then, so that he would leave me alone and so I could think quietly, I let him caress my left thigh a little.

HORACI DUC/SENYORA MIRALPEIX: "In the beginning, I would say that she not only accepted it but that she was happy with it. She liked me to tell her stories of people who had been in the war, and I may say that I invented many of them. She listened to me enraptured. She stared at me in such a way that I had to exaggerate a lot, to the point that I no longer knew what was true and what was false. In those times, to survive, you had to live in an ideal world."

"That's true of any time, Senyor Duc."

"I would get up very early, at six o'clock, and leave my room barefooted so as to make no noise. I looked at her in her sleep, like Sleeping Beauty she was, and I thought, when I come back, I'll kiss her like the prince and break the enchantment. She breathed so softly that she seemed a girl. My working hours were only a parenthesis and, when closing time came, I hurried to finish my last job, I left the counter without polishing it, my tools without sharpening, I felt so anxious. She waited for me on the balcony. The walk home from work was short, but it was a walk filled with strange feelings; I felt uneasy but all at once so happy. . . . Only when you are in love, Senyora Miralpeix, do you realize the existence of what they call time. My house was like a silver platter, I have never known such a tidy woman. The furniture looked like mirrors.

And the little balcony was so full of potted plants that pass-ersby stopped to look at it as if it were an exhibition. The asparagus plants bent almost to the ground, the carnations jutted up toward the sky, the geraniums a burst of color, the hydrangeas in bloom. . . . And she among the flowers, the princess waited for me among flowers, in that apartment like a closed-in paradise, away from the poverty outside, and now, just remembering it, I could cry. . . . Excuse me."

"Please, don't stop on my account, go on, go on. But have another piece of toast, please."

"That's how the first months went, fast as a thought. Be-cause I, Senyora Miralpeix, have been a man without any companionship. My mother died of a heart attack just as the war ended. And my father, my father left one morning at dawn when the revolution broke out, and he never came back. In the neighborhood they said that he had left with a militia woman, one of those who practiced a free life. Stories of war. During the last year they almost sent me to the front. I wanted to go, but I was only fifteen. My mother said, do you think this is an adventure? But I wanted to go because they said that the Moors behaved like barbarians and also because everything was collapsing, and my father had told me that Catalonia is a country that hides when things don't go well and that it is reborn the stronger because of the suffering, but that a day may come when the blow would be so hard that we would no longer rise. . . . And I don't know quite how it hap-pened that the day they came in, and people were shouting 'They are on Diagonal Avenue!' I found myself on the roof only wanting to look at the sky. With his hands on the roof railing he was also looking toward the sky."

"Who was he?"

"His name was Pagès. I went closer and glanced at him out of the corner of my eye. He was crying like a child. Like a child, Senyora Miralpeix. Tears came down his cheeks and he did nothing to hold them back. And to see such a strong man, so tall, crying like a child is something you cannot easily forget. I asked him nothing; I knew very well why he was crying, and he put his hands on my shoulders and, pointing to a place up in the sky he told me, they have defeated us, Horaci, but we must keep on, now we'll have to be quiet, but deep inside we must shout very hard. Remember this, Horaci, inside we must shout a lot so that they do not take away our words. And I looked toward the point in the sky and I could see nothing, but I imagined that God was there and that God had gone over to their side, He had abandoned us."

"God sides with no one, Senyor Duc. God is inside each one of us."

"God is with no one; but let's not discuss that now. I had a lot of trust in Pagès. In the very early days he had gone to the front as a volunteer. Pagès was our upstairs neighbor and a good friend of my father, even though he was younger. The day the Republic was declared they went together to Sant Jaume square with Catalan flags, and took me with them. Pagès placed me on his shoulders, and people were happy, flags were waving; grandfatherly Macià spoke to us from the balcony, he told us we had a Catalan Republic, and Pagès was shouting louder than anyone while holding my legs, and I felt like a man just like them, because I saw my father was laughing, he, a man always in a bad mood. He turned to Pagès and told him, now, now we can start working, and Pagès answered, you're right, Duc, now is our time!"

"That day I was very frightened."

"But my father left with that woman, and we stopped speaking to Pagès. My mother said that she didn't want to have anything to do with him or her husband's world. And that men had used the war as an excuse to hurt and to destroy families. I saw him when he came on leave and was dying to ask him how things were going at the front, but a mother is a mother. And so I met him on the roof, alone and crying like a child. He walked with crutches for he had been wounded in the war. I saw that he had aged a lot, even though for a boy of fifteen a thirty-year-old looks like an old man, and he told me that thing about shouting out loud inside, remember, Horaci. Since they had wounded him he did not want to escape to France and he was arrested. He spent a few years in prison, and when he came out he was once again that man from the day the Republic was declared. Was he made of stone? Once he came to see me when I was closing up the butcher shop. He said he wanted to talk to me. He had a bunch of leaflets because the Eleventh of September was approaching.* He told me, you must distribute them to the stalls in Santa Caterina market. He commanded me as if I was one of them. But years had gone by and I was very afraid. When I got home I burned them. And through this lie everything began. He had been in prison, but I had lived in the neighborhood. The neighborhood was not the same: many had disappeared, some looked like ghosts, others were just skin and bones. Nobody trusted anybody. Some had become rich by denouncing others. And my father, who never came back. The owner of the butcher shop told me, you'll have to be thankful to me for your whole life, you see, I'm giving you a job even though you are the son of a Red. But if I learn that you have dealings with Pagès, out you go. I took to being alone, as if it were a punishment. I thought, You've been condemned not because you are the son of a Red, but because your father left with a woman. That was the way things were, that's all. But I also wanted to live, I was young, Senyora Miralpeix, I had many years ahead of me, I wasn't an old man like I thought Pagès was. And that's why I burned the pamphlets. I didn't let him know. I was afraid of Pagès. Every year, when the Eleventh of September came near, he brought me pamphlets to distribute, and I burned them every year and threw their ashes in the toilet. I never dared tell him the truth because I had seen him cry like a child, he, who was so strong and tall. Those

*Senyor Duc is referring to the Catalan resistance to Castilian domination, commemorated on the eleventh of September. On this date in 1714, the Catalans lost their bid for autonomy as a result of the War of Succession.

kind of tears make one more frightened than the threat of a beating."

"I think you're too sentimental, Senyor Duc."

"During our first married year I taught Maria to write correct Catalan. At night she would ask me, do you write 'amor' with an 'h' or without? She was teasing me; she thought it was very funny that the Catalan name for the letter *h* was 'hac.' I had her do homework. She wrote it down in a notebook with grid paper. Like a girl, she bit on her tongue while doing the exercises. That's how I transformed Maria into an authentic Catalan. I had done it all by myself. I had kept my inner words for her, just for her. I thought this was my contribution so that our country would not disappear, even if it was in the basement then, or in the sewers filled with shit, forgive me. And the day would come when I would show Maria to Pagès and would tell him: See? This is my trophy, my little work to help Catalonia become once again what it was. I have transformed an illiterate hick into an educated Catalan. I've paid my dues."

MARI CRUZ: The hut where the gardener kept his tools was made of red bricks and covered with an ivy vine that never stopped growing. The ivy covered the walls and a window as well. If you wanted to see what was inside you had to draw the leaves apart. The outside leaves were light green and those inside were darker, almost black, because the sun could barely penetrate there. I don't quite recall what the gardener looked like, except that he had very blue eyes, yellow teeth, and a pockmarked face. He came to the school three times a week, he pruned the lemon trees and the pear trees; in the spring he planted summer flowers and winter flowers in the fall. He taught us to talk to the flowers, he said they had souls, souls smaller than ours because they were vegetable souls and, if we did not talk to them, they would wither and die. We told our secrets to the flowers and also whispered to them whose father was the most handsome.

I waited for the arrival of the gardener; he gave us licorice and told us news from the street. One day he called a few of us and told us to go to the toolshed during break, that he had something for us, something we would like very much, but to tell no one, for we were his pets. He closed the door and had us sit on the floor, on top of a pile of empty sacks. He showed us three pieces of candy, lollipops, round, strawberry flavor, and a bigger one in three colors blended like watercolors. We started to play with him, clapping our hands, and then we played Humpty Dumpty. We had to lie on his knees, face down, and guess how many fingers he was showing. After that he pulled up our blouses and undershirts and he pretended to play piano on our "rosary bones." He started to kiss us all over. He gave us the strawberry lollipops and he said that the three-colored one would be for the girl who took her panties off. I wanted it and took them off and then he put his hand on my little hole. I didn't complain because I was enjoying it, even though his hand was rough and callused. But it smelled exactly as I felt the day I was on the Rambla with Senyor Duc, a moist smell but warm, even though it sounds strange. And while he was caressing my hole, he told me, you have one like a flower, your little hole has soul. When you grow up they'll water it for you and you'll love it, you'll see.

We thought it was very amusing and became used to getting locked up with the gardener in the toolshed, all covered with ivy, while the other girls played in the garden. He told us not to tell anyone, that it would be a secret. We ended up calling it "the secret of the watercolor lollipop," because we all wanted it, the bigger lollipop. And we told no one, we just waited for the day the gardener came to get locked up in the ivy shed. One of the girls had a father and one Sunday she confessed to him that she had a very big secret but she couldn't tell him because, then, it would no longer be a secret. The father told her mother, and her mother wanted to know about it and spanked her daughter. The girl finally revealed the secret, the spanking was so hard. The mother told the fa-

ther, and the father told the nuns, and the nuns got very
alarmed and reported it to the police, and the police went after the gardener; but it seems that he had suspected it for he
disappeared. The nuns called a very large lady, dressed in
white, with breasts like cathedral domes. The fat lady had us
all undress and examined us very well and said I don't know
what to the nuns and what happened is that the nuns had us
get up at six in the morning for a week. We had to stand without moving, with arms stretched in front of the main altar, to
see if the Holiest would forgive us, now that we had lost our
purity. The gardener was still in hiding, and the police were
still looking for him. Everybody now knew the secret, the
nuns told the other girls that we had been stained forever,
that the stain we had would never go away because we had
been sullied by the Devil, who had come to earth in the body
of the gardener. The other girls did not wave to us or speak to
us, and chanted that jingle, I'm not your friend, to the world's
end, if I see you in town, I'll frown, and I told them they were
idiots because we were never in town and they could never
frown at us since we were always locked up in the school, and
that one day I would elope with the gardener, even if he were
Satan himself. Weeks went by, we were locked up in the classroom or in the bedroom, forced to say prayers all day long to
see if we could wash away the stain we had inside. The nuns
said I was the worst one of all and that I would burn in hell,
just like my mother. Until finally everyone forgot about the
gardener and, one day, one of the girls in on the secret of the
watercolor lollipop climbed up the moist ivy vines that covered the window of the toolshed, and she let out a scream because there she saw a dancing shadow. It was the gardener,
who had hanged himself.

I was shaking all over while we were going up to the study. I
don't know why, but the Rambla was an avenue filled with
leaves. Senyor Duc told me that for a few years fall had been
coming early, the sycamores in Barcelona had a strange dis-

ease that had come from outside, and they were slowly dying. It was almost the hottest part of summer and the streets were filled with dry leaves. It was sad. Senyora Miralpeix had told me that all those changes were provoked by the rockets they were sending into space, they were polluting the universe, and they made summer no longer summer and winter no longer winter. And the sky over Barcelona would never again be like before, it would now have a dirty and grayish patina, as if the city had put on a hat. I had always seen it like this, an overcast sky as if it were about to rain, and I was used to it. But Senyor Duc explained to me that summer showers cleaned the sky and then Barcelona would look like before, clean and jolly. And then it started to rain, a good storm with big drops, far apart; and he said it was summer heat and it would soon stop, and you'll see a truly clear sky, like a gift from the gods. From my house I can see the sky, I said. Let's go, he said, and his eyes became bigger and broader like the drops falling from the sky.

I was shaking because I felt a fire within, I was and was not afraid. While we climbed the little staircase to the study the image of the ivy-covered toolshed came to me, and I saw the gardener with yellow teeth and pockmarked face, I felt his fingers caressing my little hole and also his rusty voice saying to me, this flower, one day they will water it for you and you'll like it a lot, you'll see. And out of the blue a word Senyora Altafulla had used came to my mind: selvage. Selvage. I did not quite know what it meant, but I adopted it, as if I had invented that word. The gardener had touched my selvage, he had touched the bottom of my soul. Selvage. My little hole would get moist as I took the gardener's hand, time and again, I longed for his coarse and callused hand smelling like the moist earth.

I didn't let the poet of the phalluses touch it, nor the man who took me to Tibidabo, but I was craving for Senyor Duc to touch it. Selvage. That word came down my throat, like swallowed honey. I wanted Senyor Duc to caress my soul, I longed to feel once again my cunt moist as when I was little and the school gardener touched it.

I didn't dare ask him to do it and we remained distracted for a moment, looking at the sky that was now clear and blue as Senyor Duc says the sky always is after a summer shower. I didn't want to look at the sky, I didn't care what color it was, I would rather have captured Senyor Duc's thoughts, make them go down toward my hole, to the moist cavern, moist like the ivy on the toolshed, I was thirsting to capture them well inside me, with the word selvage tickling me all over; I said, I would like you to caress my cunt, and I don't know how I told him, but the words came out of my mouth as if it wasn't me saying them but my body. He stood there motionless like a boulder, he took a while to answer me, and when he did he just told me, in great fury, where have you learned this bad word, Maria? Haven't I taught you to speak properly? Be kind enough not to repeat it, I find it disgusting. My body answered: it's a word that comes from deep within: and I told him because the nuns used to punish me when I pronounced it, because for a long time nobody told me what it meant, only this, something that's very disgusting, that was meant to designate ugly things, that which is unspeakable, and because for a long time I thought it was a word with no object, a bad word with no meaning, empty, until I found out that the word cunt was the selvage of my desire, all of me turned into desire, and for this reason I wanted him to caress it until I would die; you're strange, Maria, I don't understand you, he told me with a sorrow beyond my comprehension, why do you want to tempt me once more? It made me laugh, the idea that I wanted to tempt him, I thought it was kind of cheap; but I just replied don't call me Maria, Senyor Duc, don't call me Maria: and I grabbed his hand, warm like the gardener's, and I made it go down to my sex, I want your hand there, Senyor Duc, right now.

Everything changed. He said kneel down, and I knelt and then Senyor Duc was transformed. He became a magus, a haughty and powerful magus, standing on a hilltop, and he pierced me with his gaze, as if the whole of him wanted to invade me, I want you to suck my sex until you die, just as you want me to do with you, I want to fill you with my strength. I told him yes, that yes I would do it and, then, I'll lick your cunt as I know you like it, and you'll taste the sky, Maria, as you have never tasted it, or like before, like when you were all mine, when you belonged to me, when you were thirsting for me to caress you. On my knees I started to lick his sex with the top of my tongue, slowly at first, as if his sex were a flower about to open, slowly, and I closed my eyes, to concentrate deeper on what I thought was a new wonder, a pleasure that had been hidden from me. I cast away the image of the poet of the phalluses, all the marble phalluses, and the great phallus in the desert, the beginning and end of all creation, because this sex belonged to me, I would suck it, I would destroy it, you are my little whore, and his whole sex filled my mouth, as if it could not get out, a piece of sky, a piece of earth, all mixed up, water and mud, teeth and tongue, inside my head, inside my head, and I no longer knew who was speaking, he or I, Maria, Maria, his sex said, I am Maria and I'll swallow you, like the bee sucks the flower's pollen and with my sting I'll kill you, Maria, Maria, you have to destroy me, and his sex was so deep inside me that it seemed as if I was all a part of him. The magus threw me to the floor, he made me open my legs and he kissed my selvage and then I tasted the sky, I wanted it to be him, all of him, I wanted him to come deep inside me, the magus was my cunt, he was mine, and I was the cave that would protect him, it was me, it was him, he-me, I-he, the two of us, the two of us until death, I wanted to disappear, and the magus told me, ride me, and I galloped on top of him as he pierced me with his sex and became a male animal and I a female animal, and in that way we lay for a while, just panting, shrieking, skin, sweat, no words, until he, all of a sudden, went away, far, so far that I couldn't catch him, come back, come back, love, but he had left without me, each one of us in a different world, two galaxies beyond understanding, irreconcilable, as if we spoke two different languages, come back, come back, love, and then he cried out frightfully, a sound that seemed to be of terror but that was of pleasure, as if he were a mortally wounded animal, and he became all distended, returning heavily to earth, as if forced, and his eyes went after mine, and he had me lie on the floor, and from behind he caressed my selvage and then it was I who shrieked with no containment, a long howl, as if an electric current ran through my backbone, an unstoppable current, unstoppable, until I felt like crying out for so much happiness and my shriek penetrated all the darkness of my forgotten past, of my demolished hometown that I had left as a child, of the nuns, of the father I did not have, and then I understood for the first time that I had fallen in love. I felt the joy of abandon, abandoned in that harmony that nobody had ever explained to me and that I, all by myself, had discovered. All I said was, thanks.

Mari Cruz/Senyora Altafulla: Distracted, Mari Cruz was cutting Senyora Altafulla's nails, and she could barely hear the old woman scream, "But, girl, can't you see you're hurting me? Where's your head?" God knows where it was. She would have gladly severed her fingers with the clippers. She felt anger as she began filing Senyora Altafulla's claws, it was as if she were filing at her own heart, she wanted to see if what Senyor Duc had left inside her would disappear, that mixture of apprehension and joy.

Senyora Altafulla again asked her why she had only one earring. She was shouting. Filing away at her own heart she could not hear her. Finally she answered that she wore only one because she wanted to, trying to hold back the tears. She wanted by all means to hide her tears from the witch, come on, hold on. Oblivious, the old woman repeated that only one earring was very ugly, that you had to keep in mind the proportion of the human face, and so on and so forth. You'll leave me without nails, girl, don't pull so hard.

She had never felt sorry for herself; she thought that her life was laughable, like all lives, if you look at them closely. She had always felt untouched by the stories of others, she thought that over time people added a good dosage of fiction. Now she had to swallow her own sadness, not let the old woman see it. But there was no danger, her boss continued to mumble, that if we have two ears we must show them off, I can't stand so much carelessness, your poor aesthetic sense, girl. Mari Cruz hit her with the file.

"Look, Madam, I wear only one earring because I damn well feel like it, and leave me alone, damn it," she shouted.

Shocked, Senyora Altafulla was left with her hand hanging down and her nails spread out. She remained like that for a while, her hand in the air, her mouth open, not knowing what to do, ready to slap her. But she lowered her hand slowly and caressed the girl's cheek.

"Forgive me, my child, it was none of my business," she said.

She took hold of her chin and, little by little, inspected the girl's face. She gazed at her eyes and eyelids and perhaps realized they were moist. But she did not persist.

"You know that you are very pretty?" she said. "Your face is a perfect oval. And I like your eyes; they are pure eyes."

She was examining her face with her half-filed nails, as if drawing all its lines.

"Your features look like a Botticelli," she added, "I had not realized it before. A fine chin, a long neck, a svelte figure . . . and your lips . . ."

She followed her lips with her fingers and, all of a sudden, she stopped.

"No; I don't like your lips, your mouth is a bit too large. Let me see, show me your teeth. . . . Yes, your teeth are also pretty. . . . But you need your eyebrows plucked, they are too thick, and also your upper lip. A mustache is very unbecoming, for a girl like you. You seem older than you are."

For the first time since she started working for the old woman, Mari Cruz smiled at her. Senyora Altafulla detected a mixture of irony and friendship.

"Well, I mean that it could look as if you didn't wash," she specified, "and that makes you look older. You are a lucky one, all you need is a clean face."

"But you yourself don't wash a whole lot," Mari Cruz answered in a relaxed way. "What you do is use a lot of perfume."

"We old women do not need to wash much," replied the old woman as she observed her nails, now completely filed. "And even more if we follow my habit of not going into the streets, to soil myself with dust, and with what they now call pollution. That way I preserve my silken skin. Have you noticed? See how soft my skin is? Touch it, touch it. . . . Move your finger on my face, my neck, my arms, you'll see how fine my skin is. The colonel often told me. Caterina, he said, your skin is like a young girl's."

Mari Cruz felt her face while Senyora Altafulla held her hand. "Was Colonel Saura a man of his word?" she asked.

"Of course!" said Senyora Altafulla, looking into the box of the manicure set. "I don't know what color to choose. What do you think? Candide is a good evening color, but Grisant Fum Rosé is more delicate."

"The pink suits you better."

"The night we both were on top of the bluff and we could see the lightning pierce the sky, we sealed a pact without words. We knew that our relationship would be different. I won't deny that, at that time, I was seeing other men. And I am sure he was seeing other women. But, how can I tell you? We did not want to mix what we felt for each other with lust. . . . It was . . . as if we were both looking for our lost youth. I found in him the ideal of the male, the ideal I had built for myself when I was still a girl and wanted to leave my hometown. Perhaps he felt the same way. I am afraid you may not understand me, dear. At the time people did not understand us either. . . . My friend Núria Campins wanted to found a family with a real man. And I did not want to be a mother, I had no wish for children. I wanted to preserve, untouched, inside me, the dreams from my early years, when you feel the world is made just for you, when you discover it in all its neatness. I resisted growing old. I was forced to, later. . . . That's why, the night on the bluff, I felt totally possessed by my colonel at the very moment when he seized me by the waist. He was the lightning piercing my sky and I had no more needs. Who knows, if things had gone differently, our dream might have cracked open. . . . And later it might have become corrupted. Then we discovered, the two of us, that people had gone crazy and they were destroying the world's harmony and killing each other with no regrets. For this reason, one evening when we were strolling in Ciutadella Park, when the birds had left the linden trees in the avenue, we said good-bye to each other so that our relationship would never become a routine. . . ."

Mari Cruz listened to the beginning of Senyora Altafulla's last monologue. She had heard it many times, but now she captured every word. A Minorcan colonel, Albert Saura, smiled at her from afar and his image, which had been blurred and distant before, grew, becoming solid, tangible, real. With him she strolled down the avenue of the linden trees, on a birdless day. And for the first time she understood that she did not have to grow up the way they wanted her to. Because now she had inside of her an image that would never fail her.

Instead of applause Senyora Altafulla heard the voice of Mari Cruz asking, why didn't you marry the colonel? Senyora Altafulla took a moment to answer, she liked to feel the ecstasy, transported to an imaginary state, and Mari Cruz's question did not fit the scenario she had created. Without changing her dreamy tone she replied, Why should I marry him? How ridiculous! . . . We were two free and independent spirits, we had an inner life, just like Verdi and his beloved Giuseppina Strepponi. They never married either. They faced the sharp tongues of Busseto, they faced the Parma authorities. In a letter to Barezzi, his father-in-law, Verdi had written: "Neither she nor I need render any account for our actions and, besides, who knows what our relationship is like? What is there between us, what ties? Who can tell if these are good or bad? Why shouldn't they be good? And in the event that they were bad, who has the right to pronounce an anathema? . . ." Senyora Altafulla sighed. We too liked a solitary life and did not have to account for our acts to anyone. . . .

Mari Cruz wanted to know more things and she spewed forth questions, without thinking much. She was so happy on account of Senyor Duc's telephone call telling her he wanted to see her. . . . And she felt no surprise at her own attention now to a story that she had heard so many times and the end of which she knew by heart. . . . She was so happy that she continued to question the old woman. And what happened to you both when the war was over? Heavens, girl, what can I tell you; Senyora Altafulla continued with her gaze half-lost; I was holed up in the Pirelli factory, working like a mule, making ends meet as best I could. I spent the summers in Caldetes, with Raul and Antonieta, who had made it and pretended to be aristocrats. . . . God, how boring they were, those summers! Until I retired and became my own mistress I wasn't able to relax. With theatrical tenderness the old woman placed her fox stole around Mari Cruz's naked shoulders. See? Who would have guessed, she said, how the picture changes with some furs over your buxom décolletage. . . . Or would the llama-wool dress suit you better?

But Mari Cruz persisted; and the colonel, what happened to the colonel? Without interrupting her appreciation of the effect of the fox stole on the buxom décolletage, Senyora Altafulla removed from one of the drawers of her Jacobean dresser an old photo album with frayed edges. In it there was an envelope of foreign origin and she gave it to Mari Cruz.

The colonel went to his island, my dear; for all his bravery and courage in the affairs of war, deep down, he was a peaceful man.... Do you know what? I think it is better if you wear the fox to go to the opera; I want you to be the prettiest of all.... But Mari Cruz had already opened the letter and had begun to read what it said. It was handwritten in an English hand, in almost perfect Catalan:

> In Mexico we live well, the worst is over. At first I myself had to do the cooking, but now I have two maidservants, can you imagine! They are very inexpensive here. We have bought a villa in Cuernavaca; Ricard makes a very good living at the laboratories. If our parents could see us; they did not want me to marry a man in the military! My sister writes often from Chile, and it seems they are also doing well.... We were very lucky, Caterina, to take off before they came in; I do not know what would have happened to Ricard as he was a career soldier.... We heard so many stories, later.... I am sure he would have ended up like that poor soul, Colonel Saura, the Minorcan.... Do you remember him? How we used to laugh at him because he was so sloppy, and stiff as a fence-post. You were always the first to make fun of him, you said you could not understand how he could be an officer, so short and small-chested. Ricard used to say that he had gotten into the quartermaster corps to avoid the front lines and that he was so naive that he did not see the disaster coming. I must say that he did not deserve that death; it was a pity for him to be executed. At any rate they shot him because he was an idiot and a coward; who told him to stay in Spain? He had never hurt a fly.... Well, you may not remember this Saura; I think you did not meet on many occasions, did you? I hope you will write now that you know our whereabouts. A big hug from your friend,
>
> Núria Campins

She read the letter twice. First because she was not used to reading in Catalan and then because she could not quite believe what the letter said. She repeated, to herself, some of the terms: "sloppy, short, fence-post, coward...." She could barely hear the rustle of Senyora Altafulla's voice. She had not stopped speaking all that while; I told you, darling, the colonel went to his island because he was a man of peace, even though he had courage to spare. You don't know how much I am looking forward to going to the opera tonight, mostly because they are putting on *La Traviata*. You and I will be the most beautiful; we each have a different style and we look so chic, don't you think? . . . At times, when I was young and felt sad, for I felt sad once in a while, I would murmur to myself the duet with Alfredo and Violeta, when they say:

> *Amor e palpito*
> *dell'universo intero*
> *misterioso, altero,*
> *croce e delizia al cor!*

For love is this way, child, at once a cross and a delight. . . . But, you are listening to me, aren't you? If you go on so distracted you won't understand a bit of the performance. In order to understand opera you must have a special disposition. You may begin with this one, this is an easy one, and little by little I'll explain others to you, you'll see. . . . I tell you, you'll learn a lot with me, you are just a young sprout and I an excellent teacher, you can be thankful for that. . . . Let's see, to begin with I'll tell you how Verdi composed *La Traviata*. He had been to Paris and had seen *La Dame aux Camélias,* and since at Busseto they didn't much like Giuseppina Strepponi, his beloved . . .

Mari Cruz came down from her thoughts and interrupted her: No, Senyora Altafulla, tonight I can't go to the opera with you, I'm busy. . . . But, what are you saying? the old lady did not quite get it; is that why you dressed up? Come on, don't laugh, you must think that going to the opera is like having a date with the colonel, with our colonel. . . . No, Senyora Altafulla, it's no joke, I can't go, I have a previous engagement with . . . another person.

Her dress was uncomfortable, the underwires were digging

into her flesh under her breasts, the fur was suffocating. She put the letter back in the album. She felt that she had to forget something that was hurting her and could not remember what, she wanted to go with Senyor Duc, Senyor Duc who waited for her on the corner of Hospital Street. The old woman, now hysterical, was screaming: what do you mean you cannot come? Do you want to miss *Traviata*? No, this cannot be, you are out of your mind, dear. There is still a lot for you to learn, you'll see what you feel when the tenor starts that part *"Libiamo, amore"* – Look, I'll translate it for you:

> Let's drink, love, for in the glass
> One finds the most ardent kisses
> That love ever offers!

Your body will fill with a new breath, she went on now with a dreamy voice, as if it were filled with air. . . . She looked tenderly at the girl; O.K. I'll let you wear my pearl necklace, I'll go without. Mari Cruz paid no attention to Senyora Altafulla's insistence – I can't, I told you I have a date. Then the old woman became her boss once more: What do you mean? I am telling you to stay here, after all I've done for you, after all that I've given you! You'll never amount to anything, do you hear me? You will go through life like a toy top, like a valise, like a . . . And right now, I want my furs back, this very minute. She looked at her with teary eyes: And besides, you smell!

Mari Cruz was laughing while Senyora Altafulla was crying like Mary Magdalene. Come on, Madam, you have no demands on my free time, the comedy is over. The old woman was still trying to retain her: Comedy? Yes, this is nothing but pure theater, nothing of what you tell me exists, it has never existed; "your" Colonel Saura, that phony, the Royal Café, the woman you say loved that man Verdi; you're way off, you're . . . dead, do you hear? They're all dead. Mari Cruz threw the fox fur on the brocade bedspread as she fled from the room.

Senyora Altafulla carefully picked up the fox stole and started to pet it. Theater? Did you hear, Colonel? She says this is all theater. . . . She will never understand opera, she will never understand life. She turned around slowly and looked at herself in the mirror with delight. Her lips insinuated a smile, a smile as soft as the grimace of a fish just caught.

MARI CRUZ: She spoke openly, until it was dark and I couldn't see her face, and I thought it was not Senyora Miralpeix who spoke but the shadows of all the old people I knew. They were laughing at me, like the gardener with yellowish teeth and a pockmarked face. They told me their secret and I felt all smeared with it.*

When she finished talking I let out a scream, it was a shriek that came out from my entrails, long imprisoned there. I went to the toilet and vomited, as if my guts came out of my mouth and, with them, all my memories.

I was enraged at Senyora Miralpeix. I didn't want to know. And she seemed to enjoy it, telling me those stories. The colonel, I mean Senyor Duc, had made me love this land almost without my realizing it. He had made me notice the color of the sky over the city and he had helped me understand that I had a body. I don't care what he had done before. Older people, at times, give that too much importance.

Senyora Miralpeix was now observing me with her gaze made out of bark and, as she held my forehead to help me vomit, she said, you see? I told you, you should have taken some herb tea. . . . I have not invented what I told you; if I know about it, you must know too; this man has left it on top of me, like a tombstone. . . . With my hand I asked her to be quiet, but she went on, you must clean it with a sponge, don't you see that he only looks at you with his memory for the other woman?

*Senyora Miralpeix has just revealed Senyor Duc's darkest, haunting secret to
 Mari Cruz, as well as the news that he has left her.

But I didn't remember what she had told me, because I know today's Horaci Duc; through him I discovered the word selvage, with him I became the mistress of words. I will look for him. And when I find him I will no longer have to stand in line to be kissed by the fathers of the other girls. The colonel will be mine alone.

MERCÈ RODOREDA

The Salamander

Translated by David H. Rosenthal

I WALKED under the willow tree, came to the patch of water-cress, and knelt beside the pond. As usual, there were frogs all around. As soon as I got there they'd come out and bounce up to me. And when I began to comb my hair, the naughtiest ones would start touching my red skirt with the five little plaits on it, or pulling the scalloped border on my petticoats, all full of frills and tucks. And the water'd grow sadder and sadder, and the trees on the hillside slowly darken. But that day the frogs leaped into the water in one jump, and the water's mirror shattered into little pieces. And when the water was all smooth again I saw his face beside mine, like two shadows watching me from the other side. And so he wouldn't think I was frightened, I got up without a word, I began walking through the grass very calmly, and as soon as I heard him following, I looked around and stopped. Everything was quiet, and one edge of the sky was already sprinkled with stars. He'd halted a little ways off, and I didn't know what to do, but suddenly I got scared and started to run. And when I realized he was catching up with me, I stopped underneath the willow with my back against the trunk. He planted himself in front of me, with his arms stretched out on both sides so I couldn't escape. And then, looking into my eyes, he pressed me against the willow and with my hair all disheveled, between him and the willow tree, I bit my lip so I wouldn't cry out from the pain in my chest and all my bones feeling like they were about to break. He put his mouth on my neck, and it burned where he put it.

The next day the trees on the hill were already black when he came, but the grass was still warm from the sun. He held me again against the willow trunk, and put his hand flat over my eyes. And all at once I felt like I was falling asleep, and the leaves were telling me things that made sense but which I didn't understand, saying them softer and softer and slower and slower. And when I couldn't hear them anymore and my tongue was frozen with terror, I asked him, "And your wife?" And he told me, "You're my wife. Only you." My back was crushing the grass I'd hardly dared walk on when I was going to comb my hair. Just a little, to catch the smell of it breaking. Only you. Afterwards, when I opened my eyes, I saw the blond hair falling and she was bent over, looking at us blankly. And when she realized I'd seen her, she grabbed my hair and said "Witch." Very softly. But she let go of me immediately and grabbed him by his shirt collar. "Go on, go on," she said. And she led him away, pushing him as they went.

We never went back to the pond. We'd meet in stables, under haystacks, in the woods with the roots. But after that day when his wife led him away, the people in the village started looking at me like they didn't see me, and some of them would cross themselves quickly as I went by. After a while, when they saw me coming they'd go into their houses and lock the doors. I started hearing a word that followed me everywhere I went, as if the air whistled it or it came from the light and the darkness. Witch, witch, witch. The doors shut. I walked through the streets of a ghost town, and the eyes I saw between the slits in the curtains were always icy. One morning I had a lot of trouble opening my front door, which was old and cracked by the sun. They'd hung an ox's head in the middle of it, with two little green branches stuck in the eyes. I took it down. It was very heavy, and I left it on the ground since I didn't know what to do with it. The branches began to dry, and while they were drying the head began to stink and there was a swarm of milk-colored worms all around the neck on the side where they'd cut it.

Another day I found a headless pigeon, its breast red with blood, and another a sheep born dead before its time and two rat's ears. And when they stopped hanging dead animals on my door, they started to throw stones. They banged against the window and roof tiles at night, as big as fists. . . . Then they had a procession. It was the beginning of winter. A windy day with scurrying clouds, and the procession went very slowly, with white and purple paper flowers. I lay on the floor, watching it through the special door I'd made for the cat. And when it was almost in front of the door, with the wind, the saint, and the banners, the cat got frightened by the torches and chants and tried to come in. And when he saw me he let out a great shriek, with his back arched like a bridge. And the procession came to a halt, and the priest gave blessing after blessing, and the altar boys sang and the wind whipped the flames on the torches, and the sexton walked up and down, and everything was a flutter of white and purple petals from the paper flowers. Finally the procession went away. And before the holy water had dried on the walls, I went out looking for him and I couldn't find him anywhere. I searched in the stables, under haystacks, in the woods with the roots – I knew it by heart. I always sat on the oldest root, which was all white and dusty like a bone. And that night, when I sat down, I suddenly realized I had no hope left. I lived facing backwards, with him inside me like a root in the earth. The next day they wrote "witch" on my door with a piece of charcoal. And that night, good and loud so I could hear them, two men said they should have burned me when I was little, along with my mother, who used to fly around on eagles' wings when everyone was asleep. That they should have had me burned before they started needing me to pick garlic or tie the grain and alfalfa in sheaves or gather grapes from the poor vines.

One evening I thought I saw him at the entrance to the woods with the roots, but when I got closer he ran away and I couldn't tell if it was him or my desire for him or his shadow searching for me, lost like I was among the trees, pacing to and fro. "Witch," they said, and left me with my pain, which wasn't at all the kind they'd meant to give me. And I thought of the pond and the watercress and the willow's slender branches. . . . The winter was dark and flat and leafless. Just ice and frost and the frozen moon. I couldn't move, because to walk around in winter is to walk in front of everybody and I didn't want them to see me. And when spring came, with its joyous little leaves, they built a fire in the middle of the square, using dry wood, carefully cut.

Four men from the village came looking for me: the elders. From inside I told them I wouldn't go with them, and then the young ones came with their big red hands, and broke down the door with an ax. And I screamed, because they were dragging me from my own house, and I bit one and he hit the middle of my head with his fist, and they grabbed my arms and legs and threw me on top of the pile like one more branch, and they bound my arms and feet and left me with my skirt pulled up. I turned my head. The square was full of people, the young in front of the old, and the children off to one side with little olive branches and new Sunday smocks. And while I was looking at the children I caught sight of him. He was standing beside his wife, who was dressed in black with her blond hair, and he had his arm around her shoulder. I turned away and closed my eyes. When I opened them again, two old men came forward with burning torches, and the boys started singing the song of the burning witch. It was a very long song, and when they'd finished it the old men said they couldn't start the fire, that I wouldn't let them light it. And then the priest came up to the boys with his bowl full of holy water, and made them wet the olive branches and throw them on top of me, and soon I was covered with little olive branches, all with tiny shoots. And a little old lady, crooked and toothless, started laughing and went away and after a while she came back with two baskets full of dry heather and told the old men to spread them on the four sides of the bon-fire, and she helped them, and then the fire caught. Four col-umns of smoke rose, and the flames twisted upwards and it seemed like a great sigh of relief went out of the hearts of all those people. The flames rose, chasing after the smoke, and I watched everything through a red downpour. And behind that water every man, woman, and child was like a happy shadow because I was burning.

The bottom of my skirt had turned black. I felt the fire in my kidneys, and from time to time, a flame chewed at my knee. It seemed like the ropes that tied me were already burnt. And then something happened which made me grit my teeth. My arms and legs started getting shorter like the horns on a snail I once touched with my finger, and under my head where my neck and shoulders met, I felt something stretching and piercing me. And the fire howled and the resin bubbled.... I saw some of the people looking at me raise their arms, and others were running and bumping into the ones who hadn't moved. And one whole side of the fire collapsed in a great shower of sparks, and when the scattered wood be-gan burning again it seemed like someone was saying "She's a salamander." And I started walking over the burning coals, very slowly, because my tail was heavy.

I walked on all fours with my face against the ground. I was going toward the willow tree, rubbing against the wall, but when I got to the corner I turned my head slightly and off in the distance I saw my house, which looked like a flaming torch. There was no one in the street. I went past the stone bench, and then quickly through the house full of flames and glowing coals, toward the willow, toward the watercress, and when I was outside again I turned around because I wanted to see how the roof was burning. While I was staring at it the first drop fell, one of those hot, fat drops that give birth to toads, and then others fell, slowly at first and then faster, and soon all the water in the sky had poured down and the fire went out in a great cloud of smoke. I kept still. I couldn't see a thing, because night had fallen and the night was black and dense. I set out, wading through mud and puddles. My hands enjoyed sinking in the soft mush, but my feet grew weary behind me from getting stuck so often. I would have liked to run, but I couldn't. A clap of thunder stopped me in my tracks. Then came a bolt of lightning, and through the rocks I saw the willow. I was out of breath when I reached the pond. And when, after the mud, which is dirt from the ground, I found the slime, which is dirt from the bottom of the water, I crept into a corner, half-buried between two roots. And then three little eels came along.

At dawn, I don't know if it was the next day or some other, I climbed out slowly and saw the high mountains beneath a sky smudged with clouds. I ran through the watercress and stopped at the trunk of the willow tree. The first leaves were still inside the buds, but the buds were turning green. I didn't know which way to turn. If I didn't watch where I was going, the blades of grass would prick my eyes – and I fell asleep among those blades until the sun was high in the sky. When I woke up I caught a tiny mosquito, and then looked for worms in the grass. Finally I went back to the slime and pretended to be asleep, because the three eels immediately came up, acting very playful.

The night I decided to go to the village there was lots of moonlight. The air was full of smells and the leaves were already fluttering on all the branches. I followed the path with the rocks, very carefully because the smallest things frightened me. When I got to my house, I rested. There was nothing but ruins and nettle bushes, with spiders spinning and spinning. I went around back and stopped in front of his garden. Beside the hollyhocks, the sunflowers hung their round flowers. I followed the bramble hedge without thinking why I was doing it, as if someone were telling me "Do this, do that," and slipped under his door. The ashes in the hearth were still warm. I lay down for a while, and after running around a bit all over I settled down under the bed. So tired that I fell asleep and didn't see the sunrise.

When I woke up there were shadows on the floor, because night was already falling again, and his wife was walking back and forth with a burning candle. I saw her feet and part of her legs, thin at the bottom, swollen higher up, with white stockings. Then I saw his feet, big, with blue socks falling over his ankles. And I saw their clothing fall, and heard them sitting on the bed. Their feet were dangling, his next to hers, and one of his feet went up and a sock fell, and she took off her stockings, pulling them off with both hands, and then I heard the sheets rustling as they pulled them up. They were talking very softly, and after a while, when I'd gotten used to the darkness, the moonlight came in through the window, a window with four panes and two strips of wood that made a cross. And I crawled over to the light and placed myself right under the cross because inside myself, even though I wasn't dead, there was nothing inside me that was totally alive, and I prayed hard because I didn't know if I still was a person or only a little animal, or if I was half person and half animal. And also I prayed to know where I was, because at times I felt like I was underwater, and when I was underwater I felt like I was on the ground, and I never knew where I really was. When the moon went down they woke up, and I went back to my hiding place under the bed, and started to make myself a little nest with bits of fluff. And I spent many nights between the fluff and the cross. Sometimes I'd go outside and go up to the willow tree. When I was under the bed, I'd listen. It was just like before. "Only you," he'd say. And one night when the sheet was hanging on the floor I climbed up the sheet, holding onto the folds, and got into bed beside one of his legs. And he was as quiet as a corpse. He turned a little and his leg pressed down on top of me. I couldn't move. I breathed hard because he was crushing me, and I wiped my cheek against his leg, very carefully so as not to wake him.

But one day she did a housecleaning. I saw the white stockings and the raggedy broom, and just when I least expected it blond hair was dragging on the floor and she shoved the broom under the bed. I had to run because it seemed like the broom was searching for me, and suddenly I heard a scream and saw her feet running toward the door. She came back with a burning torch and jammed half her body under the bed and tried to burn my eyes. And I, clumsy, didn't know which way to run and was dazzled and bumped into everything: the legs on the bed, the walls, the feet on the chairs. I don't know how, I found myself outside and made for the puddle of water under the horses' drinking trough, and the water covered me up but two boys saw me and went to look for reeds and started poking me. I turned and faced them, with my whole head out of the water, and stared right at them. They threw down the reeds and ran away, but immediately they came back with six or seven bigger boys, and they all threw stones and handfuls of dirt at me. A stone hit one of my little hands and broke it, but in the midst of badly aimed stones and in utter terror I was able to get away and run into the stable. And she came looking for me there with the broom, with the children constantly shouting, waiting at the door, and she poked me and tried to make me come out of my corner full of straw and I was dazzled again and bumped into the pails, the baskets, the sacks of carob beans, the horses' hoofs, and a horse reared because I'd bumped into one of his hoofs, and I went up with him. A whack from the broom touched my broken hand and almost pulled it off, and a trickle of black spit oozed from one side of my mouth. But I still was able to get away through a crack, and as I escaped I heard the broom poking and poking.

In the dead of night I went to the woods with the roots. I came out from under some bushes in the light of the rising moon. Everything seemed hopeless. The broken hand didn't hurt, but it was dangling by a sinew, and I had to lift my arm so it wouldn't drag too much. I walked a little crookedly, now over a root, now over a stone, till I got to the root where I used to sit sometimes before they dragged me off to the bonfire in the square, and I couldn't get to the other side because I kept slipping. And on and on and on, toward the willow tree, and toward the watercress and toward my slimy home under the water. The grass rustled in the wind, which whipped up bits of dry leaves and carried off short, bright strands from the flowers beside the path. I rubbed one side of my head against a tree trunk and slowly went toward the pond, and entered it holding my weary arm up, with the broken hand on it.

Under the water streaked with moonlight, I saw the three eels coming. They seemed a little blurred, and intertwined with one another, winding in and out, making slippery knots till the littlest one came up to me and bit my broken hand. A little juice came out of the wrist, looking like a wisp of smoke beneath the water. The eel held onto the hand and slowly pulled it, and while he was pulling, he kept looking at me. And when he thought I wasn't watching he gave one or two hard, stubborn jerks. And the others played at entwining as if they were making a rope, and the one who was biting my hand gave a furious yank and the sinew must have snapped because he carried off the hand and when he had it he looked at me as if to say: "Now I've got it!" I closed my eyes for a while, and when I opened them the eel was still there, between the shadow and the shimmering bits of light, with the little hand in his mouth — a sheaf of bones stuck together, covered by a bit of black skin. And I don't know why, but all of a sudden I saw the path with the stones, the spiders inside my house, the legs hanging over the side of the bed. They were dangling, white and blue, like they were sitting on top of the water, but empty, like spreadout washing, and the rocking water made them sway from side to side. And I saw myself under that cross made of shadows, above that fire full of colors that rose shrieking and didn't burn me.... And while I was seeing all these things the eels were playing with that piece of me, letting it go and then grabbing it again, and the hand went from one eel to the next, whirling around like a little leaf, with all the fingers separated. And I was in both worlds: in the slime with the eels, and a little in that world of I don't know where... till the eels got tired and the slime sucked my hand under... a dead shadow, slowly smoothing in the dirt in the water, for days and days and days, in that slimy corner, among thirsty grass roots and willow roots that had drunk there since the beginning of time.

ABOUT THE AUTHORS

Born in 1936 in the village of Balciai, JUOZAS APUTIS worked as a journalist before turning to short fiction. His first short story appeared in print in 1960. He is the author of the collections *Bee's Bread is in Flower* (1963), *September Birds* (1967), *Wild Boars Are Running on the Horizon* (1970), and *Dusk is Falling on the Fields* (1977).

LADISLAV DVORAK is from Czechoslovakia.

REGĪNA EZERA was born in Riga, Latvia, in 1930. A journalist for many years before becoming a professional writer, her literary output includes four novels, five short novels, and seven collections of short stories. In 1972 she received the State Prize of the Latvian SSR.

KOLDO IZAGIRRE was born in 1953. His poem "Oinaze zaharrera" (To the Old Evil) was published in 1976, and collection of short stories, *Gauzetan* (About Things), was published in 1979. Both his poetry and fiction demonstrate a constant preoccupation with language. His experimentation with language led him to incorporate different dialects and colloquial expressions in his 1981 book, *Euskal lokuzioak* (Basque Idioms).

TEET KALLAS was born in Tallinn, Estonia, in 1943. His first book (1964) was a juvenile story in a lyrical key, and the problems of youth have been dominant in his later works as well. Kallas's novels of everyday life, notably *Corrida* (1979), deal with different attitudes toward life in a successful synthesis of conventional and novel devices of form. Kallas has also worked for the theater and radio and has written criticism.

RITA KELLY writes in Irish and English. Her first collection, *The Whispering Arch and Other Stories*, was published by Arlen

House in 1986. She has won the *Irish Times*/Merriman Poetry Award and the Maxwell House Prize for short fiction. Born in 1956 in Balinasloe, County Galway, Ms. Kelly lives now in Enniscorthy, County Wexford.

DANILO KIŠ was born in 1935 in Subotica, Yugoslavia. Among his published works are *Psalm 44* and *A Tomb for Boris Davidovich*. He was the recipient of the NIN Prize in 1973 and the Goran Prize in 1977. He died in 1989.

IVAN KLÍMA, born in Prague in 1931, spent three years as a child in a Nazi concentration camp. He edited several journals until they were prohibited. In 1969 he served as a guest professor at Michigan University, Ann Arbor. He has published numerous novels and plays, including *Ma vesela jitra* (My Joyous Dawns) in 1979, and *Love and Garbarge* (1991).

Born in 1902 in Reykjavík, Iceland, HALLDÓR LAXNESS made his breakthrough in 1923 with the novel *Vefarinn mikli fra Kasmir*. He is the author of numerous plays and novels, as well as works of non-fiction and translation. He was the recipient of the Nobel Prize for Literature in 1955, and the Sonning Prize in 1969.

A professor of literature in the Escuela de Magisterio in San Sebastián, ANGEL LERTXUNDI has published several works, including many children's tales. He received the Yon Mirande Basque government prize for his 1983 work, *Hamaseigarrenean aidanez* (The Sixteenth Time's the Charm), in which he attempts to recreate the traditional Basque story. His literature explores the changes occuring in the Basque identity and utilizes forms and content that are uniquely Basque.

LAURA MINTEGI was born in 1955. She studied history at the University of Deusto. Although she contributed to various Basque periodicals, the collection of stories, *Ilusioaren ordaina*

(The Cost of Illusion), published in 1983, was her first major contribution to Basque literature.

MERCÈ RODOREDA was born in Barcelona in 1908, when Catalonia was autonomous and its citizens were allowed to speak, write, and study their own language. She fled to exile in Paris and then Geneva at the end of the Spanish Civil War, when the Catalonian culture was brutally suppressed. She regularly produced novels and collections of short stories and became a fixture on Catalan best-seller lists. When Franco died she returned to Barcelona, where she died in 1983.

Born in 1946 in Barcelona, MONTSERRAT ROIG is the best known of the new generation of Catalan writers. While much of her fame comes from her work in journalism, she is the author of four novels and one collection of short stories, *Molta roba i poc sabo,* for which she won the Victor Catala prize.

HANAN AL SHAYKH was born in Lebanon where she lived and worked as a writer and journalist on a leading Arab newspaper until civil war forced her to move to London with her family. She is the author of four novels and a collection of short stories. *The Story of Zahra* was published in 1986 by Quartet and Pavanne to critical acclaim. Her fourth novel, *The Deer Musk,* is currently being translated.

DUBRAVKA UGREŠIĆ is a member of the Department of Russian Literature at the University of Zagreb, but is better known in her country as an award-winning novelist and screenwriter. Two of her novels have been recently translated and are scheduled for publication in Great Britain and the U.S.